BANISHED

The Dragon's Game
BOOK I

H. N. Henry

Presse Dragon Libre
Free Dragon's Press

Trois-Rivières, QC, Canada

FREE DRAGON'S PRESS
Huard, Norman Henry
220 B rue Farmer
Trois-Rivières, Québec, Canada, G9A 3E6
www.hnhenry.com

Publisher's Note: This is a work of fiction. Names, characters, places, and incidents are a product of the author's imagination, except for his use of the Cree language in Roman orthography to number and title chapters and as one of the languages spoken by certain characters; and also for his use of certain Tai Chi exercise names. Locales and public names are sometimes used for atmospheric purposes. Any resemblance to actual people, living or dead, or to businesses, companies, events, institutions, or locales is completely coincidental.

Book Layout © 2014 BookDesignTemplates.com

BANISHED The Dragon's Game BOOK I by H. N. Henry—1st edition

ISBN 978-0-9958367-0-9

Dedication

To all my writer's workshop students, the immense courage you showed in choosing to write stories gave me the courage to write this one.

The world will not be destroyed by those who do evil, but by those who watch them without doing anything.
—ALBERT EINSTEIN

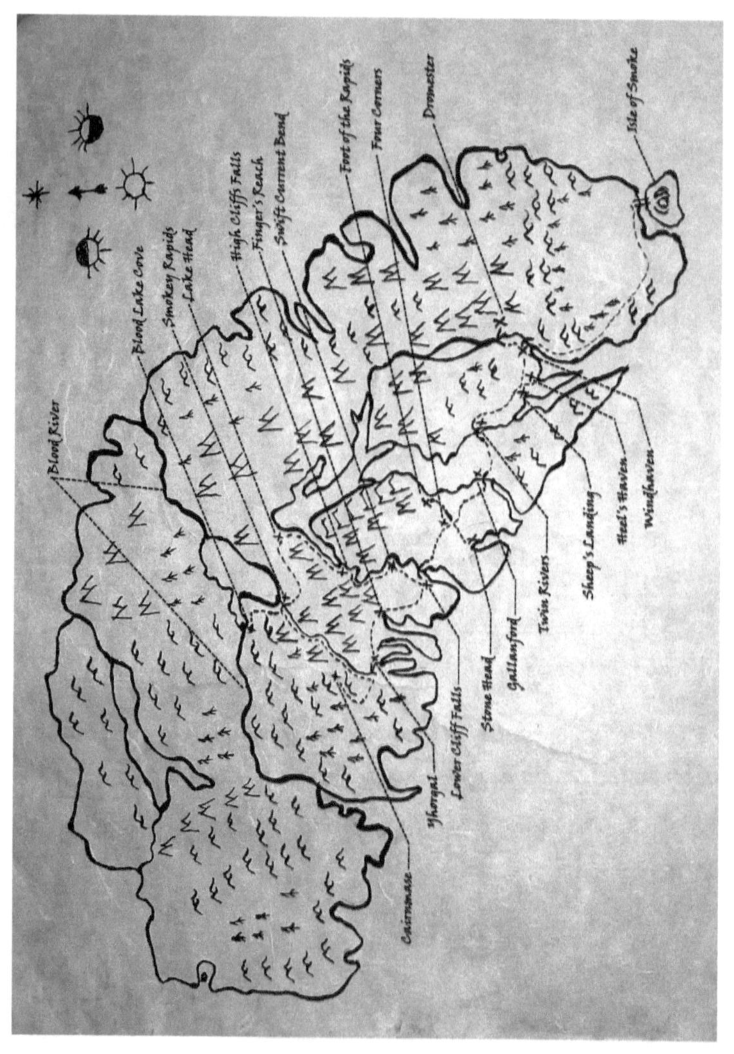

Map on hide side of Nagora's vest.

CHAPTERS

Lone Wolf — *Ka Peyakot Mahihkan* 1

Pug — *Awîyakka aspihat wecayah* 33

Banished — *Wepinikewin* 53

Ilma — *Awîyak ekâ ceskwa ka wicehtot* . 79

The Witch — *Kîskwehkan Iskwew* 99

No Longer In My Eyes — *Pâskâpiw Ôyêhâ* 119

The Prince — *Okimâwikosisân* 169

Edana — *Onâpehkâsoweyinis* 193

The Guard — *Okanaweyihcikew* 223

The Bridge — *Âsokan* 257

The Stone Standers — *Asinîy Chimataw* 271

The Chain — *Sakâpihkan* 297

Lone Wolf
Ka Peyakot Mahihkan

— ✝ —

Legend tells us dragons fly so high they see the future.

Reason tells us that to know the future is a curse.

Our hearts tell us the seeds of hope are sown in the reality of the present.

— ✝ —

Back then, dragons no longer flew above that sorry land, but the one that hoped to fly in those skies again watched over Nagora, for she was the one the dragon needed.

On the outskirts of the tiny rebel hamlet of Cairnmase twenty-three young warriors sat cross-legged around the perimeter of the sandy training circle, showing little interest in their instructor.

Most had their envious eyes on Nagora, the only female trainee among them. Her sixteen year old leather-clad body was a tightly strung set of muscles and skilled fierceness that helped her master every weapon they ever trained with. Her wavy black hair was pulled snug to the back of her head and tied into a solid rope braid that hung down her straight back all the way to the leather belt at her waist.

The few in that circle who had been graced with the warmth of one of her rare smiles longed to be touched by it again. While a few, who had never seen her smile, sought to draw her anger. Not only did she beat and hold them down with the training weapons, but she also held them at a distance with her cold, blue-gray gaze.

Nagora caught the three stones Pug's gang members had pitched at her and juggled them as she ignored the names they continued to fling her way.

"Stone."

Her callused, tar-stained hand batted the pebble away. It hadn't stopped her from catching and throwing the three she juggled.

"Loner."

This one bounced off her other hand. She clenched her teeth, didn't move from her crossed-legged sitting position, and kept juggling.

"Tar Baby."

She caught the rock Pug had thrown and held it in her fist. The three juggled stones fell from their vertical flights. Pug, you're nothing but a useless toad. I've been waiting for this one.

Randsord stepped into the circle of sitting trainees and looked around at each one of them before speaking. "Time to listen up. When we meet next, bring your staffs and bring some heart to put into your efforts." His back was to Nagora. She threw the rock at Pug with all her might. On the mark!

It struck his forehead, and he fell on his back with a scream as his hands went to his face. He rolled over and came up on one knee, pointing a bloody finger at her. "You bitch. I'll get you."

She held his eyes with hers and bared her clenched teeth in a silent growl. Inside, she wore a satisfied smile. Bleed, you bugger. She rested her hands on her knees as Randsord turned in her direction, but kept her eyes focused on Pug. He had called her "Tar Baby." I prefer "Stone," Pug. You'll never get me. Neither you nor any of your chumps. You don't have what it takes.

Randsord stood between her and Pug and shook a long, bony finger at her. "What'd I say about this bickering amongst you? It's a waste of time. No good comes from it. It starts with name-calling and ends with bruises and bloodied noses. I thought you were beyond that."

She leaned to one side to keep her scowl on Pug who stood, wiping blood from his face. Tar piss! Next time I'll aim for your eye, Pug. I could damn well blind you if I chose to.

"Well, what'd I say?"

She let her eyes roll up to Randsord's. You know what you said. She tried not to glare at him. Not our best trainer in hand to hand combat. Moves are too predictable. Wastes our time with words, putting us down, rather than demonstrating skills. She could take him in the training ring, any day.

He pivoted on his heel and pointed at Pug. "What'd I say?"

"It's her fault. The bitch!" Pug pointed to his bleeding forehead. "She threw that rock." He looked down and pointed to his minions. "You saw her. Didn't you? She threw it. Didn't she?"

They nodded.

Nagora cast her cold stare on them. Puppies. Listen to your bully bastard. Do his bidding. Don't dare think for yourselves. Keep your noses to his ass. I've had enough of you louts, wasting my time. They weren't interested in bettering their warrior skills. Did all her efforts even matter?

If it weren't for Uncle, she would be like them, just going through the motions. To be away from them, to never see them again, to no longer hear their incessant name-calling. Tar piss! I wish! Three years now, still, she was the only damn girl in training at Cairnmase. The previous few others had moved on to become mothers.

Was that how they escaped from this gang of mockers? Lay down and spread for one of them, who would turn into a defender because now she had his pup at her tit? Did it weigh in the balance of their choice? Or had they lost their belief in The Cause? Damn! I have. None of us believe in it anymore.

"Dismissed."

Nagora was on her feet in an instant and broke into a run along the winding dirt road through the tall natural stone cairns of the village to Geirador's smithy to find Uncle. She ignored the calls from the few younger trainees who ran after her. Couldn't they see she wasn't in the mood today?

Good. He's not in the forge. Her uncle, Dangor, had just finished folding a tarp and wedging it beneath the wagon bench before turning to sit. Nagora snatched the reins as she climbed up onto the wagon and dropped onto the bench next to him. His eyes were on her. He didn't say a word. At least he wouldn't waste words prodding her. She loved him for that. It would give her time to cool down and collect her thoughts. She would speak when ready and right now she wasn't. The sooner we're away from here, the better.

"I take it we're not dropping in on Geirador and Paruline?"

Nagora did her best not to glare at Uncle. Today, she had to get away. She would not impose her dark mood on Geirador, or Pare. Uncle would deal with it as he always did.

She bent her forehead to the reins on her clenched fists and squeezed her eyes shut.

Usually, she would enjoy stopping in to see Geirador working at his forge. Something about the clang of his magic hammer on a piece of molten metal spoke to her as he transformed it, made it take shape. And what he did with metal, he did with horses. Tamed them, trained them, and made them into tools for the best warriors, those who could pay. Someday she would be able to pay.

Or, if Uncle wasn't pressed to return home to the chores awaiting them, she would run over for a short visit with Pare. Pare was like a big sister, one of the few sources of brightness in her life. Pare had taught her everything she knew about riding and caring for horses. And other things women seemed better at teaching than men.

She straightened up, stared ahead, and snapped the reins. "Let's go, Patches. We're going home."

Nagora guided Patches out of Cairnmase and continued to ignore the calls and waves from the younger trainees who now play-trained with stick swords outside their stone huts. Didn't they understand she had enough of Pug and his gang? Perhaps they could. She didn't want to take the fun out of their games. Could she ever return here and find time to just have fun with them? Climb the cairns with them? If she dared answer at this moment, the answer would be no, never again.

Patches plodded onto the forest road leading to Yhorgal.

Only then did Nagora look directly at Uncle. "I've had it with training. With those useless asses. I have no challenge. Except putting up with their name-calling. I can best them all. They don't give a rat's tail about The Cause. They just complain about the beatings I give them in combat. They don't want to get better. They're as useless as teeth on a hen. They would never be able to put up a decent fight if their lives depended on it."

Uncle gave her a glance and then looked ahead, leaning his head to one side.

Today, she didn't have his patience, so she pressed. "Well?"

He took a long breath before shifting his eyes back to her. "Is that all you have to say?"

She shifted a rein from her right hand to her left to beat home each argument. "I'm done with them. I'm not going back. It's a waste of time. I'll better use my time working for you. You can still keep training me. I always learn something from you. You always make me better. You don't waste my time."

When her hand took back the rein, Uncle's eyes went back to her eyes. "That's the difference. Training one is easier than training a group."

"I don't believe that. I always learn something when you train us with our bows. They listen to you. They don't listen to Randsord. And I've not learned a thing from him. I can best him. I have to hold back not to make him look bad. I could knock him on his ass every time I face him."

Uncle scratched at his bearded chin as he took another long breath. "It may be he's letting you do the teaching, letting you show how it's done."

"I do when I beat them one on one with the training swords and the staffs. They don't want to get better. They just complain. 'Tar Baby's not fighting fair. She hits to hurt.' Chickens, every one of them. Today, they threw rocks. It wasn't the first time. I threw back and hit my mark."

Uncle looked at her. "I don't doubt it. You draw blood?"

Nagora couldn't hide her smile. "I did. Cut Pug's forehead good. Bloodied his goose-livered face."

He smiled. "So now you have a sworn enemy. Is that why you don't want to go back?"

"No, I told you before. He's the leader of a pack of cowards. I'm not afraid of him."

"They're not all like Pug and his gang. Don't put them all in the same bag." Uncle's eyes traveled along the reins to Patches' back as he shifted his jaw from one side of his face to the other. "If you don't go back, Pug'll label you a coward."

She lifted the reins with both hands. "I don't care. I'm not going back."

Uncle placed a hand on her shoulder. "Think about it until the next training session."

...

Nagora awoke in the pre-dawn darkness of her loft. Her hands, clasped together, rested on her chest near her collar-bones and still held her amulet. Her fingers ran over the tightly woven cat sinew that encased the black stone. She had worn it around her neck for almost seventeen summers now. Since the day she was born. That's what Uncle had told her.

The stone holds a mystery. I'm sure of it. It contained a blood-red crystal, visible from two of the stone's sides. When she held it up to the sunlight, a pale pink filament seemed to float within the red crystal. I swear I've seen the filament change shape at times, but it's best I keep that to myself.

And now her strange dream about the wolf lingered long enough to make her focus on her amulet and remember.

On her seventh birthday, Nagora had asked Uncle: "What is this stone? What does it mean?"

"When the time's right," was all he had answered.

From that day on, at least once every ten days, she had asked the same questions and made the same accusation: "You don't trust me, Uncle. Why? Tell me."

Uncle would shake his head to get away from her questions, find something to do, or somewhere to go.

On her twelfth birthday, after Nagora had stopped yelling her accusations, Uncle said, "I'll tell you this, child. There's power in the stone. If I tell you what it is, you'll not believe me. Trust me on what I tell you. You'll only discover its power when you have complete trust in yourself. How you go about finding that, I can't say. That's when you'll learn its true power, all on your own. I won't be the one to reveal it to you. It'll reveal itself. So stop asking."

On that day she had stopped her questioning. She had withdrawn. She became Lone Wolf, one of the names her fellow warrior trainees called her.

Who am I? There, in that simple question, lay the mystery today, stronger than ever before. In Nagora's strange dream, there were even stranger words: *Ka Peyakot Mahihkan.* Strange, yet so familiar on her tongue when she spoke them, like any other words she knew the meaning of. They mean "Lone Wolf." I'm sure of that. But how can I prove it? Is my amulet revealing its power today? Am I *Ka Peyakot Mahihkan*? Is that my real name? Is this just something I dreamed?

In the dream, she ran with a wolf, not away from it. She didn't fear the wolf. Its eyes were the color of hers. How did Pare say they were? Pale blue, almost gray, the color of wind-swept lake ice on a clear winter day.

She loved to listen to Pare speak, especially when they were alone, and she said things that touched her. "I love your eyes, Nagora. They change with the color of the sky and your mood, like pools of water." Pare always had words to make her feel good about herself. How many times had she repeated those words to herself, hearing Pare's voice as she spoke them. Maybe they would make her feel better today.

Below, the wooden door to their small stone lodge opened. Uncle dropped an armful of firewood on the dirt floor next their fireplace. He was back from his exercises. It would be

Nagora's turn. While she dressed, the crackle and pop of the kindling catching fire made her smile.

Returning to the fire for their morning meal would not only warm her body, but help her think as she stared into the flames. Thinking was easier when staring into flames. Why this was so, she did not question. It was a fact, like water is wet. I want to make clear my questions about The Cause. Later. The exercises will help me.

Barefoot, Nagora made her way down the loft ladder, inhaling the scent of smoke from the dried spruce twigs used as fire starter beneath the split birch kindling and logs. The sweet smell of the bark tickled her nose.

Without a word, she grabbed her bow, opened the door, and stepped out.

Dull twilight drizzle loaded the air with wetness. Nagora climbed up the sod roof section of their hut. It sloped down and over the part of the big rocky outcrop that made up one of the walls of their lodge.

She stretched on tiptoes and looked around. I love quiet mornings, even damp ones like this. This is better than living in Cairnmase or Yhorgal. I'm glad Uncle built our lodge away from those places, even if the nearest neighbor is a long walk away. They were near the sea. Uncle always said he had to be close to the sea, and she had grown to love being close to the sea too. And it was near enough to their beach hut where they worked, on her beach. This was her home.

Nagora walked past the lazy column of smoke rising from the stone chimney. Later, it would drift to where the sun rose, as it always did on rainy days like this when the wind picked up. The absence of the distant rumble of crashing sea waves made the dawn quiet. Only the cool wet smell of the grasses followed her.

With just enough light to make her way, Nagora ran toward her spot on the cliff overlooking the sea, almost a count away if walking. She cut the time in half. It seemed she was always counting time, though, now she did it without effort. A day's work was twenty-four counts, and a day was three times that. With the help of the sun, it was even easier.

Nagora scampered through the wet grass and low bushes until she set foot on the wet rock ledge of the cliff that reached out over the sea.

Today, she didn't bother searching the horizon for a sail. On clear days she would take the time and hope to see the sail that just might bring her father's boat back home. Mum had died giving birth to her just after Da had sailed over the horizon in search of new lands. That was all she knew. Still, she hoped to see her da someday. Would he be surprised to see a daughter instead of a son? Never mind, like it or not, I'm what he'll get.

Fog shrouded her spot on the cliff. With her unstrung bow in hand, facing out to sea, she set about the ritual daily exercises Uncle had taught her years before: ward off, rollback, press, push, pull, elbow strike, shoulder strike, advance, retreat, look left, gaze right, center balance. She repeated these a hundred times each morning session. She did them with a different weapon in hand, no matter the weather, at times deliberately slow, at times blindingly fast.

Today, as she flashed through her routine, the rain spit and splashed around her. When she finished, she was soaked in sweat, rain, and sea mist. She stripped off her leather shirt and leggings and stood naked, letting the downpour cool and cleanse her until steam no longer rose from her and her breathing became even. She picked up her garments and headed for home, calm and at peace with herself.

Their breakfast of gruel, stone baked flat bread, goat cheese, and honeycomb filled Nagora for the morning of work that awaited her and Uncle at the beach hut where they built curraghs.

As she sipped her tea from the bowl and stared into the flames, images of the day's work ahead slipped by. The stitched hide on the wooden frame of one of the small leather boats needed to have its seams tarred to render it watertight and seaworthy. That dirty work was hers.

After, they would build a new curragh frame upside down by steam-bending pieces of split ash which they would tie to a form as ribs, then lash the ribs to the longer steam-bent stringer pieces with brine-soaked leather lanyards. Teamwork.

The leather lashings would shrink as they dried to bind the curragh frame pieces to each other, ready to have cow hides stitched over them. Without its hides, a curragh looked like a big overturned basket with its crisscrossed frame pieces needing to have the spaces between them filled.

Uncle always made the tar mix. So far, it was his secret recipe. It allowed the tar to stick to the seams of the curragh and remain flexible. The seams would lose their flexibility if the curragh was used when it was cold enough to turn water to ice on the rivers and bays where fishers took them.

Nagora applied the tar mix with two wooden spoons, one bigger than the other. She would tar the inside lashings and stitched seams before tarring the outside seams. It was messy work, and she couldn't rid all the tar stains from her hands and forearms until winter. She looked at her left hand. Tar piss! But it came with the job. Like Uncle said, "Every job has its dirty side." Sometimes, dark brown tar stains covered her feet. At least she had boots to hide them in, most of the time.

Nagora tested the curraghs for leaks by rowing them out to sea, her favorite part of the work. Most of the vessels they made were for two fishers, one to sit at the oars while the other set and checked the net or hook lines.

To keep the craft afloat in case a seam ruptured, she would tie inflated leather bladders inside the bow and stern frames and row out with a killick anchor at her feet and a pronged fishing spear at her side.

In calmer warmer weather, she would anchor in shallower water and jump overboard with her spear to swim down to fish for bottom feeders. Most times, she would come back with a catch to make shore soup.

Later that morning, as Nagora stood in the wet sand next to the hut's wide-open door, she wiggled her toes and looked seaward. There would be no testing today. The wind had picked up, sending big waves crashing onto her beach. "Uncle, do we rig a tarp on the lee side of the hut?"

"Might as well. We'll set up the fire pit there too with the steam box. Once you get the seams tarred on that last one, we'll drag the form over here. Get the ropes. I'll bring the tarp out."

She had helped rig the tarp many times before, so it wasn't long before they had a roof over their heads to work out of the wind and occasional sprinkles of rain the clouds would bring.

By the time Nagora had scavenged more pieces of driftwood to feed their fire, Uncle had the tar mix on the boil and the steam box in place along with split lengths of ash ready to be softened by the steam. She dropped the pieces near his fire. "You didn't waste any time."

Uncle stirred the pot of tar mix. "I figured we'd put in a good day's work. Ready to tar those last seams?"

"I won't keep the tar waiting. Smells like it's just right." Nagora reached over for the big shell that held her wooden spoons, lifted the tar pot off the fire with a wooden hook, and set it on the sand next to the overturned curragh.

She stuck the spoons in the mix and held onto the handles with her bare hands. Better to gauge the temperature. Too hot, the mix went on too thin and ran from the seam stitches. Too cool, it wouldn't run. Just right, it filled the seam with an even bulge, as it did now. Her fingers endured it like that. Too hot the tar piss mix would burn her fingers. Only the outer seams left to tar. Won't take long to tar those.

In little over a count, Nagora finished. "There. Done with the tar piss today. I'll go tie a loop of rope on the form."

Uncle had made his form from wooden boards nailed together and cut to the shape of seven of the little boat's cross sections. He nailed them upright into deep notches cut into a log the length of a curragh. She tied the two ends of the rope to the log's end, leaving them a big loop to pull with. "Ready over here."

Like most curragh makers, the length of Uncle's curraghs was twice the span of his outstretched arms, plus the length of one of his forearms. At their widest, they measured his arm span. He had set the widest cross section in the middle, and the others in equal distance and decreasing size on each side of the middle cross section. She double-checked to make sure none of the cross-section boards was loose.

Uncle picked up the rope. "Sections solid?"

"All tight."

He stubbed the toe of his boot on the big log. "I don't think I want to know how many boats we've framed on this. Or how many fishers are still paying for them."

They still got wax-sealed jars of pickled herring delivered in the fall and armloads of dried salted cod. Some paid in firewood. Some in skeins of spun wool. Some in tanned leather hides. Some in bars of tallow soap. Any who paid in coin must've been discreet.

Nagora had never seen a piece cross to Uncle's palm. "Imagine, Uncle, if they'd all paid in coin."

Uncle laughed. "You'd have more than one bag of coins. That's for sure. And they'd be in a different hiding place. That'd mean a new hidden map because the hiding place would be much bigger."

My treasure. She had only ever seen the bag once. And only once, one of the gold coins it contained. Uncle had showed her one—a gold dragon. "Whatever's in the bag is yours, Nagora," he had said on that day, a month ago. "You've earned it, and more."

And he had laughed when she asked if she had enough to buy a horse. "Horses, Nagora. Horses." *My dream. My dream'll come true someday. Soon, I hope.*

"Well, lass, what are you waiting for? We've got work to do."

She smiled at Uncle and took hold of the rope. *I'm waiting for my dream to come true.*

After hauling the form in place not far from the steam box, Nagora went into the hut to get the two buckets of brine-soaked leather lanyards, one for her and one for Uncle. She set one down on each side of the curragh form.

Uncle stood next to the steam box. "Ready when you are."

Nagora sat in the sand and spread her legs wide on her side of the form. "Bring it on."

Uncle pulled a split length of ash wood from the steam box and bent it in place so she could lash it to the cross section board. It was the first of the curragh's seven ribs.

Once they had tied all the ribs in place at the even-spaced holes along each section's curved edge, they set to work tying on the long stringers.

Nagora placed her toes on each side of the hot stringer piece, where it crossed a rib, and leaned forward to pull hard on the wet lanyard knot to bind the stringer to the rib joint. She would tie hundreds of these knots today.

The first lanyard broke. *Tar piss!* She pulled the short end of the knot away and remade a hitch at the rib and stringer joint. It held, and she finished the four lashing loops around the joint before cutting off the remaining wet lanyard with her knife.

She stuck the blade of her knife in the sand. "*Ka Peyakot Mahihkan.*"

Uncle looked up. "What'd you say?"

"*Ka Peyakot Mahihkan.*"

"Is that someone's name?" Uncle paused on the knot he was tying on his side of the curragh.

"I don't know. I overheard it. Thought it was from the trader's tongue. Thought you might've heard it before."

"If it is, not that one. You didn't ask?"

Nagora reached into the brine pail for another longer lanyard. "No. They'd moved on. I forgot about it. It just came back to me now."

Uncle pulled the lanyard to make the knot tight. "You sure you're saying it right?"

"Hmmm. No. Probably not. That's what I think I heard. How I remember it." She shrugged. She had a piece of information. It proved nothing. Maybe it was just part of the dream, but it didn't feel that way. Not like it belonged in the dream, but was part of her, one of all the words she could speak.

Near the end of the afternoon, the tarp above their heads snapped. Uncle looked up. "Wind's shifting. It'll clear tonight. Tomorrow the tarred one will catch the sun and dry out." He finished tying his last knot.

Nagora looked up at the tarp as it snapped again, louder this time. "It's coming from where the guide star sits. It'll be cool tonight." She leaned back on her hands to rub them in the sand to try to remove the fresh tar. She rested her heels on one of the curragh stringers.

"Good, Nagora." Uncle smiled at her. "And tomorrow morning, where will the wind be?"

"From where the sun sets. It'll be warm by afternoon. The beach'll be dry by then. The piles of sea grass above the high water line will still be wet. It'll take a few days for them to dry out if the wind holds."

She let her feet fall to the sand to bring her knees up and wrap her arms around them.

Uncle's smile curled bigger at the corners of his mouth, displaying his teeth, usually hidden in his beard. "That's my girl. You're getting the weather eye. And you've worked hard today. We've got one tarred and seven framed. Couldn't have done it without you. We'll move them to their spot and call it a day."

It was the best pay for her hard day's work—Uncle's sincere recognition of her work and his smile. Now she was ready to talk. First, a rinse in the waves.

Nagora stripped off her tarred and tattered leather work pants and shirt, went to retrieve the big woolen sweater from the peg behind the hut door, and ran toward the crashing waves.

Nagora dropped her rear into the cold wet sand, where the tongues of the waves licked at the beach, and rubbed sand over the tar spots on her feet and ankles. While she rubbed her feet back and forth in the coarse sand, she scooped up finer sand from beside her hips, rubbed it into her fingers and over her forearms. When a cold wave washed in, she leaned into it, held her breath, rinsed, and scooped more sand to rub into the tar stains to wear them down.

After a dozen rinses, she stood and looked at her hands and feet. Tar Baby. She walked into the oncoming waves, watching for the next big one. When it came, she dove into it and swam out with it as it receded. The water was cold, but it didn't stop her from swimming.

How had she learned to swim? Uncle must've taught her. But she couldn't recall specific lessons. Playing and laughing in the waves with Uncle? Yes, from the time she was young. Nagora just seemed to belong in the sea. It allowed her body to move in a whole new way. Uncle said she was a fish, a water baby, able to swim before she could walk. Spinning and diving into waves. Coming up for air and disappearing again. Even today. But he taught her one thing—to respect the sea.

It came from learning to read the waves and pick out the backwashes and tidal rips. It made the difference in being able to get back to shore or not. And never discount the wind. Combined with waves and tidal currents, it could take her far out to sea before she realized it.

She loved her beach, even on a day like this. But she loved it best when the sun was hot in the sky, baking the sand on the beach so she could cover herself in it when she came out of the cold water. At times, warmed by the hot sand, she would fall asleep.

Not today. Nagora crawled from where the wave had dumped her, lurched up on one foot and then the other, to make her way to the welcome warmth of the big wool sweater. She pulled it over her head and hauled her long, stringy, wet hair out of the collar and shook it out onto her shoulders and back, gathering it as best as she could to wring as much water from it as possible.

...

Nagora ran back to the fire in the lee of the hut. Uncle had cleared away the steam box, and had brewed forest tea in the pot. He had added a few pieces of wood to the fire, and set a small cloth bag of shelled nuts with dried berries and a bowl of tea on a flat stone for her.

Nagora drew her knees up to her chin under the sweater as she sat as close to the fire as possible. Her toes peeked out from the hem of the sweater. She reached for the hot bowl with both hands hidden within the sweater sleeves. "Thank you." For a long moment, before taking a sip, she let the warmth from the bowl seep through the wool and into her hands, her eyes on the dancing flames. She took a long sip to warm her insides.

Uncle warmed his hands as he looked at her with a da's eyes. Do you look like my da? You're brothers. Da's younger. She smiled back at Uncle.

They climbed the trail from the beach to the bluff above, leaving their day's work behind them. Nagora ran, calling to Patches. She had left him to graze in the meadow. His long ears perked up, and he moved in Nagora's direction. "We're going home, Patches. Come to the wagon."

The ride home was almost two counts. The rain had stopped. The wind had shifted and cooled. Nagora had the reins and the question she wanted to ask. "Uncle, we've been training all these years. There's been lots of talk, off and on, about The Cause. That the rightful king's supposed to return someday and that we'll fight for him so he can get back his throne. But that's all we ever hear.

"No name. Nothing about his whereabouts. Nothing about his troops or fighters. If he has any or not. Or if we're the only ones he's counting on.

"Okay, we hear about the queen and plenty of whispering about how evil she is, and her mercenaries and all. And we know we're not supposed to speak a certain word, ever."

She wanted to say it, "dragon," and be done with it. But the dangers of doing so had been so often hammered into her, she didn't, even if it were safe to do so now.

"What's going on, Uncle? The trainees don't seem to care about The Cause and to be honest, right now, neither do I. What gives? You must be able to tell me something." Give me something I can latch on to. Will you even answer me?

Patches had reached the road. To the right, it went to Yhorgal. To the left, it went to Cairnmase. They would head toward Cairnmase for a short distance before turning off to the left on the trail home. Uncle's hands rested on his knees. He moved them to his lower back, stretched, and took a long breath.

After they had turned onto the trail, he cleared his throat. "Well, Nagora, we're lucky to be living in this part of the land. We're far away from the big towns. Yhorgal is small compared to the others. We see some of what's going on in other places, there."

Nagora held up a hand. "Like the defaced bridge and statues?"

"Yes, to rid them of any traces of dragon images."

Uncle said it. He spoke the word out loud. She pointed at him.

"You're not going to turn me in, are you?" His smile was wide. "The situation in the big towns is becoming dire. Food is scarce. The queen is having crops collected and, supposedly, hoarding grain for worse times to come. Some wonder if times can get any worse than they already are."

"But why would she starve her people? She'll not win their favor that way."

Uncle looked at Nagora. His face was sad. "We think it's her way of fighting against those who'd rebel against her. Food in considerable amount is the reward she uses for any who denounce anyone they hear talking of an uprising or even speaking of times past with the dragons."

"And the poisoned well water I've heard about?"

"That too. Yhorgal only has one well, and people there are learning to waste its water and no longer drink it. Word's gotten out to the other towns, but it's difficult. Many have no choice but to drink it and fall sick with drowsiness. They lose all energy and won't do anything beyond taking care of their basic needs. It's like they become slow-witted. They can be pushed to do things, but rarely take any initiative. More and more people have been wasting the poisoned water, and so it's having less effect on people. Word is the supply of poison's run out and hasn't been replenished yet."

Nagora shook her head. "I don't think I'd want to live in one of those big towns. I didn't enjoy those times you made me experience hunger for real. Four and five days without a thing to eat except for the berries and roots we could find. It hurt. I was so weak. I hated you for making me go through that."

"You were lucky to have water, most of those days."

"Damn right! Thirst is worse than hunger."

"True, Nagora. And it'll kill you faster too. So try to imagine what people in big towns go through when they're both hungry and thirsty."

"They must go crazy looking for their next meal. If they can't find it in town, they must head for the forest, lakes, rivers, the sea, wherever there may be food of some kind. Finding something, anything, to eat was all I could think about, Uncle. Except I knew you knew where we could find food, but you kept me from it. You made me look. That pissed me off."

"But you learned valuable lessons."

"Aye, I did. Planning ahead is important. Carrying rations too. Hunting on the move and eating game rather than rations. Being able to read the land to find food and water, especially water. How to hold off panic. How not to wear yourself out. You had us up high in the mountains. Barely anything at hand to hunt or forage for. It was tough, truly tough. I cried. To me you were the most heartless bastard to ever walk the land."

Uncle's eyes were smiling. "And you swore, when we'd get back, you'd never spend another day under the same roof with me."

"Until I shot that ram. You'd taught me to track. To spot goat tracks on stone surfaces. Especially near a water source. And the hunter's patience, the value of waiting in hiding. When my arrow took it down, I was so thankful. Everything you taught me fell into place. It was a revelation. You let me gather grasses and twigs and branches to make a fire. You waited for me to cut off a hind leg and roast it. You waited for me to invite you to my fire to share the meat."

"And you, Nagora, took back your words."

"You're a hard teacher, Uncle."

"No, Nagora. The lessons you learned were hard to learn. I only put you in the situation where you had to apply all the easier lessons, to solve a bigger problem."

"So we're far from all those problems in the bigger towns, aren't we?"

Uncle exhaled. "For now we are. They'll come our way, sooner or later. Mark my words, when Prince Acindor comes to settle in his fortress, we'll know evil is on our doorsteps."

Nagora had often heard talk of the progress of rebuilding the fortress on the ruins of old Yhorgal Castle on the sea cliffs. She had almost forgotten the queen had had it built for her son. "Will people still go there to pay tribute to the queen?"

"Aye, but the prince will become the tribute collector, full time, not just for one month in the year. We've been planning for that. Building caches to hide food stores. Disguising our garden plots and setting up secret pastures out of the way. Taking stock of the deer around us. Adding to the berry bushes and nut trees in the forest."

"Uncle, when you say 'we,' who do you mean? The king and others?"

Uncle looked her in the eye. "Those of us we know we can trust, those loyal to The Cause."

"You don't trust me?"

"Oh, I trust you, Nagora. With my life. There are things I can't tell you because I want to protect you. For now the less you know, the less you'll reveal under questioning, hard questioning."

"Uncle, do you mean torture?"

"Aye. The queen's inquisitors haven't showed up around here yet. They will one day. They'll question everyone. Almost everyone talks, especially when they're hungry. They'll be looking for any sign of a rebel organization."

She scratched her head. "So neighbors will no longer trust each other. They could be turned in for a misspoken word or for doing anything out of the ordinary. Won't that lead to false accusations?"

Uncle nodded. "It's like a poison chain. The falsely accused make false claims, and before you know it, the finger pointing spreads. The more fingers pointing to you, the more suspect you become, and before you know it, you're labeled a rebel. You're as good as gone."

"So anyone who knows about us training in Cairnmase could turn us in?"

"Right now there's no reason for that to happen, nothing to make it worth their while. And anyone thinking of doing so knows they're risking their own life if they do. Remaining loyal to The Cause has its price as well."

Nagora put her hand on Uncle's arm. "So The Cause is still alive. Some kind of secret preparation is going on. A possible rebellion. But given the situation in the land, organizing it isn't easy, almost impossible, if hardly anyone can be trusted. If there's an uprising, it will not happen tomorrow."

Uncle placed his hand over hers. "That's the situation. You've summed it up simply, without any names. You know as much as the queen. Raganora is fighting blind, doing her best to keep the cover on the pot and the flames low so nothing boils over."

"So if I don't go back to train with the others, will they consider me disloyal to The Cause?"

Uncle shrugged. "What do you think?"

Tar piss! Do I have a choice? "If I go back, I'm not holding anything back. Every one of them will wish they'd trained harder. I swear I'll break some bones. They'll think the enemy is among them. Even Randsord better be on the lookout."

Uncle grinned from ear to ear.

"What?"

Uncle held up his hands. "I didn't say anything. When we get home, go rinse your long mop of hair. It's caked with sand and salt. You look like a witch."

Nagora slapped one of his hands. "A witch am I? I'll put a hex on you! All tha sand 'n salt I washes off'll go into yer barley soup, old man. Tha sand'll grind yer teeth down 'n tha salt'll make yer eyes go crossed."

Uncle raised his forearms in a cross before him and leaned away with eyes wide-open. The next moment, he held his sides laughing.

She laughed too. "I know. I can't wait. I feel sticky all over. But while I go to the stream, you make the soup."

"Deal, and I'll go for a soak after we eat while you clean the bowls and scraps. I won't come back until you play me a tune."

"Deal." They touched fists.

Nagora sat on the sod roof of their lodge with a blanket draped over her shoulders. She had pulled the hood of her linen shirt up over her damp hair before playing *The Miller's Wife* on her flute as the sun set. It was a toe tapping tune. Then she played Uncle's favorite, a sad simple ballad she had composed. She called it *Lost on the Sea*.

Uncle whistled along with her playing as he returned from the stream.

"Thank you, lass. I'm going in to get warm by the fire."

"I'll play a bit longer to the stars."

He waved and smiled at her before making his way to the door.

As Nagora continued playing, she looked up to the stars. They held so many stories, stories she would have Uncle tell and retell when she was younger, until she could tell them back to him. Some she liked were about the bear, the swan, the hunter, and the tamer. Actually, he was the "dragon" tamer. But she wasn't supposed to say that word.

The Woman Waiting at her Window was her favorite story of all. The woman would spend all her free moments every day lying on her side, resting on her elbow, with one knee bent up, hoping to see her man come home.

She liked to think Mum was up among the stars and someday, when she would die, she would go to be with Mum and all her ancestors who came before her. Which star would she choose be her own star? Not easy. But it would be one of those close to where Mum was.

Nagora set her flute in her lap and spoke aloud. "What do I do, Mum? Do I go back to train with those oafs? I hate them. They're useless. They just waste my time. They don't care about The Cause. I can't say I do either. It seems so far off. It's still being planned. That's all I know about it."

She reached for her amulet. "I still wear the amulet you left me. It's supposed to reveal its power to me someday. I wish you were alive. Perhaps you could tell me about the power it has. I've told you this before. Uncle says it'll reveal its power when I have complete trust in myself."

She reached a hand up toward the stars. "I don't quite know what that means. I think I have trust in myself. I know how to do lots of things and I can do them well. So far, I haven't been in a situation that truly frightens me. Uncle has taught me to deal with so many things."

Nagora brought her hand back to her lap, and her voice became a whisper. "I had this dream about a wolf, and when I woke up I was holding my amulet. I heard strange words, *Ka Peyakot Mahihkan*. But it was as if I'd always known them and I'm sure of their meaning. They mean Lone Wolf. Would that be my real name? The name you gave me before I was born? It feels like it belongs to me. That it's a part of me. Someday, Mum, I'll take my place at a star close to you and you'll have answers to all my questions. Until then, Mum, please watch over me. And guide Da home to me soon."

She picked up her flute and played *Lost on the Sea* one more time before going in to bed.

In the cool clear air of the dawn, Nagora finished her routine exercises on the rock ledge of the cliff. While she scanned the orange horizon for any sign of a distant sail, she leaned on her staff, rested her cheek against it, and her chin on the back of her hand.

High tide pushed the sound of the gentle crash of incoming rollers up and over the cliff's edge. Already, gulls were gathering to see what the receding tide might leave them for the breakfast they were calling for. Each of them jostled for the first available place at their daily banquet table. Why can't the people of the land be as free as the gulls? They're not starving. Just doing their part to clean the shore.

Nothing on the horizon. She stood her staff an arm's length ahead of her to seaward, rose on her tiptoes, and stepped around it until she faced home. She sprinted all the way through the dew-covered grass.

"Soon as we've eaten, Nagora, we're headed to Cormac's to load the wagon with sacks of charcoal for Geirador. I'll be making several trips today. Geirador's coal bins are near empty. He says he's going to have a busy summer pumping the bellows of his forge. He wants his bins full and then some."

"You know what he'll be making, Uncle?"

"No. Something's in the works, though. We'll find out sooner or later.

"On one of those trips, I'll stop at the tanner's for a big bundle of hides. I'll leave them in the bushes next to the trail down to the hut. If I'm not back by the time you finish training, do you think you can go there and roll them down to the beach?"

"Sure, I'll run the forest trail back."

"Good. And can you untie the bundle and hang the hides in the hut?"

"How many will you get?"

"Two dozen, if I can."

"So two per pole?"

Uncle nodded.

Later in the morning, Nagora brought the wagon to the back end of Geirador's smithy. She had Patches back the load to the outer door of the coal room. She pulled the brake on the wheel and jumped down from the driver's seat to untie her staff from the sideboard.

She went over to Patches, and rubbed his nose. "Good work, Patches. You've got a few more loads to haul today. Soon as they unload the wagon, Uncle will give you some feed and water. Keep up the good work. See you later." She rubbed her nose to his before going to see Uncle.

Geirador nudged Dangor's shoulder. "Now there's a warrior who looks determined to bruise some bones with her staff." Nagora tilted her head back and returned Geirador's smile. He stepped from the doorway and wrapped a giant arm across her shoulders and pulled her to his side so he could rest his bearded chin to gently rub it on the top of her head.

She put an arm on his back and leaned against him.

"Nagora, you take care of yourself in the ring. Show 'em how it's done. Don't be too hard on 'em. I don't have time today to go set any bones." He let her go, but held on to her staff.

She looked up at him. "Geirador, when I'm done at the ring, I'll let you use my staff to make splints."

He laughed loud and shook her staff. "Go get 'em, Nagora."

Uncle smiled as he too took hold of her staff. "Take care. See you tonight."

"I'll have the soup ready for you. Now, if you two let go of this, I'll go crack some bones." Nagora yanked on her staff.

Geirador and Dangor were shaking their heads and smiling. Uncle let go of her staff. Geirador held out a big hand. "My hammer for your staff."

She smiled, pulled it from behind her back, and slipped it back into the pocket of his leather apron. "I could've used it."

Uncle poked Geirador's shoulder. "You're the one who taught her to pick pockets. Don't complain if she always practices on you."

Geirador let go of her staff. Nagora turned to leave, then faced him again, and held out a small steel file. "I won't need this, either."

Pug
Awîyak ka aspihat wecayah

As Nagora approached the training grounds at the other end of Cairnmase, the trainees had already paired off and were sparring in the big sand-covered ring. Randsord was in the middle, shouting reprimands and advice as he focused from one pair to the next. She stood on the perimeter of the ring, waiting for Randsord to notice her.

"Tar Baby's here. You're late, Tar Baby." Pug had stopped sparing and leaned on his staff, staring at her.

As Randsord turned to look at her, most of the other trainees stopped their sparring.

"Lone Wolf has showed up after all," called out Pug's sparring partner. Now all the trainees had stopped and had their eyes on her.

Randsord moved a few steps in her direction. "You're late. You know the rules." He waved his hand. The twenty-two other trainees moved to the perimeter of the big ring. It would take at least twice as many, holding outstretched hands to close the perimeter of the ring.

Nagora spit in her hands and rubbed them together. I know the rules. Why do you think I'm late? She stepped to the center of the ring, gripped the small end of her body-length staff. She set the big end in the sand, an arm's length away from her, and, as she looked at the trainees, she turned slowly to draw a circle in the sand around her.

One by one, she pointed to Pug's five toads and finally, to Pug himself.

Randsord waved to stop them from coming forward. "The rules say three against one."

"I figured because I'm so late, I deserve double." Randsord's eyes narrowed as he seemed to consider what she had said. He looked from her to the six she had picked.

Aye, I chose the biggest.

He looked back at her. "As you wish." He backed away to the edge of the ring.

Pug wore a smirk as he and his cronies approached her circle.

They took their positions. You haven't realized it yet, have you, Pug? You've just walked into my trap. Rules say you strike first.

Pug did.

Nagora warded off his blow, rolled back, pressed into the nearest attacker, knocking him on his ass. Five to go.

She pushed the next one into another, who fell. Four to go.

She pulled the staff of the one she had just pushed and took him out with an elbow strike. Three to go.

Now they had room to maneuver and strike. She didn't hesitate. A hard shoulder strike to the one waiting for Pug's orders had him reeling until he fell. Two.

She advanced on Pug.

He came at her with fury on his face.

Nagora retreated while taking a quick look left in time to ward off a blow to her back. Gazing right she braced and held her center balance to use the momentum of Pug's charge to pull him with her as she rolled back to throw him against his partner. They hit the ground. Pug was on top of his partner. Pug rolled off onto his back and reached for his rod, but she quickly pitched their staffs out of reach with her own. She planted the big end of her staff on Pug's chest and pinned him to the ground.

She looked to Randsord to declare the winner.

He pointed to her. "Nagora wins."

"Sir, what do the rules say happens next?" said Nagora.

Randsord looked down at Pug and then back to her.

She looked down at the loser. "Not your day is it, Pug? Six against one. Looks like you need some practice."

"On your hands and knees, Pug," said Randsord.

Pug spit. "Bitch!"

Nagora backed away as Pug rolled over onto his hands and knees. He crawled around what was left of the circle she had drawn in the sand. Then he crawled to the middle of the circle. She followed him and looked to Randsord.

"Head to the sand, Pug."

Pug brought his elbows down, put his forehead to the sand, and clasped his hands over the back of his head.

She looked around to Pug's friends sitting in the sand well beyond the edge of her circle. "My, oh, my! Pug, right now, your fat ass is looking pretty vulnerable. Too bad you hit the ground last. What's the rule say, Pug? Last one down takes a whack for each one the winner knocks down. Counting you,

Pug. I think you can count. Can't you? That makes six whacks, Pug. Six 'Tar Baby' whacks."

Nagora spit in her right hand before taking hold of the big end of her staff. She backed away from Pug's side until the small end could reach across his backside. She spread her legs and bent her knees slightly to center her balance. She brought her arm back so her staff pointed to the sky. Then she swung it down with all her might.

Pug screamed, and his body lurched forward onto the sand.

Tar piss! Pug, I bet that hurt you. She waited until Pug brought his sorry ass up before she raised her staff for the second whack. She didn't hold back. She put all her strength into each hit.

It sounded like Pug couldn't hold back. He put all his breath into each scream.

As Pug crawled over to his friends, she stood with the big end of her staff resting on the toe of her boot and looked around the circle at the other trainees. They were quiet. Many of them wore smiles, especially those who had suffered bullying from Pug's gang.

Randsord stepped into the ring. "A fine demonstration. Lessons learned from it?" He looked around at the trainees. "Anyone?"

"Speed of execution." The words were barely audible.

Randsord repeated them. "What else?"

"She always knew where each attacker was." These words were louder.

"Yes. And?"

"She never lost her balance and used their attacks against them." Spoken with confidence.

"Oh yes. Anything else?"

"Smart thinking. Surprise. They thought they had the advantage. But it was a trap. They were too close to each other at the beginning to use their staffs well. Nagora had a plan from the beginning. She took good advantage of their early weakness and their overconfidence. She thinks well on her feet. And she's truly strong. Her staff's an extension of her. She didn't waste any moves. She must practice every day on her own. She's so confident." Little Ben, the youngest trainee, had spoken bravely. Her ears burned from his compliments. She gave him a smile and a thumbs-up.

Randsord held out a hand. "I couldn't have said it better myself. There you have it. You don't gain that kind of skill by only showing up here to practice. Pair up and get to it."

Sixteen trainees crowded around her. "Teach us," they clamored.

Nagora held up a hand, backed away a few paces, and waited for quiet. "I can't teach you everything I do. Not today. Today, I'll give you some simple advice. It'll be your starting point. It may sound stupid to you today, but you'll come to see its worth later on." For a moment she caught herself speaking the very words Uncle had used with her years ago. They were wise words, and today she was glad she had heeded them.

She held up her staff. "Okay. Here's what I want you to do." She paused to make sure they were all looking at her. "From now on, wherever you go, whatever you do, no matter what, you're going to carry your staff with you. Bring it to bed with you, to the latrine, to your table when you eat. Bring it with you wherever you go to do chores. Sounds stupid, I know, but that's how you're going to learn the limits of the spaces you can use it to not only defend yourself, but to use as a tool to help you do all kinds of things."

Nagora stepped over to Little Ben and put a hand on his shoulder. "Ben said my staff is an extension of me. That doesn't happen overnight. You must have it with you all the time until you're completely comfortable taking it anywhere. You'll learn where to put it so it's never more than a step away from you.

"The day you realize you've carried your staff with you all day without thinking about where or how to hold it; or where to put it so it doesn't fall over and hit people or knock things over; and when no one has told you to be careful with it; that's the day you'll be able to say your staff is part of you, an extension of you.

"When that day arrives, you'll know you're ready to start learning to use it as a weapon. It won't be the same day for each of you. For some it'll happen sooner than you think. For others, it'll take months."

Nagora looked from the slack-jawed lads, who were still drinking in her words, over to Randsord who stood alone on the edge of the ring. He nodded as he looked down at the mark his boot left in the sand as it swung back and forth. Never saw it that way, did you? It's never too late to learn.

Nagora looked back to the boys. "How about working on your balance today? You've got two arms, two knees, two feet, two hands, two elbows, two shoulders, and one head. I want you to practice balancing the small end of your staff from each one of those. Spread out around the ring and watch out for those around you. You don't want to go bonking someone or get bonked. Have fun and keep at it."

As they spread out, Nagora placed the small end of her staff to her forehead and leaned back to hold it in balance for a few moments. When she let it fall into her hand, sixteen lads got busy trying to imitate her.

Pug shuffled around the outer ring. He rubbed his rear end with both hands. His eyes were to the ground. His five followers didn't seem to know what to do. They had picked up their staffs and were standing in a loose group. One of them seemed to be edging away from them. When he looked up, Nagora made eye contact with him. He had been the first to fall. She smiled as she held his gaze. He smiled back and moved to a spot in the ring where he balanced his rod. Now I've got seventeen followers, Pug. I can't wait to see if the others will remain loyal in the days to come.

Later in the afternoon, Nagora found the doors to Geirador's shop open, but only the smell of cold charcoal ash and iron from the forge greeted her. Outside, Geirador's wagon wasn't parked in its usual place near the stable, and Big Bart, his mule, wasn't in the corral. They're using two wagons to haul charcoal. Pare must be home.

Nagora headed for Geirador's hut, almost three hundred paces away, set among the trees against a high cliff wall. It looked so small from the corral. Just a poor smithy's hut. That's what Geirador wanted strangers to see. But not to her, it was her second home. The door was open, and the aroma of biscuits poured out and pulled her in. Nagora leaned her staff on the wall next to the door step.

"Pare." Her eyes adjusted to the dimmer inside light. "There you are."

"Nagora!" Pare put down the wooden spoon and bowl and moved to her with open arms.

She held Pare close for a long moment, breathing in her scent, a mix of warm bread, caraway, and rosemary. When she let her go, Pare's smiling eyes and mouth greeted her.

"Good to see you, Little Sister," said Pare.

That smile and those two sincere words made her heart swell. She held onto Pare's hands. "Good to see you too, Pare. Seems the older I get, the less I see of you."

Pare pulled their hands up to her chin as she leaned closer. "Stay for supper then. I'll not have a problem convincing Dangor to stay. He and Da'll be hungry when they get back."

I want to accept. The catching up we would have to do.

"Pare, I'd love to, but I've chores to do. Hides to hang in the hut. Soup to make. Garden fence to shore up."

Pare wrapped her arms around her and swayed her in a little dance. "Well, next time there won't be any excuses. You'll have to spend the night. We'll talk until a candle burns out. Promise." Pare squeezed her tight.

"Promise, Pare." Something to look forward to. Oh, the stories Pare would tell when they were in bed. "Can I fill my waterskin with some fresh water?"

"Of course. Let me do it for you. Sit and have a biscuit. I expect you'll be taking the forest trail. Running it as usual. You know, Nagora, I could lend you a horse. Da wouldn't mind."

Nagora held a biscuit to her nose and inhaled. "Your biscuits smell so good, Pare."

"You're supposed to bite into it, Nagora, not sniff it."

"Uncle would mind. He says I can have a horse when I can buy one, feed it, and give it proper care."

Pare looked back at her from the big earthenware crock. She held the waterskin in one hand and turned the spigot with the other. "Well, what are you waiting for?"

"We have to build a proper stable. He says Patches' shelter isn't enough. Bad enough we have to bring Patches and the goats into the lodge on the coldest nights in winter. There wouldn't be enough room for a horse too. A stable would take care of that problem."

Pare set the filled skin on the table. "Pester Dangor. He'll build one. He built your lodge. He can build anything he sets his mind to."

"What do you think I've been doing? He's got all these curraghs to build. The stable can wait he says. No rush. Besides, he says I need to be able to run long distances.

"It's that warrior way of thinking he has. You're only as good as the weapon you have at hand. A well thrown stone that hits its mark is better than an arrow that misses. Your own legs, if you know their limits, can take you places where a horse can't. Could be the difference between life and death. So it's run girl, run."

Pare leaned onto the table with both hands. "Well, Little Sister, he's talking from experience. As a scout and the lead archer in Good King Bernhard's forces, he spent more time on foot than on his horse from the stories we've heard him tell at this table. But just between us, Nagora, I've overheard him and Da discussing plans for a stable. If you ask me it's in the works and it could get built sooner than you think."

"Truly, Pare?" Nagora couldn't believe her ears. This day was turning out to be one of the best in a long while. She could bargain a good price from Geirador. Which of the mounts weren't already spoken for? He provided mounts to the queen's cavalry at a hefty price. Never talked about that openly though. When someone brought it up, he seemed to fight back a smile. Why would he smile?

I like Kimmo, the only one with three white socks.

And trusty Jarra even if she's shorter than Kimmo. Dark brown with a black mane. The black on her back ran down her sides and melded into the brown on her belly, legs and knees where it became black again. She could do anything she wanted with Jarra. She had even trained her so she could hang to the side from her saddle to shoot her bow. The sound of her bow string's thrum didn't bother Jarra in the least.

Oh! The new one Geirador hasn't broken in yet. A young stallion with Jarra's colors. He had grow to be taller than Jarra. Maybe Geriador would let her break him in. He wouldn't have that to do. Could be a deal maker. Naw, that would never happen. Tar piss! To be so lucky.

"Got you dreaming, did I? Here, open your scrip. In case you get hungry on the way." Pare had wrapped a half dozen biscuits in a piece of cloth. "And save one for Dangor. I'll check to see you did. Eat the one in your hand before you leave."

"Yes, Mum." She bit into the biscuit. "I'll have trouble sleeping tonight. How will I choose a horse? I've been spoiled, training with you and your da. Except for the new one, I've ridden them all and more over the years."

"Stable comes first, Nagora."

Her own horse. Go anywhere faster, whenever, for no other reason than to be with her horse. Something about them. They returned the love she gave them. They thrived on that as much as Nagora did. Unconditional love. They understood her. They listened to all her secrets and fears and wishes and hopes. Now she could truly dream of having one to call her own. What would she name it?

She finished her biscuit.

"Drink up. You'll run stronger with this in your belly." Pare set a small bowl of goat's milk on the table in front of her.

"Yes, Mum." She did. The smooth richness of it filled her mouth. Pare had taught her about kissing. She had said something about real kissing being sweet and warm like fresh goat's milk. But Nagora hadn't the courage to actually kiss a boy. Anyway, Pare had made her promise to save her first kiss for a handsome lad who would make her dream about him. That one hadn't come along yet.

When Nagora stood up, Pare slipped her waterskin over her head, onto her shoulder, so it hung at her back. "Thanks for the biscuits, the milk, the water, and for giving me something to dream about."

Pare smiled and gave her shoulders a squeeze before pulling her into a hug. "Little Sister, remember your promise—next time you spend the night. Good speed on the trail. Dream well tonight."

Nagora held on to Pare, breathed in the scent of her hair and closed her eyes for a moment. I'll dream of my horse and

I'll dream of the rides we'll go on together, Pare. "Time to go."

Nagora paused at the corral fence to look at the horses before heading down the road from the smithy. The new stallion. What would she name him if he were hers?

A little farther along the road, Nagora took the uphill path to the forest trail that would take her home quicker than by the road. As soon as she reached the trail, she ran with her staff in one hand. Slowly, she picked up her pace. She was light on her feet, happy with the day's events, and her growing chances of owning a horse.

Almost at the halfway point, Nagora came to the pines. She loved the smell and the quiet of her footfalls on the cushion of needles covering the forest floor there. But it was too quiet and, before she could slow down to take in her surroundings, she ran into a net.

Someone must've thrown it. It tripped her. She fell hard. Tar piss! They pinned her down, as well as her staff, and, before she could reach for her knife, pairs of hands had grabbed her wrists. Other hands held her ankles while others held her head against the ground. She could only see with her right eye as a hand pressed her cheek hard into the pine needles. At least three of them! She struggled, but they held her pinned. Four of them! "Ouch!" Someone came down heavy and hard on her back.

"Lookee the fish we caught us, lads."

"Pug!" Her blood boiled. I'll have your balls for this.

A hand joined the two already pushing down on her head. Pug put his weight on the side of her head. For a moment his fat face loomed into view. Nagora tried her best to buck and pull free. Pug held the blade of a knife to her cheek just below her eye. She froze.

"Where ya running to, Tar Baby?"

She couldn't speak. The heel of a hand pushed down hard on her jaw.

"Now, if ya don't want to get hurt, ya have to let go of yer staff. This is yer knife."

She didn't dare move. Her heart beat faster with each breath she inhaled.

Pug tapped the side of her nose with the knife's blade. She tasted the bile rising in her throat. "We've got ya. You're not going anywhere. Make it easy on yerself, Tar Baby. Cooperate. We're going to turn you over."

Nagora let go of her staff.

Pug pushed himself up off her. He took the staff. "Turn her over."

Nagora let them, but they still held her to the ground, one on each arm and leg.

"Pug, you're going to regret this."

Pug straddled her, pressed the big end of her staff against her chest, and stared down at her. "If ya know what's good for ya, ya won't say another word."

She stared back. What are you going to do? You useless toad! Keep it to yourself. You just might get out of this. Don't give him any fuel. Damn it! The stars know you've given him plenty already.

Pug let himself down until he straddled her thighs. He threw her staff a dozen paces away.

Should I breathe easier?

Pug held up the knife.

Nagora swallowed, and her breaths came quicker. She followed it as he slowly brought it down.

Pug cut through the knots of the net. "Gotta get a closer look at our catch. What do we have here, lads?" He pulled up her shirt. "Lookee, lads. Tar Baby has two raisins. No apples." He pinched and pulled one hard until it pulled away from his fingers.

She clenched her teeth. She refused to scream. But she couldn't stop herself from spitting in his face.

"Bitch!" Pug struck her face with the back of his hand and laughed.

The blood in her mouth tasted like the copper ladle in their water jar. Her tongue found the gash on the inside of her cheek. I swear, if I get out of this, you're going to pay. Oh, are you ever going to pay.

"Could be we find nuts down here." Pug's eyes were as wide as his smile.

Pug pulled the bow knot at her waist.

Nagora let her head fall back. This can't be happening. She closed her eyes and tensed every muscle in her body. He thrust his hand into her under garment and forced it between her legs. She opened her eyes in time to see the smile on his face disappear.

He withdrew his hand. "Shit." He wiped his four bloodied fingers across her face. "Flip the bitch over." He stood and helped them.

...

Nagora tried to kick and pull free, to hold back her tears. She gritted her teeth and willed the flood to stop. Be strong.

When they had her on her stomach, Pug straddled her thighs with his knees. He pulled down her undergarment.

Pug must've untied his crotch piece, because the next instant he was on her, trying to push into her.

With all her might she tensed her muscles and held her breath, the only thing she could do to try to stop him. How long would she be able to hold? She had not been trained for something like this.

Pug pulled hard on her braid and continued to grind into her bum until he grunted and spent. He went limp on her back, let go of her braid, and lay on her for a long moment.

Nagora expelled all the air from her lungs in one long growl. Pine needles beneath her face jumped. Motherless toad. I swear you'll be cockless soon.

Pug pushed himself up from her back.

She looked back. His hand reached down to his boot and pulled her knife from it. He grabbed her braid and pulled it back, harder this time. The pain from the strain on her neck almost choked her.

What in the stars was he doing?

The answer resonated through her scalp into her head as he sawed through her plait. You bastard! Just you wait. You won't believe it.

She held back her scream. You won't get that pleasure.

He tore the last strands of her uncut braid out. It made her eyes water. Her face and ears and neck were burning hot. Nothing like he'll be when I get a hold of him.

"Ya tell what we done, ya don't live another day." Pug stood and put her braid in his scrip.

The crony holding her left arm let it go. When he came back, he held a bow with an arrow nocked.

Pug stepped over next to him.

Nagora looked up at Pug while he tied his crotch piece. "We let ya go. Stay on yer belly. Count a hundred before ya get up. Get up before, there'll be arrows in yer back." He reached down to his boot, took her knife, and threw it at the tree nearest her, where it stuck. "Start counting."

Nagora stumbled into the stream behind her home. She had run all the way, fighting back her tears. But now, as she stripped off her clothes, she bawled. Her chest heaved as she struck at the water with both hands. "Damn you, Pug! Damn you!" Her arms flailed from side to side as her fists ripped across the surface until her screams turned into a wail, and she fell to her knees.

When Nagora caught her breath, and her sobs began to settle, she clenched her jaw and bared her teeth. Why didn't I see them? Why did I fall into his trap? I knew he would want to get even. Why didn't I expect it to happen on the trail? I let my guard down. Misplaced trust in myself. She struck the water again with her fists.

She dunked her head and scrubbed her face with both hands, hoping to remove the blood smears. She lifted her head and spit out a mouthful of water. She scooped up more, drank it in, and blew it out her nose. She tasted fresh blood. She touched her cheek. It was tender and hurt.

Nagora splashed and rubbed water over the rest of her body. She had stopped bleeding down there. Perhaps her run had let it all out. She stood and went to retrieve the garments she had flung to the bank of the stream. Her linen undergarment would have to soak in salt water. A plan began to form.

She rubbed silt from the streambed into her leather leggings before rinsing them clean. She rinsed her shirt, bundled the leggings and undergarment into it, grabbed her boots, scrip, and staff, and made her way to the lodge.

After hanging the wet garments to dry near the fireplace and getting into a fresh change of clothes, Nagora set two bowls on the table. She turned hers over and stuck the handle of her spoon under it, their agreed-upon sign she wouldn't be back for the night. It usually meant she had gone hunting. *I'll be hunting alright, but not for the usual game.*

Nagora climbed up to the loft to dress and get a scarf to tie her hair so it stayed out of her face. Already she missed her hair. Her habit of swinging her braid in place on her back was now an awkward toss of her head, and her hands came away empty when they reached behind her. *How soon would those old habits disappear?*

Back at ground level of their lodge, Nagora took her bow and quiver from the wooden cabinet where they kept their weapons. Before setting them on her chair, she did a quick check of the string and arrows.

Then she removed the packet of biscuits from her scrip. She put two in Uncle's bowl before going to their dry food box for raisins, shelled nuts, and several strips of dried venison. These went into her scrip.

Nagora slipped her sheepskin vest onto her shoulders, then her scrip, waterskin, and quiver. With her bow in hand, she took a last look at the table. Uncle shouldn't worry. She would hang the hides in the beach hut and spend the night there. She would be safe. Before daylight she would be on her way to track her quarry. He would not be expecting her.

The next morning, Nagora had Pug's arms wrapped around a tree, tied at the wrists. One of Pug's sidekicks knelt on the ground next to the tree with one of his wrists tied between his two ankles. His free hand held Pug's pants down.

Nagora held her knife between Pug's legs, pressing the blade's cutting edge upward. "Not a word. Say one word, Pug, and you lose it."

He cried. His whole body shook. And I've only just begun.

"Careful, you're cutting yourself." She kicked Pug's friend. "Lookee, lad. Nothing worth cutting here, is there?" She kicked him again. "Is there?"

Pug's crony shook his head. "Na … na … naw."

Pug cried louder.

Nagora pulled her blade back ever so slow. Pug cried even louder. So scared you can't even speak. You poor toad. She brought the knife up so Pug could see the tiny trickle of blood along the length of the blade. His eyes grew wider as he blinked away tears. Is that fear I see? Wait you bastard. You haven't tasted fear yet.

She walked around to his hands. "Spread your fingers on the trunk, Pug. Don't you dare tell me you can't."

Pug cried louder, but still did as told.

Nagora moved Pug's right hand so his fingers pointed up. She placed the tip of her blade against the second joint of his middle finger, hard enough to steady its shake. "This much's about what you got down there." She brought the palm of her other hand to the heel of the handle of her knife. She peeked around the side of the tree. "Isn't that so, Pug?"

His eyes blinked, and his lips trembled as he looked at her.

Nagora leaned onto her knife handle, and Pug screamed.

She looked back at the piece of finger resting on her blade. Ever so slowly, she wiggled the blade to release it from the bark of the tree.

She held it before his terrified eyes. "Pug, you got a choice. Swallow it or have your friend here shove it up your arse. Either way, it's going to come back out that way."

Try as he might, Pug couldn't swallow it.

Nagora held the blade against his trembling lower lip. "Easy now. Spit it back on the blade." He had trouble bringing it to the front of his mouth. "Bend your head forward. Open your mouth. Wider. There you go, Pug." She pulled her knife aside just in time.

Pug gagged and choked.

"Get a hold of yourself, Pug." He coughed and spit up phlegm and blood. Pug, I wouldn't mind watching you choke to death on your own fear. I bet you never dreamt payback would be like this. Never in all your bullying days.

Once he got control of himself, she held her blade out to Pug's accomplice. "I made Pug a promise. Do it."

Nagora knocked Pug on the side of his head. "Look at me, Pug. I didn't tell. Will you tell, Pug?" Just as he shook his head, his eyes became two big tear-filled pools, and his jaw dropped.

"Done," said Pug's stooge.

"Good work. Don't lick your fingers.

"Pug, I know you'll tell. I just know it. Next time, I won't just nick you down there. Believe me, next time, you'll swallow it, even if I have to make you chew on it for two days."

Banished
Wepinikewin

Two days later, Nagora returned from the stream with two buckets of water hanging from the ropes of the wooden yoke on her shoulders. She paused for a moment as she came around the side of their lodge. Geirador's horse, Caim, was tied to the hitching post a dozen paces from the door. Do I go in and face him? Act as if the matter is done with?

She bent her knees to lower the buckets to the ground, slipped the yoke off, and rested it on them.

She went over to Caim. "You're looking good, big boy." She reached up to pet the side of his strong neck. "I haven't ridden you in a while. Have I?" She rubbed his broad nose. "End of summer last year when Geirador came with Pare. You enjoyed the beach, didn't you? And the swim. That was a treat for you and Jarra. Wasn't it?" She let Caim nuzzle her neck.

"What if I take you and run away with you, Caim? Just the two of us. Where would we go? Away from all of this? Hide in the mountains? Then I'd be in deeper trouble, wouldn't I? It wouldn't be right for me to do that to you. Anyway, they'd find us." She kissed Caim's nose and gave him a last pat.

Nagora made her way to the door and stopped before going in. Uncle's voice came through the door. " … hardly a word from her since she came back. Mind you, when I saw her hair, I knew something had happened. It almost broke my heart. She loved her long hair. Loved having me braid it for her. It was our special time together. She closed right up. She won't tell her version of the events."

Pug and his lying witnesses. I would just as soon be done with them. Tomorrow I'll know.

Geirador said, "So she's lived up to the names they call her, 'Stone' and 'Loner.' Some'll say she acted like a lone wolf.

"They call her that too."

I am *Ka Peyakot Mahihkan*. I fight my own battles. Her words made her stand straight.

"There's more to what happened to her than we'll probably ever know," said Uncle.

I only have the stars as witnesses. When I die and go there, my ancestors'll come forward and speak for me. The scales will tip in my favor.

Since they were talking about her, she turned to leave, but changed her mind and returned to the door. Geirador spoke. "He wants you to tell her. He says she should know. You know, in case."

"I don't agree. It won't change a thing. She doesn't need to know. It's better she not know. I trust her. She'll be able to do it. If he wants her to know, he can come tell her himself."

Tell me what? I'm going in. Nagora turned to fetch the buckets and came back. She banged one against the door before setting it down to lift the latch.

The door swung open. Geirador handed a leather-wrapped bundle to Uncle. They both looked at her.

"Geirador. Uncle." She forced a smile as she set the pails on the earthen floor.

They returned her smile. Geirador stepped toward her with his arms open. "Nagora. Good to see you."

She took his hug. When he let her go, he was looking at her hair. She pulled her scarf from her head to let her scraggly mop spring free. She turned once to give him a complete view of the damage.

"That Pug is one sore loser. You beat him and his gang by the rules." Geirador shook his head.

She clenched her teeth, not as hard as she would have liked to. Her jaw hurt, and her cheek was still swollen. A sore loser and a pig is what he is.

Before she could speak, not that she wanted to, Geirador did. "Listen Nagora, I'll not dance around this because I think you have a pretty good idea of what your sentence will be tomorrow. This morning, after hearing the accusations against you and what the witnesses say they saw, I sat with those who'll decide your fate based on your actions. Because you didn't speak in your own defense, it looks like you'll be facing some kind of banishment."

Thanks for giving me something to say. "Even if I'd spoken, without a witness to my actions, my words wouldn't have weighed in the balance. I'm not a man. And I don't want to be labeled a liar too. Someday the stars'll speak for me. Until then I accept my fate. Pug'll have to live with the conse-

quences of his own lying words." I'm going to keep my promise, Pug.

Geirador placed a hand on her shoulder, looked over at
Uncle, and then back at her. "There's honor in your heart,
Nagora. May it prove to serve you well in the future."

I don't think it's called honor.

"Dangor, I'll be on my way. See you tomorrow morning."

Her eyes followed Geirador as he rode away on Caim. Will
I ever have a horse of my own? Right now it doesn't look like
it.

Nagora stood at the top of the training ring, at the position
of the guiding star. How fitting. This is where I'll get my direction.

Opposite her, the other trainees lined the edge of the ring,
except for Pug. He stood alone to the side of the ring where
the sun rose, to her right, holding his bandaged right hand
with his left.

Opposite Pug stood Randsord, to her left. Looks like he'll
be delivering my sentence.

Behind Randsord, many onlookers had gathered. Pare was
among them, with her smiling eyes and face showing support.
Geirador and Uncle were just behind Pare. As Nagora's gaze
moved among the others, she found some faces she recognized, mostly parents of the other trainees.

When she looked over at Pug, he hung his head. Only six
people stood behind him outside of the ring. How are you
feeling, Pug? Enjoy your cock while you have it. I'm going to
keep the last promise I made you.

She looked to the center of the ring at the line in the sand.
It extended from the base of the staff that had been planted

upright. The shadow of the stick edged closer to the line. When it did, Randsord would pronounce her sentence.

The shadow crept to the line. Now. Nagora took a deep breath and stared at Pug.

"Nagora, you are banished from Cairnmase for one hundred days for your actions against The Cause. Have you anything to say for your actions?" It was Randsord's voice.

She shook her head, but kept her gaze on Pug. He never looked up. You don't dare, do you? A long moment of silence followed. Movement caught her eye. Little Ben came forward and pulled the staff from the sand. He held it above his head with one hand while, with his other hand, he made a fist at his heart and saluted her.

Her chest swelled and, as she fought back her tears, applause erupted from behind Randsord.

She looked back to Pug. He slunk out of the ring following those who had stood behind him. They had already turned to leave.

Nagora had remained quiet on the ride home. Uncle had left her to her thoughts, most likely waiting until she opened up. She would have to. Surely, he would have something to say about the banishment. A hundred days. She could probably spend most her time at the beach, building curraghs. It would go by fast. Mostly the nicest days of summer. She would get to swim almost every day. And fish. She would practically live there.

Would Pare come to visit? She had never gone so long without seeing her. Were there rules about being banished?

...

Nagora took Patches' bridle off and released him into the pasture. She slid the two gate poles in place and went to meet Uncle.

Nagora found him inside their lodge at the table. He had her sheepskin vest spread out, hide side up. He held a fine brush in one hand and a small bowl of liquid tar in the other. The smell was unmistakable, even with the mint and mead Uncle had mixed in with it. She pulled a chair alongside him. "What are you doing?"

"Drawing a map."

"On my vest?"

"So you don't lose it. You're going to need it."

"And what if I don't want to go wherever that map's supposed to take me?"

"You've been banished. You can't stay here. I'm one of the trainee instructors. You can't be in my company for a hundred days."

"I can stay at the beach hut."

"I work there too. Besides, it's about time you see the country you'll be fighting for someday. Better you have something to do while you're away. You'll learn plenty and feel useful."

Hold on! What's this about? "Uncle. Wait. What do you mean, I'm going to have something to do? Do what?"

"An important job for The Cause."

Important? He can't be serious. She threw up her hands. "Aye! Right! I know as much as the queen and I've committed actions against The Cause. And I'm being given this important job? That doesn't make sense."

He didn't stop to look at her. "And that's why you're perfectly qualified for the job; you know so little about The Cause. That, and because of the skills you have to take care of yourself."

Hold on! So that makes me qualified? "So what is it I have to do?"

"Start by preparing a pack with at least five days worth of food rations. Then choose the biggest waterskin you'll feel comfortable carrying. You'll be traveling on foot."

Should I start worrying or not? Uncle seems so calm and matter of fact about it. What is it he always says about warriors going into battle? Focus on those things you can control, your weapons. Let the leaders worry about the big plan. Do your part to the best of your abilities. "What about weapons?"

"Prepare your quiver. Arrows to hunt with, a couple of blunt-tipped ones, three fire arrows, and a whistle arrow or two. And some war arrows."

War arrows! This is getting serious. "And my bow?"

"I've got a new one for you. I'll show it to you later. When you see it, you'll understand why."

Tar piss! I'm starting to worry. Shit. Will I remember everything Uncle's taught me? Something in the pit of her stomach churned. Still, she couldn't wait to find out more. That was Uncle. He had pricked her curiosity. A hundred days on my own, on a mission of my own.

"Oh. Nagora, do you think you can make yourself look like a boy? Dress like one? Act like one? You're going to have to try to think like one so you can pass for one in the presence of strangers."

Hold on! Uncle? Well. She scratched her head and looked at her hands. They didn't look like Pare's. Tar stained. Tar under her nails. Calloused. They were more like a boy's and stronger than most of those she had trained with. And she dressed like them, most of the time. Only rarely did she ever wear a dress with apron and shawl. "Aye, I can do that." She pretended to spit. "Shit. Shouldn't be much of a problem, aye?"

Uncle flashed her a quick smile. "Give yourself a name you won't forget. You'll have to become him. Your life'll depend on it. Now get to it so I can finish the map."

My life'll depend on it? What'll I be doing? What could it be? Who'll I become? A name to remember? Enough. Focus. The answers will come. Clothes first.

Nagora climbed the ladder to the loft and flipped open the lid to the wooden trunk at the foot of her bed. The leather leggings with the baggy knees and fat stains. The big hooded linen shirt with worn elbow holes in the sleeves and the frayed cuffs. The faded green woolen tam. She threw each on her bed. They were worn, but clean. They were to be her next set of work clothes.

She looked at them. Uncle always put out word to his customers for any secondhand clothes suitable for their dirty work. He always kept spares on hand, and she always had first pick. For any that didn't fit, he found takers for them in Cairnmase. Who's the guy that's going to wear these?

Next, she chose three clean undergarments, three pairs of wool socks, and three rolls of linen strips for her bleedings.

She changed into her boy clothes. After tucking most of her hair under the tam, she pulled out strands to let them hang over her forehead and sides of her face. The sole of her boot provided her with dirt to smudge on her chin, nose, and neck.

Nagora chose a leather pack. What was left on the bed went into it. Slinging it over her shoulder, she reached for the ladder.

Nagora walked over to the table. "G'day, Dangor."

"Good day, Na—What'd you say your name was?"

She crossed her arms in front of her and stood with her legs spread wide. "Tars is my name. Buildin' curraghs' my game." The name had come to her just as she climbed down the ladder.

"You planning on being in these parts for a while?"

"Nope. Movin' on. Goin' to see if I can make my luck elsewhere. Why you askin'?"

"I could use your skills. I'm going to be short-handed for a while."

"You pay well?"

"A hard coin for a solid day's work. And I'll feed you and give you a roof to sleep under."

"If ever I'm back this way, I'll take you up on your offer."

"Good, Tars." He looked her up and down. "Now get your rations packed and quiver filled." He dipped his brush into the liquid tar.

Let's go, Tars. We can do this.

From the dry box Nagora pulled dried beef strips, dried berries, shelled nuts, a small bag of buckwheat flour, another of ground oats, some salt, and a palm size piece of honeycomb. There we go, Tars. We'll get these wrapped and then prep the quiver.

She filled a small copper cooking pot with most of the food packets, capped it with a smaller copper bowl, and shoved a wooden spoon in along the side. She easily wrestled these into her pack.

Nagora set her pack on the floor next to the hutch where they kept their weapons. She retrieved two arrows, both of which stood with their tips pointing up. These, Tars, are whistle arrows. She pointed to the tip of one. This is the whistle's reed. Uncle makes these in secret, so you'll keep what I tell you for yourself.

Shoot it up in the air. She held the arrow higher. When it's done its climb, it tips over to come back down. She tipped it. The reed slid forward on the tip of the arrow's shaft. A small chip of wood fell to the floor. When that happens, the reed opens. As the arrow starts coming down faster, the whistle starts to scream until the arrow hits the ground. She brought it down fast. Believe me, it screams fierce. I've heard it. We can use it as a signal or to create a distraction. Or like Uncle says, to scare the shits out of people. They have no idea where the scream is coming from, and it just gets louder until the arrow hits.

She readjusted the reed and put the chip back. She sighted down the shaft and ran her thumb along the sides of the feathers with enough pressure to check that their glued string whippings held them tight to the shaft and were intact. She placed the two whistle arrows tips up into one of the side separators of her quiver.

She checked ten hunting arrows before adding them to their section. And then a dozen broad tipped war arrows, like the one she had used to persuade Pug and his friend to go to the forest with her. She pointed to one of the broad tips with its razor-sharp barbs. Hurts like you wouldn't believe, Tars. Does lots of damage because to get one out, it has to be either pushed on through, if it can be, or cut out of the wound.

That's why Uncle limps. Got hit in the calf muscle with an Outlander arrow when fighting for Good King Bernhard's forces years ago. Lucky for him a medic came across him. That was Geirador. Broke the feathers off, smeared the shaft with salve, and then hammered it out the other side. Uncle says it hurt so much, he passed out. Woke up on a wagon with a bandage on his leg. He and Geirador are best friends since that day.

She had a special place in her quiver for them. It kept their tips from nicking each other.

Nagora reached back into their weapons hutch for two blunt-tipped arrows. Tars, see these flat leather covered tips. There's a small pebble inside to give it some weight and this blunt surface. Hit a horse's rump with one of these, you can bet it'll buck. Could even surprise the rider and knock him off his mount. Get hit on your arse with one, Tars, it'll smart for days. I'll be back in a moment.

Nagora leaned over Uncle's shoulder. "So Dangor, how's that map comin'?"

He glanced up at her. "How's your packing going, Tars?"

"Clothes done, rations done, quiver's near done. Just the fire arrows to add."

"Leave the sand-covered outer strip on. You don't want a fire arrow to stay stuck in your quiver."

Uncle pointed to the map with the handle of his brush. "Almost done." Then he pointed it at her. "Did I tell you to prepare a bedroll and a rain cape?"

"No, but I will. How about a small tarp instead? It'd be lighter than a big waxed woolen rain cape."

He scratched his chin with the brush handle. "True. Since you'll be on foot. Wrap your bedroll in it. Tie it the bottom of your pack. And bring a net, in case you have to sleep in a tree."

Nagora winked at Uncle and gave him a thumbs-up as she backed away. "Will do, Dangor."

From the hutch, Nagora pulled out the bucket of sand containing the fire arrows. Burying the tips in the sand helped keep the smell of their damp, tar-soaked cloth strips to a minimum. And it reduced their chances of accidentally catching fire. Tars, when one of these is lit, it can be lethal. Wherever it sticks, it can't be put out by dousing it with water. Nope. It has to be pulled out and dunked under water or jabbed into the ground. Don't even think of stamping on it to put it out. Ha! The molten tar'll stick to your boot and set you on fire. Bloody dangerous they are.

She pulled three from the sand, gently tapped them on the edge of the pail to knock off the excess sand. See Tars, you just have to pull this outer strip off, nock it to your bowstring, hold it to a flame, and shoot at your target.

Nagora walked to the saddle room at the far end of the big room of their living space. The narrow bed Uncle slept on was right next to the curtained doorway. She pushed the curtain aside and crossed the small space to open the outer door. It would give her more light.

As she looked around for a tarp, she rested her hand on her saddle. I've got this, but no horse. She would only used it on horses Uncle borrowed from Geirador when he took her on long training rides to scout forest trails, and to hunt for deer to shore up the meat larder they shared with Geirador at his place.

Geirador had a huge cold room and root cellar under his hut. There was even a tiny underground stream that puddled to the surface in there. Obviously, that's why he chose to build there. Cold drinking water right at hand. It rarely froze over. Only on the coldest days of winter.

Tars, you're going to have meet Paruline. I call her Pare. She's my best friend. We're close. I'm sure you'll fall in love with her deep brown eyes. I'm going to miss her. We'll make up for lost time come winter. That's our visiting time. Pare's the one who's taught me the most about reading and writing. I still have lots to learn though. She makes it fun.

When they come here, it's to ice fish in the bay. They stay for a few days and then we go visit them a while later. We cook and eat and knit and tell stories.

Wouldn't you know it, Tars. It's right here. Her saddle was on the tarp. Her bedroll was on the shelf next to the inner door. She took the tarp and two coils of rope, one smaller than the other. Rope's always handy to have, Tars. I'd bring more, but the load's already getting heavy.

She rolled the canvas tarp tightly around her bedroll before tying it to the bottom of her pack. It would make a lean-to just big enough for her to sleep under. She could cover herself with it in a downpour. And it would dry out quick enough.

...

Nagora rested her quiver against her pack and slowly walked over to the table. She was just about ready. Questions at the back of her mind came forward. What is it Uncle doesn't want me to know? Who's the person that thinks I should know it? Know what? She hadn't the slightest clue. Should I ask? Uncle said I didn't need to know, that it was better I not know.

"Map's ready." Uncle stood and went to put away the tar pot and brush.

Nagora leaned on the table and looked at the map. She had heard many of the names she read. Other than Cairnmase and Yhorgal, Windhaven was the one to come up most often. The biggest town. "So these are all the towns and villages of our country?"

"Most of them are there. Some of the smaller hamlets aren't." He stood next to her.

She leaned over to place a finger on the map. "Will I be going to the Land of Skulls? I've wondered about the Blood River. It sort of lends itself to the reputation the people from there have." She sensed a longer than usual pause, as if Uncle was considering her question. Or was he weighing his reply?

"No, you'll not be going there." He moved his finger on the map to the mouth of the Blood River.

She sensed the pause again.

He cleared his throat. "The Blood River got its name a long time ago when the kings of the two countries joined forces to defeat Outlander raiding parties that had landed at the mouth of that river. Twenty-five Outlander ships had poured a thousand raiders ashore."

"A thousand raiders! How'd the kings know they were coming?"

"Dragon patrols in the sky spotted them days before their arrival."

So the stories Pare had told her were true.

"They were all slaughtered after following the shallow riverbed inland. Their skulls rest on stakes lining the riverbank on that side. The alliance has held since then."

Uncle cleared his throat again. "Where would you place our beach hut on the map?"

"Easy, Dangor," Nagora said in her best Tars voice. "This is Cairnmase. Yhorgal here. And this finger of land, as you've drawn it, looks just like Sandy Hook. So that's our bay, and our hut would be right about here. Our lodge here. I see no other hooks of land on the map. Lots of bays. What's this—*Wacikâpahkitek*—island down here?" She did not speak the strange word that had come into her mind.

"The Isle of Smoke. The queen's summer fortress is there. You won't be going to visit her."

Another strange word she understood. "It's a volcano."

Uncle looked at her. "How'd you know that, Tars?"

"Why else would it be called the Isle of Smoke?"

His brow furrowed as he leaned his head to one side and nodded. "Mostly steam and a bit of smoke now and then still escape from it."

"Isn't it risky to be living there?"

He sighed. "Some have their reasons. They like living on the edge of danger. Wouldn't be my choice."

She made a fist and tapped his shoulder. "Say, Dangor, just what am I going to be doin'? You know, for The Cause?"

He pointed to the map. "See the town names on the map, Tars? There are quite a few. Eleven of them have a common mark. Can you spot it?"

She looked carefully from name to name, searching for a mark they all shared. *Tar piss! I can't see it. Damn it! What am I missing?* "I don't see it, Uncle."

One by one he placed his thumb on the heel of the first letter of each name.

It was the tiniest of hooks at the foot of each letter. It looked like it belonged on those letters, but other towns with the same beginning letter in their name did not have it. The little hook in the letter could be considered as part of the scribe's brush stroke.

Nagora repeated what he had just done. "The hooks on the letters."

"Aye. Good. You'll be looking for the blacksmith loyal to The Cause in each of those towns." He must've anticipated her question because he held up his hand and pointed to her neck. "Show me the knot that holds the ends of the leather lace of your amulet."

She pulled the knot from behind her neck to her front so she could see it.

"Like you, they'll be wearing, at their necks, a thin leather lanyard with its two ends tied together in a double figure 8 knot, and each separate end will have its own figure 8 knot. Look for the four 8's. They'll be expecting to see four 8's at your neck too, so when you approach one, make sure your amulet hangs down your back."

She looked from the knots to Uncle. "Then what?"

He pushed her vest aside on the table. "Put your scrip on the table."

While she did so, Uncle went to the counter at the wall on the other side of the table. He opened the bundle Geirador had handed him the day before. He brought back another scrip, a little bigger than hers. He dropped it on the table with a loud thunk.

Something heavy in it?

"Empty yours on the table."

Nagora did.

"Now empty this one."

Two pieces of horseshoe fell from the bag, but it was still heavy. Whatever was left in it didn't fall out. She held the flap open, but the pouch appeared to be empty. She moved a hand to the bottom and touched an object within. She took a closer look inside and saw a tab. "Aha! A false bottom."

She reached in and pulled the tab. A piece of chain lay beneath the false-bottom flap. She held the flap aside and, as she poured the chain onto the table, she looked at Uncle.

"So Tars, when you find a smith wearing the four 8's, you'll pull out the broken shoe. The smith'll ask who made it. You'll pull your knife and say, 'The same one who made this blade.'" Uncle motioned for her knife.

Nagora pulled it from the sheath at her belt and set it on the table.

"He'll look for Geirador's brand." Uncle turned the blade over and pointed to the etched circle. It contained three rune symbols. Algiz appeared to hold Raidho on one of its arms and Jera on the other.

Geirador had once told her what the symbols meant to him—*Courage* on the *Journey* brings *Reward*. The circle represented a wheel, as on a wagon, one of the most essential items a good smithy builds and repairs throughout a lifetime.

"A loyal smithy wearing the four 8's will say Geirador's name and then hold out his hand. Tars'll reach into his scrip and pull out the chain." Uncle handed it to her.

The chain was the length of her forearm, eleven links in all, and each big link had a different symbol on it.

"The smithy'll find his link, take the chain to his anvil, and hammer markings on his link with a steel punch. It's in code. Don't ask me what it is or what information it'll convey. I have no idea of the code, and can only guess at what the marks'll mean. Your guess'll be as good as mine.

"You have a hundred days to find those smiths, get their marks on their links, and get the chain back to Geirador. You're not to show the chain to anyone else. No one. Under any circumstances. Understood?"

"That's it? Nothing else?"

"Stay out of trouble. Keep a weather eye on the trails and roads you travel. Find safe places to sleep. Your best bet'll be in the forests and hills outside those towns. Don't hunt on an empty stomach. Use snares as much as possible. Save your arrows for sure shots. Only drink water you find from a stream or spring. No water from town wells."

"So I'll be better off sleeping out of town? I'll aim to get in as early as possible, find the smithy, and then out and away as soon as possible?"

Uncle nodded. "Yes, because most towns have curfews. No one comes in or leaves after dark. And they have guarded checkpoints. Only answer questions the guards ask. Don't volunteer any information. If they ask what your business is, pull out the horseshoe. Tell them your grandfather sent you to get it repaired. If they ask how you'll pay for it, it'd be best if you have a rabbit or a couple of partridge to show them. Tell them if the smithy won't take it, you'll offer to work for the smith to make payment.

"If the guards want your rabbit, sell it to them. Bargain for as many coppers as you can get. Don't let them take it without paying. If it comes to that, turn away. Find another way into town. Don't badmouth them. Always be polite, respectful, and humble."

"Anything else?" She figured he had covered just about everything.

"Don't trust anyone. Trust yourself, no one else."

Easy for you to say. Comes a time you have to trust a stranger. Trust yourself that you can trust them. That's what he must mean.

Nagora picked up her vest and looked at the map. "A hundred days." She tried to gauge the distance she would have to travel in that time. "If all goes well, I should have plenty of time. Maybe I could even go explore some other places."

"As long as you bring back the chain. Be careful though. Don't let your guard down."

Tar piss! I hope I've learned that lesson.

A question still nagged Nagora as she looked at the map Uncle had drawn on her vest. Well, Tars, do I ask or not? What is it he doesn't want me to know?

Uncle returned to the package Geirador had brought. His back was to her. She heard some clicking sounds. When he turned around, he held an unstrung bow in his hands. He handed it to her. How could that be? It was too long for the package she had seen Geirador give Uncle.

"It's beautiful. These recurve limbs are—"

Uncle spoke for her. "Made from ram horn tips, cut in such a way as to allow them to be glued and lashed to strips of ash and hickory."

"From the one I killed?"

Uncle smiled and nodded.

Nagora spread her thumb and middle finger over the curve of the horn. The joint with the pieces of wood was the length of her finger. The limb tip notch in the horn had been made with a file and was perfectly smooth. She would not worry about the bowstring wearing out there.

"String it."

Immediately, the extra effort to string it told her it would be powerful. She held the strange grip and pulled the string back to her cheek. "Wow! It's right on the limit of my strength. I'll have to practice with it to feel comfortable. I can't wait! This grip makes it heavier than what I'm used to, but gives it a balanced feel."

She examined the bow grip closer. "It comes apart."

"You'll thank Geirador for that brass piece. Unstring it. See if you can take it apart."

Nagora found only a single hardwood piece, no bigger than her little finger, which could be pushed out from one side of the long brass handle piece, allowing the limbs to be re-moved.

"Good, Nagora. If you put the limbs together, they can be inserted into one end of the brass piece."

She did this. So this is where the hardwood piece fits. It locks the straight ends of the limbs in place in the brass han-dle.

"Uncle, the pieces fit together small enough so I can fit the bow in my quiver."

"That's the idea."

Nagora went to pick up her quiver. Uncle handed her the new bow. She was able to fit it into the hunting arrow section of her quiver. Just the curved ram horn tips curled over the rim of the quiver, like two crooked fingers resting one on top of the other.

"I'm impressed, Uncle. When did you come up with the idea to make this?"

"Sometime last winter."

"You knew then I'd need a bow like this?"

"Not at the time, no. It was just an idea Geirador and I had played with. He wanted to see if he could cast a metal piece strong enough to take the strain a bow's limbs would put on it. And I wanted to use the ram's horn tips to make you a new bow. Geirador will use the remainder of the horns to make tool and knife handles."

"Thanks. I'll have to thank Geirador too."

Uncle returned to the counter and brought back what looked like a roll of leather. He laid it on the table. "These are from Geirador. He said you've earned them. They're the first set he's made. He'll want a report. What you like, don't like, suggestions."

Nagora unrolled the piece of leather to reveal a small sack, a small leather case, and a leather sheath the length of her forearm with her hand held open, but wider. Two adjustable leather straps were attached to the brass rings at each end of the sheath, and each strap held two smaller, molded leather knife sheaths.

The visible halves of the cherry handles of the four small blades, held by their holsters, begged to be grasped. She pulled one out. It would throw well and find its mark. She pushed it back into its tight place.

Then Nagora pulled the big blade from its sheath. "Wow!" It was a long, double-sided, leaf-shaped blade the length of her forearm. From the hilt, the blade edges curved outward and then inward until they met in a sharp point at the tip.

The crossguard curved upward on the handle where the thumb would lay and downward on the finger side to protect the hand.

The U-shaped brass flip latch riveted near the mouth of the sheath now made sense. It was made to slip over the thumb side of the cross guard to hold the big blade in place, especially if the sheath was worn on the back, upside down.

Nagora examined her hold on the handle. She looked to Uncle.

"Walrus hide. Remember, when you were about five, the big winter storm? It piled ice blocks high as the cliffs on your beach. Geirador and I got ropes on the five dead ones we found. Come a good thaw, we were able to skin them and have the thick hides tanned. Those hides were two to three fingers thick. It'll be hard to lose your grip on it."

Several thick layers of hide had been pressed tightly together over the tang of the big blade, along with the pommel that was riveted to hold them in place. Obviously, shaping the handle's walrus-hide grip had been the last step.

She wet a finger on her tongue and touched the side of the blade. "What kind of metal is this?"

"Blue steel. Made from skystone. Geirador traded with the Little People for it. For what? You know Geirador. He just smiles. We'll never know. Do I believe him? Can't prove otherwise."

She laughed. She hadn't done so in a long time. Geirador and his stories.

"There's a flask of oil in the sack. Geirador says to pour a line of oil around the mouth of the sheath. Do so. Then I'll explain."

Nagora did.

"There's a whetstone and a flint in the leather case. First, put the blade back in the sheath. Then slowly pull it out. Hold it up facing you."

The Tiwaz symbol, for a higher cause, was engraved between the two edges near the cross guard on the side of the blade.

"Easy with the flint on the edge."

She made her touch feather light. She gasped as the blade lit up with a bluish green flame. "A blade of fire!"

"Let it burn out. Geirador says it'll help season the blade. He put some of his mead in the oil. Him and his secret recipes. Apply and light once a day until you run out. He'll have more oil for you when you come back."

"If I come back." Nagora slipped the blade back into the sheath and slipped her arms through the leather straps. She adjusted the side straps so the big sheath was comfortable on her back. She moved the two small knife sheaths on their straps so they rested just above elbow height under her arms. Aye, I could stop an attacker with one of these.

She reached behind her back, just below her neck, and pulled the big blade out. With care, she returned it directly overhead so the tip of the blade found the brass plate on the sheath to guide the tip into its mouth. It sunk into place with an easy push of her fingers that found the U-shaped brass flip latch to lock the big blade in place. She did this again, three times. Satisfied, she looked at Uncle and turned once, as she pushed her chest out and stood tall.

"You'll come back. They fit you well and will hide easily under your hooded shirt."

"I don't deserve these." Nagora had never seen a set of blades so beautiful.

"Not a question of deserving. You earned them."

"But my actions against The Cause?"

"Might improve the lout's skill with a bow. No real harm done to The Cause. Your skills earned you these blades. Blades like these work in skillful hands."

Truly armed as a warrior. But she would be on her own, for real. This wasn't to be a training exercise. She would be away for a hundred days. How dangerous could it be? Would she actually have to use her new weapons? Only to defend herself if it ever came to that. And her bow to hunt for food. But still, the question nagged at her. I'll ask.

Before she could, Uncle spoke. "You know what you can carry. Fill a waterskin and try everything on. If you have to lighten your load, do so. I want you ready to leave at first light after you've filled your stomach."

"What is it you don't want me to be told?"

Uncle sat down, looked up at her, and slowly crossed his arms. "What do you mean?"

"I heard you talk to Geirador. The other day when I brought water in."

Uncle held her gaze. He seemed to be waiting.

"Geirador said someone wanted you to tell me something. You said it wouldn't change anything, that I didn't need to know, that it'd be better if I didn't."

"What else did you hear?"

"Just that." She put her hands on her hips. "I want to know."

Uncle's eyes searched Nagora's face for a long moment. "Very well." He rested his forearms on the table, looked away from her, and then back. "Others have gone before you, for The Cause, but haven't returned."

"How many?"

"Two."

"With a chain?"

He took a deep breath. "No. But the smithies will be expecting a chain this time."

"How do you know that? Maybe the first two didn't make it past the first blacksmith. It could be not all of them are as loyal to The Cause as you think."

"True enough, on both counts. You'll be showing up within the time limit set for gathering the information. The smiths were told the information could be collected up to three times, to confirm and to have the latest information."

Nagora crossed her arms as Uncle leaned back in his chair. "So this is fair warning. I better watch my back?"

Uncle pursed his lips for a moment. "Of course. You're on serious business. The other two were much older than you and, in hindsight, knew too much about The Cause. The information they gathered was by word of mouth, and they recorded it in a code of their own. With the chain, the smiths'll use their own code. They'll not tell you anything."

"That's good for me. I won't be able to tell what the markings on the chain mean. At worst, for whatever reason, I won't be able to deliver the chain to Geirador."

Uncle spread his hands, palms up, in front of him and nodded.

"Could it be those two died for The Cause?"

Uncle shrugged. "Could be. So far, we don't know anything other than they've not returned within their allotted time."

"And you think I will?"

"I do, Nagora. I know what you're capable of. I have complete trust in you."

Again, something churned in the pit of her stomach. Do I have complete trust in myself? "The information on the chain is going to be important."

"Very important."

Nagora took a deep breath. She had never been given such responsibility. And for a moment, a tiny voice spoke up inside of her. You're not up to this. You don't have what it takes. You won't come back either. Do like the other two. Disappear for your own good. You don't care about The Cause anyway.

Nagora didn't want to listen to it. It would only make her doubt. To shut it up, she pulled the big blade from its sheath and looked at the etched Tiwaz symbol. She held it over her heart. "For a higher cause."

"Yes, Nagora, for a higher cause."

Ilma
Awîyak ekâ ceskwa ka wicehtot

Seventy-five days later, Nagora had visited eight smithies. In that time she had rarely skipped her morning exercise ritual, alternately using her big blade, two small throwing knives, or her bow. She hunted often with her new bow. Just about every rabbit that she took aim at, she had been able to kill. This morning's kill was, again, proof of her skill with the bow she had grown to love.

With the dead rabbit tied to her waist and the dejected shuffle Tars had taken to using when approaching guards, she made for the checkpoint ahead of her with the broken horseshoe in hand. She usually waited to join a line of other people going into a town, but not today.

Two towns previous, she had learned that enduring the smell of fresh horse turds she had smeared on an old scarf she wore helped to get her waved through the checkpoints. Would it work here as well?

The guard looked at the broken shoe. He didn't waste time. He pointed over his shoulder with his thumb. "Across the bridge, lane to your right, at the end. Can't miss it."

Tars, is it our luck, or this broken horseshoe? The stink, you say? Could very well be.

The stone bridge, which would take Nagora into Gallanford, was long and wide, as was the swift-flowing River Gallan it crossed. Two work gangs were busy ahead. She stuck to the middle so as not to come too close to them and keep a safe distance from the guards overseeing their work. She had tasted the bite of a whip once when she stopped to give a sip of water to a young girl.

To her left was a group of mostly women, children, and elderly men. They were all on their knees, facing the stone wall of the bridge, hammering with stones at what was left of the artwork. The children scraped up the fallen stone chips and sorted them by size into wooden buckets.

How many groups like this had she seen in the other towns? All the forced laborers most likely accused and convicted of speaking of dragons or of committing some petty crimes were serving their sentences. No rebels among them.

From what she had overheard days before, such suspects were taken away and rarely, if ever, seen again. And if they did return, they came back crippled or blinded with their tongues cut out, living reminders to those who would chose to become rebel sympathizers. The hair on the back of her neck prickled. Best we not worry on that, Tars. We've done well so far.

Those to her right stood as they hammered and hacked at the artwork. Many had hammers of some kind. Only a few used stones, the hungry volunteers working the day for an extra loaf of bread. Some dared to stare at the rabbit dangling at her hip.

Getting closer to Windhaven, the towns were bigger, and more work groups chipped away at the carved artwork under the close watch of mercenaries with whips. At least such scenes no longer left her wide-eyed. Now Nagora would shake her head and clench her fists.

It had started years ago with the dragon images, and then a second decree ordered all the surrounding artwork removed. How long would it go on? What then when nothing was left to deface? Queen Raganora's decrees were leaving a bleak mark on the towns and villages, and their people. Seeing how the destruction of beauty was carried out made her want to cry.

Most of her own rations had run out. Would the smithy let her keep the rabbit? If no other customers were hanging around, most likely. We could forage for wild onions, Tars. A stew to my liking. Nagora sighed. It's not in my pot yet, is it, Tars? I just hope we won't have to join one of those volunteer gangs to earn a loaf of stale bread. We should spend some time hunting. Dry and smoke some meat or try to sell what we bag, then buy some oats and flour. Or nuts.

Near the other end of the bridge, just beyond the sound of the beating stones and hammers, a mule-drawn wagon with high-canvassed sides and roof stood parked to one side. A group of people had gathered behind it. Some of them had hand carts and barrows.

Nagora stopped on the outer edge of the group and pretended disinterested curiosity in what was going on by looking off, now and then, in the direction the river flowed.

A woman pushed a young girl closer to the wagon's rear. Her small face was red and tear-stained. A simple white smock covered her to her ankles. The child didn't want to go. She kept reaching back to the woman. "No! Mum! Please!" Her voice was hoarse with her plea. She must've been crying since the night before. What was going on?

After the big man next to the wagon had lifted the girl onto the tailgate, the child cried and shook as she stood barefoot. She's terrified. He pulled the girl's smock down from her shoulders so it fell at her feet. The girl was naked. Not more than eleven. The man motioned her to turn. The girl wiped at her tears and obeyed. Trembling, as she forced her shaking arms to stay at her sides, the girl tried not to step on her dress.

When her back was to the man, he ordered her to stop turning and bend over.

The girl pressed her thin legs together and bent. The man reached up and spread her cheeks to examine her.

No damn it! This can't be! Nagora took a determined step in the direction of the wagon.

"Hold on, friend. Are you looking for a boat by chance?" The grip on Nagora's arm was firm and turned her away, while pulling her closer to the side of the bridge. "You don't want to interrupt a sale, do you? It's not worth it." He spoke these words in a hushed voice.

"Tar piss! Let go of me." She turned on the one who had grabbed her. A young man, her age. His face was sincere. She pulled and shook her arm.

He didn't let go, turned Nagora away again, and pointed. "See over on the point. For a coin you could get a curragh for a day and fish for your meal." His voice became a hush again, closer, almost in her ear. "You're not from these parts, are you? What're you goin' to do? Throw your broken horseshoe at him?"

Nagora shook her head.

"The mum's sellin' her daughter for food. If the giant takes her, she'll end up a virgin at the Temple of Fire in Windhaven. Stick your nose in that sale, both the seller and buyer'll have your stinkin' hide. Trust me. Nothin' you can do about it."

She glanced back at the sale in progress. The girl was dressed again, wiping her eyes. The large man had climbed up into the wagon. He was bent over, pulling things forward.

"You sure you want to watch that? If the mum's lucky, she'll get three months of food for her runt. Flour, salt, dried smoked fish, maybe cabbages, last year's for sure."

Nagora looked out over the river. I wish I were away from here, on my beach. The stranger was right. She turned away to leave.

A hand touched her shoulder. She waited.

"That rabbit for sale?"

"No."

"Lookin' for someone to share it with?"

"If you let me go about my business, and I come back this way, and it's still tied to me, I'll share it." He'll be long gone. Won't he, Tars?

But he wasn't. The chain had a new set of markings. The smithy hadn't wasted time. Nor had Nagora. And now, Tars had a new friend. But could he be trusted?

"That was quick. Business done already? Smithy not want to repair your shoe?"

"You followed me?"

He shook his head. "Naw. No other business down that way. You had the pieces in your hand."

Nagora put her hand on her scrip. "He wouldn't take the rabbit. Said the shoe wasn't worth repairing. Wanted two coins for a new one. Don't have a coin to my name." She lifted the rope the rabbit was tied to. "Be lucky to get a coin for the hare."

"You got a pot to cook it in? What's your name?"

"Pot's in my pack. Name's Tars. Some wild onions would make it tasty."

"I'm Maton. I know where we can find some. Not far from where we could build a fire. Let's go."

Nagora glanced over at the wagon as they passed by. Two other mothers had their daughters in line, and they were even younger. How can this be? Why do people stand for it? What are the leaders of The Cause waiting for? Tar piss! What's going to happen to those girls? Those two can't be a day older than eight.

Maton tapped her shoulder. "Tars, you go on ahead. I'll meet you after you're out of sight of the checkpoint."

She nodded as she slowed down to look at him. Worry was in his eyes.

"Go on. Don't look back."

She did as he told her. She took out the broken shoe pieces and took on Tars' disheartened walk.

"No luck?" said the guard.

She shook her head and kicked at the ground.

He waved her past.

· · ·

Nagora didn't look back until she rounded a bend in the road. No sign of Maton. Maybe he wouldn't show after all. She continued on her way to the spot where she had come out of the woods earlier in the morning.

Just as Nagora was about to leave the road, someone whistled. Maton waved with one hand and ran toward her. Is that an unstrung bow in his hand? She waited.

Maton held up a hand as he caught his breath. "Had to be careful leavin' town. Waited for a group. Did my best to look like I was with 'em." He wiped his sleeve across his nose. "Then I had to get my bow."

He bent and laid it across his knees to rest his hands on it. "I hide it on this side of the river so I can come to hunt." The quiver on his back rose and fell with his breathing. "Glad I caught up to you. I'm hungry."

"So am I. Am I headed in the right direction?"

"Aye, fine. I'll follow you."

Nagora motioned him ahead. "I'll follow you. You know where the wild onions are."

He looked up at her, took a breath, nodded, and stepped into the woods.

Nagora was talking to the friend Tars had made. Not only did they find wild onions but some mushrooms too. While she had lit the fire and set water to boil, Maton had gutted, skinned, and cut up the rabbit. Now they sat near a small stream, savoring the last of the stew.

She had spotted it earlier. Should I reveal mine? He wore the four 8's at his neck. To trust or not to trust? "Maton, is your da a blacksmith by any chance?"

He laughed, almost a scoff. "No. If only we were so lucky. He's been long gone. Most of us hardly remember 'im. Just as well though. One mouth less to feed and his was a big one. Always open for food and wine. Mostly sour wine. A useless toad he was. Mum upped her courage and told 'im to leave or else. She had enough to care for six brats. She didn't need a seventh."

Poor lad. Happy his is gone. I wish mine would return.

Earlier, while the stew was cooking, Maton had whittled a slim spoon from a branch. Now he scraped the sides of the pot with it. He paused. "You need coins for a new shoe. I bet you can climb good."

"What makes you say that?"

"You're sure-footed, got strong hands, and you carry a coil of rope."

"Aye, I can climb good like you say. Is that going to get me some coins?"

"Could, if you're willing to climb, work hard, and risk your life. Too, it depends where you're headed. You going to Twin Rivers?" He brought the pot up, tilted it so he could scrape the last of the stew into his mouth.

In her mind Nagora saw the map. It was one of the two destinations left. "It's a little out of my way, but if there're coins to be made, I could go that way. What's the work?"

Maton wiped his mouth with his sleeve. "Twin Rivers has twin—" Maton looked around before whispering, "dragons." He winked and crisscrossed his arms and hands to mime his words. "A tall stone sculpture of two dragons with intertwined necks. It stands in the middle of the town square above the only well in town. The two heads can be seen from the opposite shores, at the far ends to the twin bridges leading into town. The wings and tails have been hacked away, as well as the scales on the backs and bellies, and part way up the necks. The queen's idea is to change the dragon heads into snake heads. No one wants to climb to even try to do the work. The few who did, died trying."

"They fall?"

"You could say that, with an arrow in their backs."

Nagora looked at Maton, mad at what he had just told her. "And you think I would take that risk for a horseshoe?"

He laughed. "Apparently, a pouch of gold coins is to be had for whoever completes the job. Look, Tars, I'm not expecting you to risk your life. I just wanted to let you know how things are in these parts. You must be from one of the loyal Outlander settlements way up." He pointed in the direction of where the guiding star sat, where she was from. "Yhorgal, or, something 'maze.' Not much excitement up there. Is there?"

"No, there isn't. You're right." At least not yet. Uncle must be right. It'll come our way too. "So a lone archer in Twin Rivers protects the statue?"

Maton lowered his gaze. "Aye. Queen Rag's guards have tortured a lot of people in their efforts to find out who the archer is. Many died claiming they didn't know who the archer was. Every house and building's been searched. Not a single arrow or bow found. No one knows anything. Rumor is it's a ghost archer."

She set her bowl and spoon down. "Maton, you look sad."

He took a deep breath and exhaled. "Aye. I had a good friend who lived there. They tortured him. I won't describe it. It would just ruin the fine meal you've had. It's best he died."

His eyes filled with water. "Anyway. Time for me to go." Maton stood and picked up his bow. "I've got a wagon to intercept. Try to save my little sister's skin."

It was a slap in the face. She was on her feet and had a hand on his arm. "That—she's your sister?"

"Aye."

"I'm going with you."

"No, Tars. It's not your fight. Bad enough I'll be the one they'll be looking for once this goes down."

Nagora reached into her shirt and pulled the knots to the front of her neck. "What if I make it my fight too?"

His eyes widened. "No. No, Tars. You'll just get into trouble."

"Let me decide that. Tell me what we'll be facing."

Maton shook his head and raised his hand.

She batted it down. "Tell me."

"That giant drove his wagon into town three days ago. He had a single escort. He might have more when he leaves, depending on how many girls he has."

As Maton spoke, Nagora reached under her shirt at her lower back. She unclipped the strap of her quiver and took hold of it as it slipped out from under her shirt. She placed it between her knees, removed her bow parts, and assembled it.

"He'll be headed to Twin Rivers." Maton's fascination with her bow slowed him down. "Looking for more virgins for the Temple of Fire."

"So what's your plan? Give me the details. Do we kill the driver and his escort? What do we do with the wagon, the mule, the escorts' horses? Do you have anyone else who's going to help you?"

"Look, Tars, I don't have a plan. All I want to do is save Ilma."

It wasn't right. It was a plan for disaster. Nagora re-clipped the loose end of her quiver's belt and slipped it over her head onto her shoulder so it rested on her back over her sheepskin vest.

Nagora grabbed Maton's arm. "Maton, you haven't thought this through. Chances are Ilma won't be alone in the wagon. You won't be saving just her."

Possible scenarios played out in her mind. She needed details.

"First, you seem to have picked a spot where you're going to intercept the wagon. Will we have a clear view of the road in both directions?"

"Yes."

"Will others be traveling the road?"

"Possibly."

"Are there trees along the road in that spot?"

"Yes."

"From what side of the road would I have a clear view to both directions?"

He blinked a few times, bent his arm at the elbow, just enough to create a blind curve. "This side." He touched his outer elbow. "From here you could see in both directions."

"Plan one: If no one else is on the road in either direction, we take out the driver and the escorts. You get the driver and then get control of the mule. I'll take care of the others.

"Plan two: If others are on the road, we stop the wagon. One of us has them in our sights. We warn them not to move unless they want to take an arrow. I'll cover them. You pull the brake lever. Have the driver come down to make like he's checking the mule's hooves. We let the other travelers go by before we take them out. You sure you want them dead?"

"If you knew what they do, you would want them dead too."

"Don't tell me. I trust you on that. Maton, have you thought about the food in the wagon? Is there somewhere you can stash it until you can come back for it? Same goes for the mule and the horses. They could be butchered for meat and feed a lot of hungry people in town."

"I hadn't thought that far. You're right."

"Think about that. I have other questions. How're you going to get the girls back in town?"

"Row them across the river at night."

"Have you got a boat ready? A safe place to cross? From what I've seen, the current's pretty strong. And when you get the girls back, what are the chances someone doesn't rat you out? You're going to need something to buy their silence. The food in the wagon might do. But sooner or later you're going to be a marked man. You said so yourself."

He hung his head. "I didn't think of all those things, Tars."

"It's not a blame, Maton. I'm trying to help."

"I know that. I have a boat. I know about the current. I can make it across. I won't be fighting the current, but using it to ferry across and down the river to the point I showed you. And I know where I can hide the wagon, for a while at least."

"Good, Maton. Are there people you can count on to help you? Do they know what you're going to do today?"

"There are, but I didn't have the time to tell them."

"Okay. Would the girls be safe with me at the place you want to hide the wagon? I could stay with them until you get help. It'll be less of a risk if you go by yourself."

Maton held onto his chin. He seemed to be thinking about what she had said.

Nagora picked up the empty pot. What mattered now was to get to the bend in the road. "Maton, enough talk. Douse the coals. I'll take care of the pot. Then take me to your spot in the road. We'll prepare our ambush. After we free your sister, we'll decide what to do."

As the wagon approached in the distance, Nagora kept her eye on the single mounted escort who followed. "Tar piss! Change of plans, Maton. The guard's moved from his horse into the back of the wagon. I'll run ahead through the trees to get behind it. Wait here. Get the driver to stop the wagon and climb down as planned. If he leaves you no choice, take him with an arrow."

Nagora was in the trees about three hundred strides from the bend. The escort had tied his horse to the tailgate. She ran from the trees with her bow and a nocked arrow in one hand. A girl screamed.

Nagora pulled herself up into the horse's saddle to see what the escort was up to. Tar piss! Only one girl! Ilma! The bastard was on his knees, straddling her and pulling his pants down. Nagora didn't hesitate.

The arrow struck brute between his shoulder blades. His head arched back, and a hand attempted to reach back as he fell over onto his arm. Ilma didn't stop screaming.

The driver yelled something as Nagora let herself down from the horse.

Nagora ran behind the wagon, grabbed the tailgate, and climbed aboard. Ilma's screams turned into panicked heaving sobs.

"Don't stick it in 'er. Make 'er use 'er mouth. Shut 'er up."

Tar piss! Nagora pulled an arrow and nocked it. You'll wish you had never said that aloud.

"Whoooaaa!" The wagon lurched to a stop. "Mind yerself, mate, we've got company."

He can't hear you.

"Climb down from the wagon. If you value your life, you'll do as I say."

Good, Maton.

"You sure you know what yer doin,' lad?" said the driver.

You're damn right he knows what he's doing.

"Oh, I'm sure. If you don't come down, my arrow'll bring you down. I'm givin' you a three count, starting now."

"Okay. Okay." The wagon bed tilted to the left as the big man moved to climb down.

Nagora held a finger to her lips to warn Ilma to keep quiet. She stepped over and past the packs of food to get closer to the canvas flap behind the driver's seat.

When the wagon settled, Nagora pushed the flap aside, planted a foot on the seat, and drew her bowstring. "Hands on your head. Do as my friend says. Things are fine up here."

The burly man looked up in surprise and slowly brought his hands up.

Maton held the driver in his sights. "Into the trees. That way. I'll tell you when to stop."

Nagora made sure the brake lever was set, returned the arrow to her quiver, and pushed the flap aside.

"Are you okay?" Ilma sat back on her legs, bent over, with her arms wrapped around her belly, whimpering. "Ilma, I'm your brother's friend. We've come for you. Maton'll be here in a moment. We'll take you to safety. I'm going to untie the canvas and pull it down. Don't be afraid."

For a moment, Nagora looked at the man she had killed. She swallowed to hold back her insides. What've I done? All Uncle had said was each person reacted differently the first time they killed. And it didn't get any easier afterwards. Her insides churned, and her mouth was dry. It was justified. I had no choice. Now she had to remove the arrow.

"Ilma, look the other way." It had pierced the escort's tunic and shirts, and was lodged in the backbone. She didn't want to cut it free.

Nagora grasped the shaft as close to the tip as she could. She pulled. It did not come free. She worked it from side to side, matching the entry cut of the barbs. It loosened and came free. Her fingers and hand were covered in blood. She swallowed again to hold in the stew. She had to use her other hand to keep the barbs from catching the material to be able to pull her arrow clear.

She set it aside and reached back for her waterskin to rinse away most of the blood from her hands and the arrow's tip.

"Sis, are you okay?" Maton appeared at the tailgate and let it down.

Ilma cried again and made her way to him on her knees with her arms outstretched. "I wanna go home."

He held her close and rocked her in his arms. "You're going to be fine. I'll take you home."

Nagora returned the arrow to her quiver, released her coil of rope, and began to tie the dead man's feet together. "The big man?"

"He fell hard. Not so big now."

"Take your arrow?"

Maton nodded.

Nagora jumped from the wagon, untied the escort's horse, and tied the end of her rope to the saddle. "Careful, he's coming out. Going to join his friend."

Maton brought his cheek to his sister's and turned her away.

Nagora climbed onto the horse. "Gee yap!" The body hit the dirt in the road face first, but she didn't stop until she had come around the right side of the wagon and dragged the carcass into the trees to the spot where she found the driver's corpse.

Nagora untied her rope, coiled it, and walked the horse back. Before coming out of the trees, she stopped to retch, but nothing came out. Why? Maybe later.

Before stepping onto the road, Nagora looked along it in both directions. No one was in sight. Tar piss! We're lucky.

Maton had untied the canvas and was pulling it from the wooden frames. His sister sat on the driver's seat.

...

Nagora tied the horse to the wagon, climbed up, and pulled one of the wall and roof frames from the wooden brackets that held it in place. She laid it down in the wagon.

With Maton, they had the frames put away and the wagon's box covered in short time.

"Maton, do you know how to turn this rig around?"

"Haven't learned that yet. I can drive it forward though."

"Untie the escort's horse. I'll turn it around for you."

Nagora climbed up next to Ilma and patted her hand. "You've been a brave lass, Ilma. You're safe now." She took the reins, released the brake, and, with the mule's cooperation, in three movements she had the wagon pointed in the right direction.

After, she handed the reins to Maton and pulled herself up onto the escort's horse. "Take us to where you want to hide the wagon."

Nagora followed the wagon off the road onto what must've once been another road of the same quality, except it was now partially hidden by the overgrowth of bushes and trees on each side of it. These were taking hold on the hard surface of the road, but they didn't offer much resistance to the wagon. The road followed the contour of a hill to its top, where a large clearing came into view.

Maton jumped down from the seat and reached up to take Ilma down. "Come, Tars. I'll show you."

They didn't have to go far before coming to the edge of a cliff.

Maton pointed down to the water in the big rectangular basin. "It used to be a quarry. When Queen Rag took the throne, the Stone Standers refused to cut and move stone for her. They abandoned their quarries, and left with their tools and stone working secrets. They swore loyalty to the dragons and haven't been seen since. This was one of their quarries."

Nagora had never heard of the Stone Standers. "Is that why Raganora ordered all the dragon images and statues to be defaced?"

"Yes, in retaliation against the Stone Standers since they also sculpted those images. And to hammer home her slaughter of the dragons—to kill any hope the people might have of their return."

"So where did the Stone Standers go to?"

Maton shrugged. "Some say they've left the land. Some say they're hiding in the high mountains, in a secret place they defend. A place where no one can set foot, other than a Stone Stander."

"And they've given no sign of life since then?"

"Not that anyone's aware of."

"Well, I've never heard of them until now." Why hadn't she been told about the Stone Standers? What else had been kept from her?

Nagora looked around. "So do we leave the wagon here?"

"If you could back it up over in the copse, it would be out of sight. There's a small pasture on the slope on the other side of the quarry. We can leave the horse and mule there to graze. There's a tiny stream over there too, so they'll have water.

"Tars, I don't think I could've done it on my own. Thanks. I'll not say a word to anyone about you helping me. You can trust Ilma. She'll keep it secret too." Maton touched the knots at his neck. "I know who'll help me. I've got a plan now."

I hope it's a good one. When those bodies are found, a lot of questions are going to be asked.

"Don't tell me." Nagora placed a hand on Ilma's shoulder. "Take care of your sister. Make sure she'll be safe. I'm going to help myself to a few things from the food supplies and then be on my way. You should too. You've got a good hike ahead of you. I'll bring the animals to the meadow for you. Good luck to both of you."

The Witch
Kîskwehkan Iskwew

Nagora had taken flour, a few pieces of dried fish, and some barley. She traveled in the woods parallel to the road and put as much distance between her and where they had ambushed the wagon.

Ilma's tear-stained face was still in her mind. They'll need more than the luck I wished them. Nagora ran at a comfortable pace, intent to go as far as daylight would permit. She would find a safe place to hide. A place where she would be able to sleep. She would eat in the morning. That was her plan.

She hadn't planned to listen to the worries as they crept into her head. She couldn't stop them. What if they had been seen? What if Maton and his sister get caught and they're tortured and they tell about Tars? Can I do anything about that, Tars? No, not a thing. You're right. Worrying about that isn't going to do us any good. Two more smithies to visit. We'll just go about our business as usual. So far, it's worked. Tomorrow we go to Twin Rivers. We'll be extra careful.

I better double-check the map. Nagora put her bow down and shed her pack and quiver so she could remove her vest. I should be just about here. The river forks to create the long island Twin Rivers is built on. If I could enter the town from the other side, I would feel safer, less likely to be seen as a possible suspect running from the scene of the ambush. Was the wagon even on a schedule? Was someone expecting it to arrive today? Is there a way to cross the river before it forks? Uncle didn't draw a bridge, except for the one I crossed this morning, and the twin bridges to come. I'll just be wasting my time if I go looking for another bridge.

Okay, Tars, we stick to our original plan. We'll continue on, find a place to lie low, set some snares, and get some sleep. Come morning we'll be on our way to Twin Rivers.

Nagora had gotten little sleep. In her dreams, she relived her first kill, over and over in different ways, searching for a different outcome each time. But it always ended in blood, warm coppery-smelling blood. It jerked her awake, and she would almost puke. If only she could, it might purge the dream and the tears accompanying it.

The twin dragon heads rose against the morning sky in the distance. If Nagora hadn't learned about them the day before, she would be guessing what they were from where she stood. She had fallen in behind two wagons on the road, keeping step with their steady advance until they came to the checkpoint at the bridge entrance to Twin Rivers. The one she stood behind held manure, the one ahead of it, livestock.

Piglets squealed and goats bleated as a guard circled it. "Tribute?"

"Aye, sir. And m' lad's got a load a manure fer tha gardens. And these, sir, are fer you. Fresh laid this mornin'." The farmer held out a kerchief, its corners tied together, obviously bulging with eggs.

Nagora hadn't had one in well over a month, now. Her mouth watered. She could almost smell one frying in butter.

The guard made his way alongside the wagon to collect his bribe. He waved them on with a big smile.

She lowered her head, placed a hand on the back of the shit wagon, and pushed. The guard didn't stop her. Thank the stars! He's more interested in protecting his eggs. She slipped by him onto the bridge.

Nagora kept a hand on the wagon and her eyes on the twin dragons, trying to estimate their height. *They stand tall, Tars. We'll go have a look after we've been to the blacksmith's.*

They were almost across the bridge. She skipped alongside the wagon with the horseshoe pieces in one hand. Soon as she caught the attention of the farmer's son, she held up the pieces. "Say, mate. Ya know where I can find the smithy?"

The lad lifted a rein and pointed off to the right. "See the black smoke risin' from that chimney o'er there?"

"Aye, I do."

"That's where you'll find 'im."

"Thanks, mate."

Nagora found two customers waiting on the smithy's services. He was shoeing a workhorse, replacing a worn rear shoe. He wore the four 8's at his neck. A young boy held a pitchfork with a broken tine needing mending. Nagora sat on the ground with her back to one of the big open doors of the shop.

Once the horse's owner had led it away, Nagora stood to watch the smith work his magic on the broken tine. In little time, he had it heated and fused to its fork on his anvil where, with a few hits of his hammer, he completed the repair. After cooling it in the trough, he pounded the tine of the fork back into its handle end and tested it by pressing it from both sides against the earthen floor of his shop. "There you go. Should be good for some more work."

As soon as the boy left, Nagora handed the broken pieces to the smith.

He held them up and joined them at the break. "Who made it?"

She pulled her knife and set it on the anvil. "The same one who made this."

The slightest of smiles appeared as he said, "Geirador."

How is it all these blacksmiths seem to know Geirador? What's he done that's so special, besides making weapons like my blades? What role does he play in The Cause? You know, Tars, Geirador has a mysterious side I'll never get to know.

He held out his hand.

She placed the chain in it.

The smith returned her knife to her and the pieces of the broken shoe. He laid the chain on his anvil and went over to a shelf, rummaged in a box, and returned with a handful of punches. He looked around before going to work with his hammer. It didn't take him long. He placed the chain in her hand. "Good luck, lad. You be careful, now. Your journey's not over yet."

Nagora read the sincerity of his words in his voice and his eyes. "I will." Did he want to tell her more? He turned away to return the punches to the box on the shelf. Probably not, he had the opportunity. Before he could turn around again, she left to make her way to the town square through the narrow dirt streets of Twin Rivers.

A hundred strides from the forge, a lone flute beckoned in the distance. It pulled at Nagora's ear and tugged at her heart. Even if her heart knew it wasn't going home yet, it could not resist the melancholy sound that made her wish she was. She reached under her vest and touched the outer pocket on her quiver. It held her flute. She had to get closer so her ear could better commit the tune to memory.

It stopped and then started a second time. She followed it to the edge of the town square. The twin dragon heads towered above her. Her ears showed her the direction of the music just before it stopped again. Her eyes caught sight of the young man tucking the flute into the sash at his waist.

He bent and picked up a tambourine, with three red apples resting on red silk scarves covering its skin. He tapped the underside, making it ring. "Who wants to win these three ripe apples? Juggle 'em like me and they're yours." He juggled the apples high in the air for a few moments, spun around once, and caught them as they came down. Then he looked to the gathered audience for takers. None came forward, so he took up the scarves. "This is how I learned. Anyone want to learn before trying the apples?"

Well, Tars, you think the other merchants are happy with the crowd this minstrel has drawn to the square? How do you think they pay him? In coin or in goods? Fancy an apple, Tars? Nagora stepped forward, took the scarves, and feigned to struggle with them.

The juggler offered her the apples.

Nagora juggled them high, juggled them low, high again, spun around twice and caught them as they came down, and placed them in her pouch. The audience clapped and called out: "Good work, laddie. Good show." Nagora winked at the stunned young juggler, smiled, turned on her heel, and crossed the town square, whistling the minstrel's tune.

Easy pickings. Right, Tars? Last fall's apples. They're getting a bit soft. Must've come from someone's root cellar.

Nagora paused at the well and looked up at the intertwined dragon necks, remembering Maton's story. Her eyes roamed over the defaced parts of the tapered necks until they found the untouched scales. The craftsmanship was remarkable in its detail. So many overlapping scales gave the necks a realistic appearance.

As Nagora walked around the well, she let her eyes come back down over the rough chipped surface of the stone. She had not spotted a single seam. The dragons had been sculpted from a single block of stone. Impressive Stone Stander skills, Tars.

When had its artisans erected it? Before or after sculpting the dragons? Probably after. What was now the rim of the well must've been the dragons' intertwined tails. A timber frame structure must've been built around the sculpture to be able to stand it in place.

Nagora backed away from the well with her head tilted back until the profile of the two dragon heads came into view. Do dragons actually look like this, Tars? They're fiercely beautiful. How else could she describe to Pare the snarled grins of their bared teeth as the dragons stared into each other's eyes? Pare had once whispered a story to her in the dark of night about a fire-breathing dragon. Surely these two could, at any moment, blow giant flames from their flared nostrils, if they were alive.

Beyond the twin dragons, down the wide street, stretched the bridge Nagora had crossed earlier.

Now Nagora turned to go in the opposite direction, toward its twin. On the other side of it, she would find the road leading to Windhaven. Only one more smithy to visit, the one on the outskirts of Windhaven. After, she would be on her way home. The tune still played in her head, conjuring up images of her bed, her spot on the cliff, her beach, and Uncle. Never thought I would feel homesick, Tars. What about you?

Nagora was about to step on the bridge when she stopped to look back at the twin dragons. What a sight. Aye, Tars? Imagine the winter sun low in the sky just behind their heads. It would look like they're spitting fire at each other. Can't wait to tell Uncle about this.

As Nagora neared the halfway point on the bridge, a cold gust of wind licked at her neck. At the same moment,

Kiskwehkan Iskwew entered her mind. The meaning was clear—witch.

"Child."

A hand was on her arm. Nagora froze for a moment, and then looked back.

"Your name, child?" The old woman was short of breath.

Be strong, Tars.

"Tars." She looked at the old woman's hand. Her eyes followed the red silk that wrapped the hand and disappeared along its pale arm into the sleeve of a black woolen cloak. It reappeared again at her neck, circling it three times, to disappear again under the other sleeve and reappear, wrapped around her other hand. She placed that hand in Tar's.

Easy, Tars. Nagora looked into the ancient eyes.

"Your skills won our midday meal from my grandson. Please, child, if you surrender the apples, I'll read your fortune with my rune tiles. I'll let you pick three tiles for each apple, and one for each of your skillful hands. That's one less than I would grant the queen seeking to learn what the future holds for her. What say you?"

The eyes of the teller of good adventures pleaded, one heart to another. When Nagora's eyes returned to the teller's red silk-wrapped hands, they were holding open a leather bag of tiles.

"Choose eleven tiles. Cradle them in your hands. When I give the signal, let them fall between your fingers to the ground."

Nagora moved to reach into the bag.

"The apples first, child, if you please."

Do as she says, Tars. She's hungry. Nagora reached into her scrip for the apples.

The old woman pulled open a pocket on the inside of her cloak.

Easy, Tars. Nagora held the old woman's gaze as she placed the red apples in the pocket, one at a time, while sneaking two from the neighboring pocket into her scrip.

The old woman smiled, closed her cloak, and then reopened her rune bag. "Reach in with both hands. Take not one more than eleven."

Eleven, Tars. Nagora reached into the bag, counted and placed five tiles in one hand and six in her other. She joined her hands to make a cradle and pulled them from the bag.

Don't even drop one, Tars. It was a tight exit, but she managed.

"Keep your hands like that. Close your eyes. When you feel me blow on your hands, spread your fingers and allow the tiles to fall."

Nagora closed her eyes and waited for the old woman's breath to touch her hands. It was quiet, as if time itself had stopped. The tiles grew hotter and hotter. Still, she held on and waited. The tiles grew so hot she moaned and, when she could no longer hold them, air colder than a winter storm's wind soothed the backs of her hands.

Nagora spread her fused fingertips as the tiles slipped through, like midnight icicles against her burning fingers. When the last of the tiles had slipped through, she opened her eyes to gaze at them where they had fallen near her feet.

The old woman was on her knees before the tiles, arms out at her sides, red silk-covered palms skyward.

Easy now, Tars. Nagora let her eyes step from one tile to the next before taking them all in. The blood-red rune symbols on the white translucent pieces of bone whispered to her.

You hear that, Tars? Nagora understood the whispers. But would the old woman dare to tell? If she dares, Tars, I don't want to hear. But I won't have that choice, will I?

The old woman looked up from the runes.

What's that look, Tars? One of pity or one of hope?

The old woman bent over her tiles. With a deliberate hand, she drew the shape of an egg around the tiles. With the same hand, she picked one tile at a time to place it back in her rune bag.

Nagora kept her eyes on the old woman's hand.

When the old woman had finished, she brought her hands together and held them out.

Take them, Tars. Help her up. Nagora stared into the old woman's eyes for a long moment.

The old woman stared back for a moment longer.

I think she knows I'm not you, Tars. When Nagora turned her eyes away, the old woman stepped closer, put her arms around her, and drew her close. Her ancient voice was a whisper. "Child, a dragon awaits you." The old woman stepped back and held Tars' eyes with her own, one last time, before shambling away.

I think we're good, Tars. Nagora marched toward the checkpoint on the other side of Twin Rivers Bridge. She had a dream of a dragon in her heart and two green apples in her scrip. So, Tars, what was that all about? *Ka Peyakot Mahihkan* meets *Kiskwehkan Iskwew*. No one knows what the future holds. Right, Tars?

The checkpoint guards were busy with a line-up of wagons. One of them gave her a brief glance and waved her by even though she hadn't reached them yet. Must be this month's tribute day, Tars. We're not worth their time. We've nothing to grease their palms. So she marched right on through to the road.

Three counts later, Nagora spotted a small bridge down the road. A green apple with salt, Tars? Makes the sour taste easier to take. She climbed down the embankment and sat on a riverbank stone beneath the bridge. As she stared into the water, she took the apples from her scrip.

She set one in her lap, reached for the knife on her belt, and cut the apple in half across its core. She examined the two five-point stars. With the tip of her blade, she flicked the seeds into the water, one at a time, and counted them as they sank.

Five.

She did the same with the seeds from the other half.

Six. That's not right, Tars. Never more than ten.

A single seed floated away inside an oily ring on the current of the river. The seed count of the second apple yielded the same result. She turned the apple halves over, tugged on the stems. They gave way easily. Tar piss! Tars, she let me pick her pocket.

Nagora tossed the green apple halves into the river and her eyes followed them until the last star disappeared with the current.

She found the flint in her scrip and dragged her small blade across it. The sparks set the invisible oil on her blade on fire. A red flame glowed along both sides of the blade. Poison oil is what that is, Tars. She's a witch for sure. Don't trust anyone but yourself. Why would she want to poison me?

In turn, Nagora held each hand above the flame to cleanse it of any of the residue. For a moment, two of her finger tips flamed red. Tar piss! It doesn't hurt! It doesn't hurt! It's only like hot tar on a seam.

Nagora dug her hands into the mud on the river's shore and pulled out wet handfuls of it. She rubbed the mud over her palms and fingers and the blade of her knife.

She rinsed her hands and looked at them. Not a tar stain in sight, Tars. Poor Uncle, he's building curraghs on his own. His tar baby's not there to help him. Could be the trainees will miss out on his archery lessons.

All because of me, Tars. The Cause can wait. It's been waiting all these years anyway, right? A hundred days more or less won't matter. Though, from what we've seen so far, Tars, something needs to happen soon.

Nagora threw a stone into the river. Best we be on our way, Tars. A dragon awaits us. Ha! She almost laughed. It started to rain. Is that going to last, Tars? Do we wait it out?

Do you hear that? Thunder? The sound grew louder and approached faster. Horses, Tars. We'll let them go by.

Nagora sat on the rock and looked to the wooden beams and floorboards just overhead. The hooves rumbled across, shaking damp dust down on her. Four of them, Tars. They're in a hurry.

I think we'll travel off the road from here on. We'll be traveling upwind. Let's see what we can hunt. She removed her pack, unclipped her quiver, took out her bow, assembled it, and chose two hunting arrows. As soon as the shower passed, she was on her way.

· · ·

Three days later, Nagora awoke to a misty morning, high in the hills above and well away from the busy road to Windhaven.

She sat up on her bedroll. Time to get moving, Tars. I hope you slept as well as I did. Two nights of bad dreams about that witch had my legs as weak as rags. We'll make good time today. She slipped out from under the tarp she had hung from the big stone projection the night before. The space was dry and just big enough to be comfortable.

After tightly wrapping her bedroll in the tarp, she donned her quiver and bow, and climbed the hill with a big piece of the stone bread she had baked the night before. She chose a slight depression just below the top, out of sight of the road below.

She bit into the bread.

The day before, while climbing up here to look for a sheltered spot that would afford her a safe place to spend the night, she caught sight of an armed, mounted contingent as it rode by in the direction of Twin Rivers. She had seen smaller contingents on patrol. They didn't travel as fast as this one. This contingent was on a mission, most likely to investigate rebel activity.

Would Maton and his sister be safe in Gallanford? How long before they were found out? The dead bodies had most likely been found. The search would be on in earnest. Many would be questioned.

Too late to worry about that. She would just have to keep on being careful. For the past three days she had been hiking well away from farms, keeping to the forest and the hills, taking her time and scouting the way ahead for anyone who might see her. Up to now she had kept herself invisible as she traveled and hunted.

So far nothing worth drawing an arrow on had come across her path and the snares she had set turned up empty the following mornings. Maybe there'll be something in one today.

Yesterday, she had waited until nightfall to light a cooking fire in her protected spot. The dried smoked fish and barley went into her pot for an edible soup she would never offer to share with a guest.

She took a sip from her waterskin before biting into her bread again.

Will we have enough rations, Tars? You're right. We can stretch what we have for three more days. Though, with luck, we'll be at the last smithy's forge in two days.

One road to cross and then the next road would take her to her destination. The first road, coming from what Uncle had labeled as the Lake Country, met and crossed the road below to become the main road into Windhaven.

Tars, it's the one we saw in the distance yesterday, so we'll be on the other side of it well before nightfall today.

Tomorrow she would reach the next road. Only then would she travel the road. It would bring her to the smithy's hamlet.

Again yesterday's contingent rode past in her mind. The checkpoint guards would be questioned too. See any strangers go by here recently? A guard worth his salt would surely remember Tars. The broken horseshoe. The smithy he had visited. There would be more questions. Had she put The Cause in danger?

Best I do my exercises to clear my mind.

Deliberately slow, with bow in hand, Nagora focused on each movement and each breath she took to ward off, roll-back, press, push, pull, elbow strike, shoulder strike, advance, retreat, look left, gaze right, and center balance. A hundred precise motions.

At the end of her routine, she stood tall and pushed her chest out. A single chain link waited to be marked. On the road back home she would stay away from towns and travel as close to the coast as possible. Food is always plentiful along the shore. Don't dwell on the past. Stay low. Bring the chain back. Your job will be done.

Before checking her snares and going on her way, Nagora climbed to the top of the hill and surveyed the road below, the woods, and the farmlands around. Even the disguised crop fields of Cairnmase didn't look this neglected. Tars, Windhaven Road lies ahead. We cross it, then come to Dromester Road. We'll find our last smithy down that road.

Of the wagons Nagora had watched heading for Windhaven from her hiding spot along the road from the Lake Country, not a single one of their drivers wore a smile. Obviously, the queen's unjust tributes weighed heavily on their shoulders and painted the grim look on their faces. What happened to those who gave up? Did they join The Cause? Did they dare? Were they aware of its existence? Did they have hope for the future?

Nagora crossed the road and stuck to the forested hills, using the rocky, tree-covered terrain to hide her progress to the next road. She kept her bow at the ready. Risk the loss of an arrow to bag a red squirrel? No, they could have the run of the woods. She would not waste time building traps. Anyway, what could she put in them to lure the squirrels? These woods too had been over-hunted and over-trapped these past years.

Nagora took her time, often stopping to listen and watch. She crouched behind a big rock, sat on her heels, and rested her back against it. Her eyes slowly did a sweep from right to left, watching for any movement.

Her ears listened for the snap of a twig, the scuff of a boot on a stone, or footfalls on dry leaves. She turned so her shoulder pressed against the rock.

She peered around one side, then the other, before peeking over the top. She would not let a two-legged predator catch her again.

Other than her weapons, she had nothing of value to make her a target. But such hunters have other motives. Don't they, Pug? She placed a hand on the knife at her belt, spit on the brown pine needles at her feet, and continued on her way.

In the distance, a dog barked. Was it chasing another sound? Nagora looked in the direction of the barking and closed her eyes. A single cow bell. It was late afternoon. Milking time approached. Chances were it was a small farm. Most likely near the road she was headed for. Do I go around it and try to make it to the smithy's before dark? Not a good idea. Find a safe spot for the night.

Nagora's frustrating search took her to a tree where she would have to use her rope and net to make her bed. It was always her last choice. Other than birds, no other creatures would come across her, hidden up among the branches and leaves. She just might sleep well.

First, Nagora did a slow sweep of the perimeter. She counted three hundred strides away from the oak before moving ahead. She kept the tree in view to her left as she circled it, scanning the terrain to her right and left. She found only a single path crossing the perimeter well away from her chosen tree. It didn't show any signs of recent use.

Her plan was clear. A cooking fire now was out of the question. Perhaps, if she awoke before the light of dawn and the forest was filled with mist, she would make a quick fire. Better to be safe. Tonight, a piece of dried smoked fish washed down with water would be her fare. Better than being hungry. She would eat well away from the tree and wait until it was almost dark before climbing the tree.

In the meantime, she prepared for the possible morning fire, gathering small dry branches, a few stones for a fire pit, and a flat one to bake a big flour and oat biscuit while water boiled her forest tea. She was proud of herself. Uncle would be too if he were watching her. In a way he was. You taught me well.

Nagora put away her big blade after completing her exercises in the dark mist of dawn. She had done them fast to warm her body. She had woken with a chill, earlier than usual. Another reason she didn't like sleeping in a net. It was fine if the night was warm. That was rare. She could count summer nights like that on the fingers of one hand.

The milkweed silk fire starter, wrapped in a bundle of the smallest of spruce twigs, caught on the first strike of her flint.

She piled on small branches and sticks. The silk was magic. It repelled water. It was ideal to light a fire when firewood was wet. She only had to use more of it. She and Uncle harvested it to use in their winter beds. If she had had a mat of it to sleep on in her net, she would still be asleep.

With hot tea warming her insides, Nagora put out the last embers of the fire and set off with dawn's dim light to find the road. She bit off a chunk of her biscuit as she traveled away from where the small farm was. Far enough to not attract the dog's attention.

Nagora had found a stick, near the road, almost the size of her staff though not as straight, and with most of its bark and two small branches still on it. It made a good walking stick and it could help keep a dog away, or a person with wrong intentions. And it added to Tars' appearance as a traveler from away.

Nagora followed the road downhill on its gentle slope past the occasional small farm. The rocky land had given up parcels of tillable soil where the now neglected small farms struggled to provide for those who had chosen to settle.

What were proud stone fences years ago were now being invaded by the brush that had already recaptured land that, in a better time, had been cleared and tilled and cared for. Now their most frequent caretakers were the few sheep or a rare cow set to graze in the stone enclosures. It was farming to survive, on the edge of despair. Wherever Nagora looked, signs of hope were absent, crushed by unjust tributes.

The huts of Cairnmase, disguised to look poor, appeared rich compared to the hovels she passed on the road. The road, where it didn't cross rocky surface ledges, had become rutted and overgrown with bushes, especially in the earthy depressions that couldn't be avoided. Obviously, the farm families living along it were no longer providing the labor required to maintain it. Why would they? There was no incentive.

Did anyone dare whisper about The Cause in these parts? If they did, Nagora could detect no sign of it. Would the last smith provide a hint of it?

No Longer In My Eyes
Pâskâpiw Ôyêhâ

It was well into the afternoon when Nagora reached the hamlet of Dromester. The barefoot children, playing with sticks and small stones on the road, scattered at her approach. Their happy voices disappeared with them. She turned to look back the way she had come. No one else was on the road.

Tars, you scared them away. See the chimney over there? Bet you that's a forge chimney. No smoke. Let's hope he's there.

The two doors were wide open. No one was in sight. She stood in the doorway and looked around before setting foot inside. A metal triangle hung from a piece of rope tied to a horseshoe nail on the beam above. Next to it, another cord held a big nail. Not as big as Ôeirador's, aye Tars? She reached for the nail and struck the triangle three times.

She waited and was about to strike it again.

"What can I do you for?" The voice came from the doorway. She spun on her heel to face it.

A grim-faced man, the size of Geirador, stood with hands on his hips. He wore a big leather apron as dirty as it was patched. He obviously owned the place."

The entrance shrunk as he stepped closer. He stopped near her.

The four 8's were almost lost in the hair where his neck met his chest.

Nagora reached into her scrip for the broken horseshoe. "Can you fix this?"

He took the pieces, one in each hand. He would most like-ly be able to break a shoe with his bare hands. He didn't move away. She held her ground and tilted her head to look up into his eyes, eyes that were reading hers, and her. Each intake of breath expanded his barrel chest like a steady pull on a bel-lows. "Who made this?"

She swallowed. "The same one who made this." The squeak that came out didn't sound like Tars at all. She fum-bled for the knife at her belt.

The hint of a smile dented his broad, bearded face. "Say again?"

Nagora cleared her throat and held out her knife. "The same one who made this." More like it. Tars, where were you?

He looked at both sides of the blade. His smile broadened. "Geirador."

She took a deep breath and bit her upper lip as he returned her knife and held open his big palm. She stuck the knife back in its sheath and reached deep into her scrip for the chain.

When it was in his hand, he walked over to his forge and threw it onto the cold ashes of the hearth.

"What—? Wait! What are you doing?"

He glanced back at her and held up a single finger. He took a big poker and pushed the chain deep under the ash pile.

What was going on? Was she going to have to fight him to get the chain back? Nagora's breath came faster as she clenched her fists.

He turned to face her and reached one hand up to the pivoting handle that allowed him to work the bellows. Still smiling, he calmly stared at her. "It'll be safe there. You know where it is. I know where it is. Unless you tell, no one else will."

"I don't understand. Aren't you supposed to—?"

"Mark it? Aye, I am. And I will, when I'm ready. I'll be ready in six days."

"But—."

He held up a hand. "I need a few more important pieces of information before I can. When I get them, I'll mark my link and then you'll get the chain back. If you insist, I can give it back to you right now, unmarked. And you can be on your way."

She exhaled and crossed her arms. "Very well, then. I'll wait until you're ready."

"That'll be a long wait. You're a skinny piece of shit. You look like you could eat something. Moreena'll be happy to have some company." He stepped over to her and placed a big hand on her shoulder. "You'll come with me. Wait here."

He closed the doors to his shop, taking his time to do so, as he looked around the street outside. Now it was dark inside.

Nagora stepped over to the post less than two paces from where he had left her standing. She spread her legs, balanced her weight, and put her hand on the handle of the knife at her belt.

A shadow within the darkness hulked before Nagora's eyes and then a door to her left opened, spilling daylight into the shop. "Sorry I left you in the dark. I should've opened this door first. I'm usually alone when I close shop. Haven't had a customer in days." He waved her through as he held the door.

She breathed easier and steadied herself as she stepped toward the light.

"To the door on the other side of the yard."

A few hens skittered out of her way as Nagora crossed to the other side to wait for him.

"I didn't get your name. I'm known in these parts as Bardas." He held out a hand.

His grip was light, gentle even. "Tars."

"Tars. Besides hauling that chain around, you work?"

"Build curraghs with my uncle."

He smiled and nodded as he opened the door. "Go ahead. Moreena, we have a guest."

Nagora stepped past Bardas into a room lit by the light of one candle lantern, the light from a small open window across from her, and the glow from the fireplace just around a corner to her left. She let her pack slip from her shoulders and looked for a place to set it on the floor near the door.

A wooden spoon struck the lip of a pot and then a heavy lid slid into place. As the smell of fresh baked bread and a stew invited her in, she caught sight of a person in silhouette coming toward them.

"Father, who is it?"

Bardas had just lit a candle lantern and was hanging it on a hook on the beam overhead. "This is Tars, a curragh maker from away. From where exactly, I haven't asked yet."

Nagora followed Moreena's steady, upright approach. Her left hand had reached out to touch the edge of the table. When it did, she turned slightly and moved forward, a deliberate step at a time. What was she looking at?

"I live not far from Yhorgal, right near the coast."

Moreena's head turned ever so slightly as she came forward. "That is far from here. You must've been on the road for a while." She wiped her hands on the knee-length apron she wore over her green dress. She held out a hand at chest level and came closer. "Tars, you've probably guessed by now I don't see well. I see you as a shadow. You'd be so kind if you would allow me to touch your face, so I can better see your features in my mind."

"Please do, Moreena." Nagora let the hand of the beautiful red-haired young woman find her. It came to rest on her sheepskin vest. She left it there as her other hand reached up to her face. "You'll want to remove your vest. It's warm in here."

As soon as the left hand found Nagora's chin, the right came up to settle next to it, and their warm finger tips explored. Moreena's hands smelled of bread dough and fresh battered butter, like Pare's often did.

Moreena's smiling face twitched for an instant as her fingers paused on the lips. Her smile disappeared as her fingers brushed over the lips again. "Smile." The word was a warm whispered command.

Nagora obeyed. She would do whatever this woman asked her, so taken she was with her, like her dear friend Pare, perhaps older.

Moreena's fingers explored the smile, and then moved to the nose, up over the bridge and back down its sides. Then on to the cheekbones, up the sides of the face, across the forehead, and down to the eyebrows. "Close your eyes."

Nagora did and held Moreena's lips in her mind. They, like the rest of her face, were sprinkled with freckles. To explore those freckles with my lips would be a pleasure.

Ever so lightly, her fingertips roamed over the eyelids and lashes then paused on the cheeks below. Her fingers spread wide and took in the whole face for a moment. "Open your eyes."

Nagora did.

Moreena took a quick breath and nodded as she let her hands fall to the shoulders. Her warm smile returned. "Thank you. Now I see you. Give me your hands."

She took each one in both of hers, feeling each finger, the thumb, the palm, and the wrist. Then she crossed her arms and held out her hands. "Take my hands."

Moreena squeezed and pulled on Nagora's hands and relaxed her grip. "Do what I just did to you."

Nagora did. Moreena's grip was strong.

"You are a good person. Welcome to our home, Tars. Please stay and share our meal with us."

"Thank you. You're most kind."

Moreena turned to her father. "Father, please keep an eye on the stew, while I show Tars where he can wash off some of the dust from the road. Stir and taste. Don't eat. Wait for us."

Bardas winked. "Don't worry. I won't even taste."

"Tars, wait right here. I'll get you a clean piece of linen and some soap."

Moreena went over to a wooden cupboard on the same wall as the door. When she returned, her arm held more than a piece of linen. "I imagine you carried a bag or pack. Bring it."

As Nagora picked up her pack and slung it over a shoulder, Moreena reached to unhook the candle lantern from the ceiling beam.

"Follow me." Moreena led Nagora out the door, along the side of the house, and into the small stable. It housed a mule, a horse, the chickens, and a goat. To their left, they came to a door.

Moreena stopped and placed a hand on the door latch. "This way."

The door opened onto a walled garden compound. At the other end was a tiny hut. Two wolfhounds came to greet them as they stepped past the door. "Meet Keng and Quinn."

The dogs were large, bigger than any Nagora had ever seen. Keng's head came almost up to her chest. "They're huge, Moreena." How could they afford to feed them? "How long have you had them?"

"For as long as I can remember, we've always had dogs. Keng and Quinn are seven-year-olds. Their pups have just been weaned. Make sure you pet Quinn. If you do, she'll show you her pups."

"So you're a mum, are you, Quinn?" She scratched the dog's neck and patted it on the back. Keng came close for like treatment. "And you're the proud da, Keng? I'd love to see your pups." Quinn's tail wagged as she barked to show the way over to the corner, where two waist-high boarded walls placed against the stable and garden walls formed a corner pen.

"They're not barking, so they're asleep. But not for much longer."

Nagora peered over at the ball of furry little bodies piled up against one another.

Moreena placed a hand on her back. "We'll be going to Windhaven in a few days where we hope to sell them all down at the docks. We have two traders who pay well for them. If they're in port, we'll sell them."

"Do they pay in coin?"

"Oh yes. Otherwise father wouldn't sell them. It's one of the few ways to get our hands on coins these days. Lots of people try to sell to the traders. Anything from fresh vegetables, berries, nuts, meat, or quality crafted goods, like knit sweaters, woven cloth, leather bags."

"One of them's woken up. The little red-haired one."

"That's the runt. We'll go now. He might go back to sleep. If not, he'll wake the others."

Moreena pointed. "That's the well house over there. Clean water. You'll be safe to wash up there."

Moreena led the way through the garden over a path of wooden planks between the two long rows of string beans.

Inside, Moreena set her bundle on a narrow table next to the glazed pottery basin. She also set her lantern on the table before reaching for another hanging above the basin. Moreena opened the hinged glass doors and, with a twisted piece of straw she had pulled from an apron pocket, she lit the second lantern before hanging both above the table. "There. You'll have plenty of light."

Moreena took a step to the edge of the stone well and pulled on the rope that, with the help of a pulley hanging from the ceiling beam, brought up a bucket of water. She pulled it over and rested it on the broad lip of the well.

"Tars, can I touch your hair? To complete the picture I have of you."

Nagora set her pack on the stone floor and took a step closer. "Sure. Do you want me to turn around?" I can only guess what her fingers will see.

Moreena's hands were already up at the sides of her face. "Not yet." Her fingers fluttered up over the hair to the top of her head and then worked their way down the back.

Moreena's face was a tempting kiss away. Her breath was warm and sweet and steady, coming at times from her nose to caress her cheeks and eyes. At other times it came from her mouth, almost hot on Nagora's lips and chin.

Moreena's hands pulled at the ends of the strands, from the center all the way to the sides. Moreena's breathing quickened. She moved her hands away. "Turn around."

The whispered words almost made their lips touch.

I want our lips to touch, but does Moreena? Nagora closed her eyes as Moreena's fingers caressed her neck as they lifted the hair from it. To lean my neck against her fingers, I don't dare.

And then Moreena brushed hair away from an ear and rested her lips against it to whisper. "I don't know what your true name is. I know you're a strong warrior maiden, skillful with a bow, and I don't doubt you can build a curragh. And you know how to use the weapons you carry on your back.

"Your hair was once as long as mine. You wore it in a braid. Someone cut it in violence, to hurt your beauty, to steal your strength. I would not want to be the one who did that to you.

"You are here, far from home, for a reason. My father knows why. Your secret is safe with us."

I guessed she would tell me some of these things, but not in such detail. Nagora leaned her head back so Moreena's lips grazed her ear as they came to rest on her cheek. "You see me so well, Moreena. Like a dear friend."

Moreena kissed her cheek and wrapped her arms around her waist. "I'm happy to be your friend. I will continue to be that while you're here. But you must never tell me your true name. Do it for your own safety, Tars, please."

"I will." Their lips touched in the softest kiss of a promise.

Moreena pulled away and reached for the bucket. She emptied it into the basin and dropped it back into the well. "I've brought you some clean clothes and a sweater."

Moreena reached out with a foot to touch the bigger basin under the wash table. "There's a wash board in it. If you want to wash some clothes, do so. You can hang them in the garden to dry."

Moreena held out her hands. "Tars."

Nagora took Moreena's outstretched hands in hers.

"Take your time. Wash your hair. We won't eat until you come to our table. You won't have to wear your weapons. You'll be safe with us. And don't let Keng and Quinn keep you." Moreena hugged her close, then left.

...

Clean, refreshed, and hungry, Nagora stepped from the well house to hang the shirt, socks, and undergarments she had washed. Keng and Quinn were waiting for her.

As Nagora hung her wet clothes on a line running from the top of the compound wall near the well house all the way back to the stable wall, she inhaled Moreena's scent. It was mixed in with the lanolin of the sweater's wool. Like Pare's scent when she wore one of her sweaters on a visit in winter. Pare, I miss you.

She shook out her wet hair and gave it a last rub with the linen cloth before hanging it to dry alongside her clothes. She returned to the well house to rinse and empty the basins in the narrow trough that took the water out to the barrel filled with gravel. Uncle had built a similar arrangement for their lodge.

Another trough from the bottom of the barrel took the filtered water out to the garden. She took down one lantern, blew out its candle, and returned it to its hook. She took the other along with her blades and pack and made her way to the stable door, again under escort of the hounds.

Nagora knocked on the door before opening it. The aroma of the stew greeted her just before Moreena's words. Was it pork? Perhaps the way of cooking it was different?

"You must feel so much better. Come, let me see you."

Nagora hung the candle lantern before setting her pack and her blades down next to the hutch where Moreena had fetched the linen. She shook her head and reached for the braid that wasn't there. The angry image flashed as she jabbed at her still damp mop, trying to place its curly tangle into something presentable.

Moreena stood waiting at the table, the knuckles of her left hand rested on its edge.

"Soap hasn't touched me in such a while. I was forgetting how good it feels to be clean." Nagora stopped just short of Moreena's outstretched hand. She took it in hers.

Moreena pulled Nagora closer and reached up to her damp hair. "Now Tars, you smell good. Not much to do with this broom until it dries. Will you let me brush it when it does?"

"Sure. I'd like that."

Moreena's hand left the hair it had been touching and came to rest on her cheek. "So will I. Father'll be back any moment now. We can fill the bowls."

"Moreena, does your da know—you know, about me?"

"Aye, Tars, he does. You'd never have gone beyond his forge if you truly were the lad you made yourself out to be. His keen eye is quick to take the measure of anyone new setting foot in his shop. Rare is a stranger who comes by here. That's why you and I'll be gone before first light tomorrow."

Well, Tars. Do you think the others know too? Where will we be going?

The door opened. She looked in time to see Bardas step inside.

"Can we eat?" Bardas patted his belly.

Nagora hadn't eaten so much in a long time. It wasn't pork, but wild boar. Close.

Bardas too had left his bowl clean. "So you liked it, Tars? Almost tastes the same as pig meat, doesn't it? Most likely would if it were raised like pigs. But that's not what happened."

Nagora brushed aside a strand of her now dry hair. "What do you mean?"

"Some farmer got a few live ones from a trader at the docks in Windhaven about a dozen years ago. Started raisin' 'em like pigs."

He set his big forearms on the table and crossed his fingers so his hands formed what looked like a pen. "A couple a years later, some broke loose through a fence." He uncrossed a few fingers. "Tried to find 'em. Couldn't. Figured they'd die of cold come winter. But no. They're a hardy bunch. They survive in the wild and grow in numbers like you wouldn't believe. Any farmer without fences to keep them out pays the price in crop losses."

"I haven't come across any yet."

Bardas pointed. "They spread all the way down to the coast, direction of the midday sun. The past two years they've spread up to these parts. I often get paid with their meat. Only so much boar a man can eat. I trade it if I can, or give to those who've given up on their own farms. Sometimes I can sell some in Windhaven."

"Aren't they preyed upon by other animals?"

Bardas reached into his scrip. "Ever see a black, hairy pig with these stickin' out each side of its snout?" He placed them next to her bowl. "Tusks. They dig in the ground for food with 'em. A gang of twenty of them'll uproot a field's crop overnight."

She held one in each hand. "They're sharp."

"Aye. And as gentle as they are when raised in pens on a farm, they're fierce in the wild. Have your bow ready or start runnin' if you don't."

Nagora set them back on the table. "At least they're providing food to those who hunt them."

"Aye. For those brave enough to hunt. Not everyone's skilled enough with a bow to do so. You, Tars, probably are."

"I've been trained to hunt. But not for four-legged animals that'll attack me. I guess if I weren't taken by surprise, I'd be able to stand my ground and take one down."

Moreena smiled at her.

Bardas put his big hand flat on the table. "I see your quiver over there. Where's your bow?"

Nagora stood. "I'll show you." When she returned to the table with her quiver, she pulled her bow and handed it to Moreena. "If you don't mind, Bardas."

"If this is a bow, Tars, it's a strange one. Does it need to be put together somehow?" Moreena held it out to be taken.

"Here, I'll show your da."

Bardas held it in both his hands, turning it over as he examined it. "Geirador make this?"

"Yes. He and my uncle made it for me. The ram horn tips are from one I killed."

Click. "Aha!" Out came the hardwood piece that held the limbs in the brass handle. "I think I've got it." He slipped each one into the opposite end of the handle. "And this holds everything together." Snap. He unraveled the string, backed his chair away from the table, and strung the bow. He gave it a pull. "You can pull this?"

"Sure."

"I told you, Father. Tars is strong. And an archer."

"You build a lot of curraghs, Tars?"

"Over the years, yes."

"That would help build your strength. You shoot a lot?"

"Almost every day."

He handed the bow to Moreena. "That settles it. You'll be leaving with Moreena before the light of day. The hounds'll be with you. They know the way. So does Moreena. But they make it easier for her. You'll be three nights away. Come back on the fourth day.

"You can set snares, maybe hunt a boar. You'll have food. And salt. Gut whatever you hunt. Rub salt on the insides. Leave the skin on unless you have time to smoke it. Anything you bring back, you can sell at the docks in Windhaven, if you come with us. Get yerself some coins."

Moreena reached over and touched Nagora's arm. "Father makes it sound like we're going on a hunt. Not so. It's for your safety. Instead of staying around here. Patrols come by and question people. Someone's surely seen you."

Bardas cleared his throat. "I put word out. A cousin from the Lake Country came for Moreena to see if she can help an ailing aunt."

"Mother was from the Lake Country. Her sisters still live there," said Moreena

"Are you a healer, Moreena?"

"Mother was. I learned some things from her. Some say I have healing hands." Moreena's face became sad. She looked at her father. She must've detected the slump in his shoulders and could read his sadness.

"I'm sorry for your loss. I didn't know your mum had passed away."

Bardas stood. "Moreena'll tell you if she's up to it. I can't. It pains me to talk of it. I trust you'll take care of my daughter?"

"Count on me. It's the least I can do. You're looking out for me."

He grunted and drew the back of his hand across his nose. "I'll see you off in the morning." He left.

"It's been hard on Father. Tars, I'll tell you about it tomorrow.

"We've got things to prepare for tomorrow. Go get your clothes outside. They'll finish drying by the fire."

Nagora had slept soundly in her bedroll under the table. No reliving her first kill in repeated dreams this night. Moreena had let down her red mane before giving her a good night hug. Nagora had nuzzled her face in Moreena's hair to capture her new friend's scent and bring it to bed with her. It had made falling asleep easy.

The dark morning mood was quiet and solemn at the table, each with their own thoughts.

Bardas didn't speak until they had reached the outskirts of the sleepy hamlet. "You take care, now. See you in four days."

He bent to the hounds and scratched their chins. "Keng. Quinn. Eyes, ears, noses. Alert. Protect Moreena. Protect Tars." He hugged Moreena.

"We'll be fine, Father."

"Tars." He placed a hand on her shoulder. "I'm counting on you."

"I'll keep a weather eye."

A sliver of daylight followed them along the cart track at the edge of a fallow field. As soon as they came to the forest, it became a trail. Keng led the way. Quinn stayed at Moreena's side.

The trail had taken them up the lower slope of a mountain in a gradual climb through the rock-strewn forest. Now they stood at the edge of a clearing. Half of the morning had gone by. They hadn't come across anyone else and, from what Nagora could tell, no one had followed them.

Moreena pointed across the clearing. "Do you see the scree over there?"

"All that pile of slate pieces come down from the steep, stony flank over there?" asked Nagora.

"That's it. We'll cross at the tip of the pile and begin our climb through the trees on the other side. It'll take us above and across that bare flank. It's usually an easy climb. Slow-going. We keep following Keng."

"Do we go much further beyond that?"

"A ways further. We'll arrive just after midday if all goes well. We'll be just above the tree line."

At the edge of the scree pile, Moreena stopped. "Do you hear it, Tars?"

Nagora listened, but noticed nothing different. "What am I supposed to hear?"

"Close your eyes. Turn your head slowly from side to side."

Uncle had taught her to do that too. *Why didn't I do that first?* "Water! It's a spring."

"Right, Tars. The water's cool and sweet. We'll refresh our waterskins and have some nuts before the climb."

Nagora looked back. Moreena had been right about the climb, slow and easy. Only once did Keng disappear to go around a stand of uprooted trees, most likely brought down with spring thaw runoff and rains. It hadn't taken him long to find an alternate route for Moreena.

The wind had become more apparent, and the sun was ahead of them now. As it rose, its beams snuck through the treetop leaves to find them and warm their faces. Soon it overtook them and led them past the tree line.

"We're almost there, Tars. Rabbits like the scrub brush around here. You might have some luck with your snares."

"Do the dogs chase them?"

"No. Father trained them not to. If they spot one, they'll lay down with paws pointing in its direction. Often what they see, Father can't. Anyway, hares rarely come to feed in broad daylight. Hawks and eagles hunt them too."

Why is it only the two-legged animals are so cruel to their own kind? Whatever happened to our kind, Tars? She didn't want to share that with Moreena. It was a question she often asked herself and could never find a satisfying answer to.

"Straight up from here, Tars. Do you see the three big boulders ahead? The smallest one is in front of the two bigger ones. The last one is the biggest. It'll be home for three nights. Careful of the loose stones. Stay on hard rock.

"Sorry, Tars. I know I don't have to tell you these things. I sound like my father."

"No harm in reminding me, Moreena."

When they reached the first boulder, Moreena stopped.

"Take my hand, Tars." As Nagora did, Moreena turned her around. "Look. Tell me what you see."

"Wow!" She took a moment to take it all in. "In the farthest distance, the sea. It's dark blue, almost black. Then the coast. There are mountains on a stretch of it, then a long inlet of water opens into a protected bay. There's a big walled town at the bottom of the bay. I can make out boats at the docks. One is under sail and headed for the inlet."

Da, could that be you?

Moreena squeezed her hand. "What town do you think that is, Tars?"

"That must be Windhaven. The main road out of there brings me to a crossroad. I traveled on that one from Twin Rivers. It's not visible from here. The main road out continues on to become the road to the Lake Country. I crossed that one and came to the next one. It brought me to you. I think I can see your da's smithy. I see the surrounding farmland fields. Difficult to tell their state from here. And then the blanket of trees we climbed under to get here."

"Do you think you could come back here on your own, Tars?"

"Aye, sure. Why?"

Moreena hugged her. "No reason. I just wanted to confirm what I was thinking. Come. Let's see if you can find my secret place.

"Keng. Here. With Quinn.

"Up we go, Tars. We'll follow you."

Nagora's experience climbing the coastal cliffs along the shore of her beach and her excursions into the mountains with Uncle had taught her rock formations rarely were what they appeared to be on a first look. A cave entrance could be easily overlooked or one could appear where one would never imagine it could be.

This being the case, Moreena would most likely win the "find-my-secret-place" game. Unless I can spot a sign of unusual wear on the surface of this rock. Slip marks or something dragged over it.

"Do you come here often, Moreena?" It was a dumb question to ask. Most likely not. A secret place doesn't stay secret for long if it's visited regularly. Creatures of habit make easy prey. I learned that lesson the hard way.

"Not since last year. I never know when I'll get a chance to come. Da always decides. He'd only let me decide to come on my own if it were to save my life. I couldn't make it without the dogs. If we three were missing, he'd know. There's nowhere else I'd want to go by myself."

Nagora couldn't see a single trace that might lead her to Moreena's secret place. She looked at all the seams. No sign of an opening yet. She rounded the last and biggest boulder. It towered over her by at least ten body lengths. Now she looked at the steep rock wall against which it rested. A mouse could squeeze through that seam, but not a hungry cat.

"We've gone past it. Haven't we, Moreena?"

Moreena had a hand on the big boulder and a huge smile on her face. Missing the secret entrance was worth it just to see that smile.

What's she hiding in that secret place? Whatever it is, it's making her happy. She's so beautiful with that full smile.

"Come back this way, Tars. It's between the two boulders."

Sure enough, it was at Nagora's feet at the back of the seam. From where she had passed, the raised lip of stone hid the hole behind it. She had to be almost on top of it to see it.

"Be careful, Tars. Sit on the edge, keep your hands on it as you let your bum slide off. Your feet'll touch the first ledge. Let yourself crouch down so you can sit on it. Let your feet hang over and they'll touch the next ledge. Sit on it and the next time your feet touch, you'll be on the cave floor. Wait for me."

In the dark, Nagora fished for her flint in her scrip. When she found it, she sparked it with the blade of her knife to light the taper Moreena held. The light it cast showed the natural ledges they had come down on. What wasn't natural on their faces were the footholds carved into the rock.

Moreena pointed to them. "My Father carved those. Makes it easier to climb out, especially for the dogs.

"See that crack? Any water coming in flows out that way."

"I'm surprised it doesn't smell dank in here." Nagora looked around. "Is this all?"

"Oh! No! Looks like it though, aye? Over here, Tars. You'll soon see why the air is fair in here."

The closer the taper got to the back wall, the depth of what was actually there took shape, an opening to a passage behind the wall. And about six paces later the passage opened to a bigger chamber.

"Hold the taper."

Moreena's fingers found the wall and guided her to a set of shelves made of twine-lashed tree branches. She took a candle lantern. "The taper, Tars." Moreena touched a small tube of bark to the flame and lit the candle with it.

Moreena held it before her and stepped slowly, obviously counting her steps. "Beds here." She touched the post of one of the two resting against the wall.

"Table and chairs there." The tabletop was small, most likely brought here. Branches had been bent and lashed to-gether with leather lanyards to make chairs, much like the ones Uncle had made for their lodge.

They stepped past the table. "The fire pit. Look up at the high roof. You can feel the air from the entrance moving up to that crack. It vents high up the mountain. Gives us a good draft for a clean fire that doesn't smoke up the place. So far, no water has come down it. Father doesn't know exactly how that works. Most likely, another crack channels it away from this one."

What's she not telling me? She's holding something back. Something I'm not seeing in here. Maybe it's hidden. Later, maybe.

"What do you think, Tars?"

"Well, it is a secret place. A good place to come to hide from those chasing you, I guess. Someone with enough supplies could hold up here for a good while.

"Err … what do you do for a latrine?"

Moreena laughed. "A cedar bucket. But I'm afraid we didn't bring enough water to swell its boards. I'll show you where you can go outside.

"Shall we eat outside? After, you can set some snares. Only if you want to."

"Latrine first, for me. Then I'll be ready to eat."

Keng accompanied Nagora as she set a dozen snares, six in the scrub near the tree line, and six right on the border between the two, on possible paths the hares might take. She would've hunted, but didn't want to leave Moreena on her own for too long. Maybe tomorrow. We're here for two more days. It'll be one way to pass the time. It would be handy to have a few coins in my scrip for the trip back.

Moreena sat watching Nagora approach as she cradled Quinn's big head in her arms. "You're done already, Tars?"

She sat next to Moreena. "Done for today. I'll see what I catch tomorrow. I could end up setting twice as many or go with a dozen again. They're out there. Keng found their turds. I hope my snares find them."

Moreena reached out to touch her arm. "Tars, have you ever heard of the Isle of Smoke?"

"Only recently. The queen lives there this time of year is what I've heard."

"That's right. Can you see the castle inside Windhaven's walls below?"

Nagora looked. "I can. Up in a corner from the main gate to the town. It's on a hill of its own."

Moreena spit. "The queen's bastard son lives there now. Either she doesn't see the cruelty he does, or she doesn't care. Either way, he's learned his tricks from her, and her witch."

"Her witch?" *Kiskwehkan Iskwew*. Could I have met her?

"You don't know Queen Raganora's story, do you, Tars?"

"To be honest Moreena, I'm ignorant about so many things you wouldn't believe it. So many things have been kept from me, supposedly for my own protection. The less I know the better is what I'm told. Coming from where I do, at the other end of the land, news is scarce. At least it doesn't reach my ears. Not much excitement out there is what someone said. That person is most likely right."

Moreena grabbed her arm. "Tars, don't be offended if I ask you this question. Do you know the name of the land we live in?"

"I know the one we're not supposed to say. And from where I come from, people don't ever speak the name of the one we're supposed to use."

Moreena leaned her head on Nagora's shoulder. "I'm not going to turn you in for speaking it, Tars. And I know you won't turn me in for telling you a story."

"Of course not."

Moreena shook her arm. "Well, say it, Tars."

"Say what?"

"You truly know how to act the part, don't you? Don't play the dumb boy. What's the name of our land?"

"The Land of the Danu."

"You know what that means, Tars? Do you?"

Nagora turned her head away. "I'm not sure. I don't remember."

Moreena placed a hand on her cheek. "Look. It's okay. Don't feel bad. 'Danu' means 'Dragon'. We live in the Land of the Dragon. But damn Queen Rag is trying to make us forget. She wants us to call the land 'Innisfhail.' That has no meaning for us."

Now I remember. She looked into Moreena's blue eyes. If only you could see me as well as I see you. She didn't tire looking at this beautiful woman. As much as Nagora's own eyes tried to explore the paths of the freckles highlighting Moreena's features, a single blink of a blue eye would pull them away to make them swim in Moreena's eyes.

But her ears wanted to hear the story, hear Moreena's voice tell it.

"So tell me about the queen and her witch. I promise, I won't turn you in."

Moreena pulled Nagora closer and pointed. "You see the castle. Move up this way from it, beyond the walls. You see the big hill?"

"The one where you could look out over the whole town, its castle, and take in the whole bay and see all the way down the inlet?" said Nagora.

Moreena gave her arm a squeeze. "That one. Yes. Good King Bernhard and his queen, Julianna, are buried there."

"How'd they die?"

"That's the heart of the story. Raganora, who is Julianna's cousin, was one of the ladies attending Julianna. Raganora was jealous of Julianna. She wanted to become queen. Hag, an old witch, showed up one day. She predicted Raganora would become queen and give birth to a son who would produce the first of many heirs to a long line of kings. And the witch, Hag, offered to help Raganora get the throne. But there was a condition—that all the dragons in the land be killed.

"Raganora agreed, but on a condition of her own. That the last dragon would be killed as soon as her son produced an heir."

"I believe you, Moreena, but how did this become known?"

Moreena held up a hand. "I'll be getting to that. First you need to know a bit more about the dragons. I'm sure on your way here, you've seen all the defaced sculptures and images of dragons."

"Impossible to miss."

"The dragons were protected in our land. In return, they shared certain secrets with us, especially with those working with the fire arts: the blacksmiths, glassmakers, potters, the candlemakers, charcoalmakers, and even the beekeepers. Our land prospered. Our borders were protected by dragon-rider patrols. All this was done through a Dragon Talker, a person who could communicate with the dragons in their language, tame and train dragons to accept riders, and transmit the secrets of the fire."

The hair on the back of Nagora's neck prickled. Tar piss! Could it be? She took hold of Moreena's arm. "This Dragon Talker could actually speak to the dragons? In their language? Did no one else try to learn that language?"

"Tars, I asked that very question to Mum. The way she explained it was the Dragon Talker actually spoke only to one dragon, the mother dragon, but not in the way you and I talk to each other with words out loud."

A shiver shook Nagora. Had Moreena felt it? "Through their thoughts?"

Moreena pulled back her head as her eyes opened wide. "How'd you know that?"

If I told you, you would not believe me. "How else? If it can't be learned."

Moreena smiled. "Yes, that's what Mother told me. It was by thoughts the Dragon Talker spoke to the mother dragon, and the mother dragon spoke to the other dragons."

If only I could be sure. "But how does the Dragon Talker learn the language in the first place?"

"Tars, you amaze me. I asked that question too. My mother said somehow the Dragon Talker passed that skill on to an apprentice."

I'm not an apprentice to a Dragon Talker.

"At that time, the Dragon Talker had died before he could take on an apprentice. His death was mysterious and within a year, the dragons had secluded themselves on the Isle of Smoke. The tamed dragons no longer obeyed their riders."

"Did the witch kill the Dragon Talker?"

"Most likely it was the start of her work. But there was hope. These events had been foretold, and it also had been predicted a man from away would come and talk to the mother dragon."

But the future can't be known. Or can it? "Who foretold this? And did it come true?"

Moreena reached for Nagora's hands and held them tight. "Tars, promise you won't laugh at me. I'm just telling you what I've been told. It was the Little People."

Can she see the smile on my face? I'm not laughing at her. Geirador swears they exist. I suppose, if anyone can see into the future, it would have to be them.

"And yes, it came true. Almost two years later, three drakkars sailed down the inlet. They could have been brazen Outlander invaders, since word had spread that dragons no longer protected our borders. We had once again become a prized invasion destination.

"But the crew of those three boats were not bearing arms. They anchored at the top of the bay, out of range of our weapons. Three of their people, two men and a woman, came ashore, each in their own strange craft. They paddled them with long, double-bladed paddles."

Nagora touched Moreena's arm. "But weren't they Outlanders? People mustn't have welcomed them outright."

Moreena placed a hand on hers. "True. But the woman who came ashore with the two men won the hearts of the crowd gathered at the beach, where they landed their long, slim, pointy crafts."

"Moreena, were their pointy boats covered in skins with only a hole on top for the paddler to fit in?"

"Yes, from the story I was told, they were. Do you know of this kind of boat?"

"I've heard tell of them once."

Uncle mentioned such boats once when I asked him why we built curraghs and not other kinds. He had called them qayaqs and said he knew how to build one. But they were more complicated to build than a curragh. Where did he learn to build one of those?

"Sorry, Moreena, you were saying about the woman ... "

"Yes, well, it's said the woman spotted a young girl clinging to her pregnant mother's dress. The woman went to her knees, took out a doll from her shirt, and held it out for the child to take. The girl's mother encouraged her daughter to accept the gift. The girl went to the woman to get the doll. She took it in one hand and with the other took hold of the woman's hand and brought her over to meet her mother.

"The woman took the mother's hand and placed it on her own belly along with the child's hand. The mother did the same with the woman's hand. Not a word spoken.

"They say it was a good-luck charm doll the women on her boat had given her. It brought luck that day. With the help of the common trader's tongue and someone who could speak some of their language, our king learned they were looking for a place to settle so their women who were with child would have a safe place to spend the winter and give birth.

"King Bernhard agreed to let them stay, on condition they help fight off expected Outlander incursions."

"So who turned out to be the one who talked to dragons?"

"One of the two men who'd come ashore. He was the woman's husband and the leader of the three-boat expedition. Originally, six boats had been on their voyage of exploration. Three of them had set up a colony in the Ice Islands. The remaining three he now led were looking for land to settle, with kinder winters than those of the Ice Islands. Apparently they'd been drawn here by the stories of our dragons."

Nagora shifted and looked at Moreena's profile. "What were their names?"

Moreena put a hand to her mouth. "Oh! My! I know I've heard them before. I'd have to ask Father. Most times when I've heard the story told, the one who talked to the dragons is referred to as the Rider and his wife as—the Rider's Wife. Father could tell you their names."

Nagora scratched her head. "The Rider? Not the Dragon Talker?"

"I'll tell you why after we've climbed a ways higher. It's a clear day. You'll be able to see the Isle of Smoke. You might not get that opportunity in the next two days. Better we do it today. Help me up, Tars."

Nagora stood and reached for Moreena's hands. The dogs were up, tails wagging, ready for whatever came next.

Moreena scratched their necks. "Keng, Quinn, we're going up to the lookout. To the lookout, Keng." Keng barked and led the way. "In close to three counts we'll be there."

They had followed the sun to that side of the mountain. Now Nagora sat on the wide ledge next to Moreena, looking off into the distance. If she held an acorn on the tip of her thumb on her outstretched arm, it would be bigger than what she was looking at. Beyond the thin line of smoke that escaped from the tiny island, the blue sea stretched away to the edge of the sky as far as she could see ahead of her.

To be a bird, to fly over that blue and then up into the other. What would it be like, Tars? Take it all in. Remember it all. You may never see this again.

Moreena took Nagora's arm and pulled her close. "Be my eyes, Tars. Tell me what you see."

"It's so small from here. As if I were standing and looking at a spot of tar fallen on my big toe. A slim line of white smoke is rising from it. Below, where the smoke comes out, I see a shape I'm guessing is a building."

"That's Queen Rag's fortress."

"And a bridge connects the island to the mainland. A vast plain lies opposite the island and forested hills surround it. Beyond the hills, in the distance where the sun goes down, high mountains stand. From the bridge, a road comes this way, to Windhaven."

"What impresses you the most, Tars?"

"The color of the sea and the sky. I've never seen them this way. They're beautiful, but not as beautiful as the blue of your eyes, Moreena."

Moreena squeezed Nagora's arm and reached up to touch her face. "Tars, you're too kind."

"So why The Rider?"

"It had been over a year since losing the Dragon Talker. The one who was to become known as the Rider had asked to be shown where the Dragon Talker lived. He asked to be left alone, saying he'd make his way back to Windhaven on his own. Well, twelve days later he flew over the town on the back of a dragon. He had it land in front of the castle gates."

"No one must have expected that."

"That's right. And from that day on he was called 'The Rider' or 'Rider.'"

"So no one knows how he trained that dragon?"

"No, that's still a mystery. Not any dragon either. It was the mother dragon. But we know that he reached an agreement with the dragons. With their help, he'd build a bridge to the Isle of Smoke to log trees that had fallen due to storm winds. The dragons would allow this in exchange for cattle to give them something other than fish to eat, and it would quiet fears of farmers in the region who had lost animals to the dragons.

"And they also agreed to allow Rider to re-tame a dozen dragons and train their riders."

"So he was like the Master Rider and Dragon Talker too?"

"Yes, he was. And for giving the people back their dragons, he was a hero to the people of the land. But it didn't happen all at once. The warriors from his boats joined Bernhard's troops and proved to be a deciding factor in defeating Outlander forces that attacked late that summer. By the next spring, Rider had dragons patrolling our skies once again."

"What about Raganora and her witch all this time?"

Moreena turned to Nagora. "They were biding their time, waiting for the right moment. Rider and his wife were getting plenty of attention. Raganora was getting even less from Julianna and Bernhard. So her jealousy most likely increased until her opportunity to strike came.

"Three years later, all in the land seemed to go well. Rider, a born explorer, was itching to take to the sea again. Most of the people from his boats had settled in the land. Many of them married locals.

"Rider had set to refitting one of his boats, the Sea Wolf, and had assembled a good crew of those still wishing to follow him over the horizon.

"King Bernhard and Queen Julianna had a son, Raynhard. He admired Rider, and had convinced his parents to allow him to sail on the Sea Wolf with Rider on his first preparation cruise, to make sure everything was ready for a longer journey. It was to last two months."

"How old was this Raynhard?"

"The prince was twelve. But when he came back, he said he felt like a man. Rider had treated him just like any member of his crew and had expected him to pull his weight on board.

He had to bend to every task in all conditions. He had fallen in love with life at sea and wanted to leave on the Sea Wolf for the three-year journey Rider had planned."

"I bet he pestered his parents until they let him go."

"That's what he did, Tars, and because they trusted Rider so much, they let their only son go."

"What about Rider's wife?"

"She'd lost two babies before they were born. Each of those pregnancies had gone well until the eighth month, when she gave painful birth to a baby who'd died in her womb. So she was in a sad state and went to sea to try to forget the loss of her babies."

"That poor woman, Moreena. Two wanted babies lost like that. She must've been heartbroken."

"Surely, she must've been. And the events that followed caused many to question what, and possibly who, had caused the deaths of her unborn infants. Within a month of their departure, Julianna and her closest attending lady became ill. Julianna was bedridden. Raganora had the lady removed, accusing her of bringing on Julianna's illness. With the witch, Hag, Raganora cared for the sick queen. But her condition only worsened and within six months, Julianna died."

"The king didn't suspect any wrong doing?"

"He may have. But Raganora must've had some kind of control over him because, within a month of Julianna's burial, she announced her upcoming marriage to Bernhard. Three months after crowning his queen, Bernhard announced Raganora was with child and, in return for her royal gift, he was building a fortress for her on the Isle of Smoke."

"Raganora didn't waste any time, did she?"

"No, she didn't. It only gets worse. Bernhard falls ill. Raganora says she fears for her unborn child. She blames the illness that's struck the castle on the dragons. She takes up residence on the Isle of Smoke in the first completed part of the fortress.

"Know this, Tars. Soon we learn the one overseeing the construction of the fortress is actually the commander of a mercenary force that arrived by boat in Windhaven. That force came to hunt the dragons with their ballista."

"But didn't the dragons fight back?"

"Without Rider, the Dragon Talker, they could not organize. The twelve trained riders couldn't do much more with the dragons than patrol our borders. So guess who the mercenaries rounded up first."

"Obviously the twelve riders."

"Yes. The dragons they rode were the first to be slaughtered. They were the easiest targets. Then Raganora had the twelve riders hung from the Isle of Smoke Bridge. Our king was too feeble to know what was going on. Powerless, as were the people.

"Before we knew it, Raganora relieved the King's Guard of its duties and replaced it with a mercenary contingent. New conscripts replaced any of the regular troops not submitting to their command.

"Once they'd gotten complete control of Windhaven, they took over the garrison towns in the same way. It was the beginning of the spread of evil in the Land of the Danu.

"With the birth of her son, Queen Raganora declared the country's new name. She was now Queen Raganora of Innisfhail. Her son was Prince Acindor of Innisfhail. Hag was always at her side. Whispers from the Isle of Smoke said the mercenary commander shared Raganora's bed and he was most likely the true father of her child."

Nagora shook her head. "And the poor king lay sick in his bed unaware of all this? What happened when Rider returned?"

Moreena sighed. "Yes. When we thought things could only take a turn for the better, they just got worse. When Rider returned, he brought news that savages, from an island country they had stopped to explore, had taken the king's son prisoner. He wanted to mount an expeditionary force to go free Raynhard. Raganora would only lend support in the way of arms for any allies who would help Rider.

"And Rider brought news of his wife's death at sea while attempting to give birth. Once again, her unborn child had died."

My mum died giving birth to me. I guess I'm lucky to be alive.

"So did Rider succeed?"

"No. Not in the way you think. He approached allies for help, not to go free Raynhard, but to overthrow Raganora instead. No help came forward. They all said she had lawfully gained the crown and concluded favorable treaties with them. If Rider felt Raganora had done something wrong, he'd have to work with the people of Innisfhail to convince them of this to fight for change."

"If he did that, it means Raynhard could still have been alive."

"Yes, Tars. Based on what Rider did next, we think so too.

"It was a desperate plan. If only it had worked. He and the crew of the Sea Wolf were able to climb the seaside cliffs of the Isle of Smoke and take control of the fortress. Unfortunately, Queen Rag was not there. Some of the fortress troops were able to take control of the Isle of Smoke Bridge and get word to Raganora and her mercenary commander.

"They returned with a sizable force and the last captured dragon. Rider had no choice but to negotiate. If Rag would let his crew leave the way they had come, she could keep him prisoner with the last dragon, since he could control it. However, Rag's mercenary commander wanted to fight Rider to the death. If Rider won the fight, Rag could do whatever she wanted.

"And so, Tars, the two of them fought on the bridge. It was a long bloody fight, but Rider prevailed and knocked Rag's champion from the bridge to his death on the rocks in the strait below the bridge." Moreena rubbed her hands over her face and brought her palms together so their pointer fingers rested against her lips.

Nagora waited. The breeze pushed a red curl across Moreena's forehead. "Raganora probably wanted Rider dead, but it was in her interest to keep him alive. Did she, Moreena?"

"Yes. That last dragon was a young one, much smaller than the adults. So on the Isle of Smoke, they had built what they called a vent house over the vent hole the dragons once used.

"Apparently, deep down in that vent hole there are caves along it where dragons laid and hatched their eggs. In the vent house there is an opening in the floor, much like a well. Over it, they installed a crank on which they attached a chain. On the end of the chain, they fastened a cage."

"So they had Rider coax the dragon into the cage?"

"Yes, and Rider had to get in the cage too. Fortress guards lowered them to a cave below. Raganora used to have Rider bring the dragon into the cage and then she'd have the cage raised to show the dragon to guests. But the dragon has since outgrown the cage.

"People wonder if Rider is still alive. If he is, he doesn't show his face. Food, animal carcasses, and water still gets lowered to the cave, but only the dragon's huge head comes out of the cave to take whatever's in the cage. At least that's what we've heard."

"Moreena, I'd go crazy down there alone with the dragon. I can't image Rider still being alive."

"Neither can I."

"So once Prince Acindor produces an heir, all Raganora has to do is starve the dragon to death to keep her bargain with her witch. Is that right?"

"That's it, Tars."

Does Moreena know about The Cause? She must.

"So if Prince Raynhard is still alive, that makes him the rightful heir to the throne. And if that's so, he must be planning to get it back some way or other. How old would he be now, Moreena?"

"Let's see. He left for the three-year voyage on his thirteenth birthday. Possibly came back three years later. Sixteen. That happened fifteen years ago. He'd be thirty-one. I'm twenty-four. I would've been six when he sailed away."

"And I wasn't even born. I'll be seventeen soon."

"No wonder you've not heard any of these stories. Being from far enough away, by the time you were old enough to understand, the people who brought you up knew enough by then to keep you ignorant of it all so you wouldn't speak of dragons, especially this last one. Better for your own safety and theirs. So be careful who you tell what I've told you."

"I will, Moreena. And I'll never speak your name as the one who told me. To anyone. You can trust me."

"I trust you. I don't trust the ones who'll torture you if it ever comes to that. I wish you can stay strong and keep all your wits about you if ever that day comes." Moreena took Nagora in her arms and held her for a long moment.

"Best we be heading back down, Tars. I'll need your help on this steep part."

They were in the cave at the fire pit. The dogs guarded the entrance in the approaching cold night air. They had eaten. Moreena had asked Nagora to face away from the fire and close her eyes. She said she had a surprise for her and she couldn't wait to show it.

What could it be? As Nagora sat with her back to the fire, she listened and tried to remember what she had seen earlier. Was there something she had missed? Perhaps that rack of blankets and skins. They must be for the beds, those bare frames with woven-rope sleeping surfaces, waiting for bedding to cover them. Maybe something is hidden behind that rack.

Shuffling footsteps, and the muffled sounds of something being set on the ground behind her, made their way to Nagora's ears.

A chair being pulled in place.

And then it came. A wondrous sound filled the cave all around. Her whole body shivered. Wow! What a sound! I want to hear it again. What made that sound? It was musical. But from what kind of instrument?

"Look, Tars."

Nagora spun her chair around to see Moreena sitting in hers before an instrument unlike any she had ever seen. "What's it called?"

"It's a harp. A dragon harp."

The proud dragon was all made of gold, from its rearing head, down along its neck and belly, to its clawed feet. The dragon's gold, spread-back wings joined along their pointed tips and extended to the top of the long wooden box that rested on Moreena's shoulder. Gold strings were strung from the edges of the wing tips to the harp's box that ran down to the cushioned stool between Moreena's knees.

"Please, Moreena. Make the sound again."

"It's the dragon chord, played by plucking the strings with these three fingers." Moreena held up her right hand with her two middle fingers pressed to her palm so that the remaining fingers and thumb spread out. She pulled at the gold cords with the three of them in a single smooth motion, causing the sound to resonate from the harp's wooden box.

Nagora sat wrapped in a shiver left by the combined notes as they danced through her body and died away. She held her hand up as if to prepare her own fingers to play the chord.

"Don't move, Tars. Look on the wall behind you. See the dragon shadow you've made. A dragon in flight, the head on the long neck and the two spread wings."

It was easy for Nagora to imagine the shadow as a dragon in flight. And it reminded her of the dragon in the star stories Uncle had told her.

"Moreena, your dragon harp is beautiful. It must be worth a fortune. That is gold, is it not?"

"It is gold, Tars. It's worth more than a fortune to me. It belonged to my mother. She started to teach me to play it when I was four, even if I couldn't reach all the strings. I'll never part with it."

"You must miss playing it. Will you play a song for me?"

"I'd love to. This tune is called *When Dragons Soar*. It's the first one Mother taught me. As custom before any song on the dragon harp, we play the dragon chord first, before the actual song. It gets the listener's attention."

The tune was joyful and painted dragons in flight, gliding and sweeping across the sky, higher and higher until they turned to swoop down fast and then pull up into graceful spirals. I'm sure I can match every note with my flute.

As soon as Moreena stopped playing, Nagora stood and clapped. "Can I play with you? I have a flute."

"Of course! Get it. It'll be fun."

As Nagora walked over to her quiver, she couldn't get over her excitement. The last time she had played with someone was last winter when Pare played her lyre. It was always more exciting to play with someone else. "Do you know *The Miller's Wife*?"

"Of course. That's a traditional."

Nagora tried to match the dragon chord with her flute, but came nowhere close.

"If you had a double flute, you'd be close. Or two more flute players here with us."

After *The Miller's Wife*, Moreena adjusted a few cords. "Have you made up any songs of your own, Tars?"

Nagora lowered her gaze and scuffed her foot on the cave floor. "Only one. I call it *Lost On The Sea*. I wrote it for my da. I've never seen him. He's somewhere at sea, lost to me. I hope he'll come home one day."

"I'd love to hear it, Tars."

Moreena didn't play along. She listened and wiped tears from her eyes. "Tars, that's beautiful. I feel your sadness in every note. Please, play it again. I have to learn it. Then I'll teach you one of mine."

It took everything to get through Nagora's song the second time, such was the beauty of the harp's support of her tune.

"I wrote this for my mum. I call it *No Longer In My Eyes, Always In My Heart*."

Like Moreena, Nagora listened to her play it. "If you have words that go with it, they must surely tell a sad story."

"Aye, they do. I cry whenever I try to sing them."

"Let's see if I can learn to play it."

Now Nagora had two more songs to practice. "I heard this one in the town square in Twin Rivers. I don't know what it's called." She played and almost immediately, Moreena joined in.

"It's another traditional, from these parts at least. It's called *A Red Apple For My Sweet Love*. It's usually played around harvest time."

"The young lad who played it had three red apples on a tambourine. He'd be very lucky to have three sweet loves to offer them to." I'll not bother you more with that story. Making music with you is too much fun.

They had played late into the night. Before they took to bed, Moreena had made sure Nagora had at least ten of the many new songs perfectly committed to her musical memory. Nagora helped Moreena put away the dragon harp.

Now they sat at the table, drinking tea and watching the flames of the fire die down.

"Moreena, tell me something about Windhaven."

"Have you ever heard of the Centre for the Dragon Arts in Windhaven?"

"No."

"How about the Temple of Fire?"

"Yes, I've heard of it recently."

"And what else do you know about it?"

"Not much, except in Gallanford, I witnessed mothers trying to sell their daughters for food. Their young girls were to be taken to become virgins at that Temple of Fire."

"Tars, if only you knew the half of it. You know, I have great difficulty believing mothers will resort to selling their daughters to get food to survive. Possibly, those people who do have been so shunned by their community for making false accusations, now they have no one else to turn to for help. It's all been caused by the hunt for rebels who would plot against the queen, and by her unfair tributes placed on crops and cattle.

"What is now the Temple of Fire was once the Centre for the Dragon Arts. If you come with us to Windhaven, you'll see what's left of it. It is eight-sided, and it could hold over five hundred people sitting on the tiered stone levels around the three sides of its big main stage. People could come in by the main entrance and leave by it, or by one of the seven smaller exits beneath one its seven great stained-glass windows.

"Now only one stained-glass window remains, the one of the dragon, opposite the main entrance. Raganora had all the others destroyed. Only their empty frames remain.

"Inside the temple over the dragon window hangs a black curtain on which young virgins are now embroidering flames with copper, silver, and gold threads. Queen Raganora says she'll destroy the last stained-glass window the day after the last dragon is executed."

"Moreena, you said the last dragon would be executed when Raganora's son produces an heir to the throne to seal her pact with the witch, Hag. Why call the Centre for the Dragon Arts a temple now?"

"It's Raganora's twisted way of laughing at the dragons' secrets of the fire arts. She taunts people to come and pray at the Temple of Fire to receive the benefits of the secrets of the fire arts. But they're no longer allowed in. Only the virgins live there.

"To assure people show up, the virgins each have a portion of the bones of the virgin who died that month and was burnt in sacrifice in the temple fire. They sell these bones back to the parents, or to those people wanting to buy them for the parents."

A sacrifice! "Is a virgin executed each month?"

"From what we understand, one virgin is starved to death each month and her body is burnt in the temple fire. So I guess you could call that an execution."

Tar piss! "It's the cruelest of executions."

"That's why the virgins also beg for alms to buy food. That's why people go to sell things to the traders at the docks—to get coins to give to their virgin daughters so they can buy food, and wood and straw for the fire."

"Moreena, where do they go to buy the food?"

"The food vendors come to them. The virgins are forced to buy it from the prince's authorized food vendors at unreasonable prices."

"Prince Acindor is a tyrant. Being a virgin at the Temple of Fire in those conditions does not sound like an honor."

Moreena shook her head. "He makes it seem like it is to the virgins, by choosing one true strong virgin each month to lavish favors upon. But we know what he truly does is abuse her for his own pleasure. After all, he reasons, she forced the other girls in the temple to do such things to make sure they had enough wood for the fire. That pig, Acindor, has turned it into a game to amuse himself and to add to the suffering of the people.

"Inquisitors say things like this: If you are not guilty of the charges brought against you and you have nothing to hide, then you won't object to your daughter coming to serve at the Temple of Fire, will you?

"And from one time to the next, the price for which they can sell the bones changes. As do the prices for food from the authorized vendors. The prices are never the same. The reasons for the price changes are always different, depending on the mood and whims of Prince Acindor.

"So imagine what that does to the people wanting to help the virgins survive. Imagine what it does to those girls. Imagine what it does to the parents wanting to get their daughter's bones to lay them to rest."

"And no one has done anything to stop this?"

"No, any requests to change anything just make matters worse the next month. Food prices go out of reach. Parents are forced to beg strangers to donate money to their daughters.

Someday, though, this is all going to blow up in Acindor's face."

Nagora reached for Moreena's hand. "I've lived all these years far from all of this, not knowing anything about it. It's not right. This is no way to live."

"We call it surviving, Tars. It's what we do, each day."

Moreena reached for a candle lantern. "Shall we go to bed?"

Nagora held Moreena in her arms. "Moreena, you've given me so much. I don't know how I'll ever thank you. I feel like I've always known you. I want to know one more thing about you, if you don't mind telling me?"

Moreena pulled back. "You want to know about my eyes. You don't want to hear. Not that story, Tars. It's too painful."

She took Moreena in her arms and rested a cheek on hers. "You don't have to. Know that I truly want share in your pain." For a long moment Moreena held on to her, swallowed, and breathed deep several times. When she spoke, it was with tears in her voice.

"Don't say I didn't warn you." Moreena took a deep breath moved to sit up in bed. The outline of her face was just visible in the light of the candle lantern. A single teardrop hung on her cheek and fell before Moreena could wipe it away.

Nagora sat before her with her legs crossed, and reached out to hold one of her hands.

"Mother used to play the dragon harp with other harpists at the Centre for the Arts in Windhaven, before Raganora came to the throne and outlawed all images and talk of dragons. When she did, the hunt for the dragon harps was on. Mother had hidden her harp here. We knew she had hidden it, but not where. And she'd not tell us. Only later did our dogs lead us here.

"Raganora summoned the twelve harpists to the Temple of Fire. They were to bring their harps. If they didn't, they were to bring their families. Three brought their harps and were allowed to leave. Then Hag questioned the others, always starting with the family members. One at a time, she had them place a hand in a silver dish of water.

"Hag has a staff with three intertwined silver snakes. Their open mouths come together at the top to hold an amber stone that resembles an eye. She'd hold the eye over the hand of the one she questioned and she could tell if that person knew where the harp was or not. If they knew, she ordered them to go fetch it at once. If they didn't, Hag would order the harpist killed."

Does Hag know who I am? She didn't have her staff with her. I guess not.

"Six more harps were brought in that way. The questioning came down to Mother and two other harpists whose family members didn't know where they'd hidden the dragon harps.

"Since they refused to tell, Hag had a cauldron of oil set to boil. She threatened to have mercenary troopers break the harpists' arms one at a time and then plunge them into the boiling oil.

"Two more dragon harps were recovered. Mum suffered the promised torture. Father fought to stop it. Troopers over-came him, knocked him out, and took him away. I didn't know if I'd ever see him again. Hag broke his spirit and his heart that day."

Moreena wiped her eyes and took a breath.

Nagora squeezed her hand. Would she continue the story?

"Hag ordered the men to cut off the fingers of Mum's left hand, one at a time, and force me to watch. She passed out several times, but would not tell.

"Then Hag ordered them to cut off her hands. I closed my eyes. Still, she would not tell.

"Hag said, 'Your daughters will live with these images of your torture in their minds for the rest of their days.'"

Daughters? Moreena has a sister?

"'If you don't tell, they'll live with your beheading seared in their memories.'

"Mum refused to tell. Hag gave the order. A man forced my eyelids open. But I didn't watch. I stared at the sun instead. Erin watched. She hasn't spoken a word to anyone but me since. At nightfall, Hag sent Father to collect us and Mother's body."

Where was her sister now? Let it not be at the temple. Nagora was on her knees, crying as she reached out to take Moreena in her arms. "Is … is Erin where I think she is?"

Moreena nodded and cried at the same time. "Yes. Two years ago, day for day on the tenth anniversary of Mum's execution, they came to get her. She's your age, Tars."

Moreena cried herself to sleep. Nagora held her in her arms, her own tears did not stop until early morning, when she crept out of bed to go check her snares.

Keng climbed out of the cave entrance ahead of Nagora.

How can my heart still hold such anger? Somehow it did, and raged inside her. If she could find a way to strike back at evil, she would, and she would do it as soon as possible. But right now, here on the mountain, she was powerless.

...

Nagora picked her way down to where the scrub met the trees. Mist shrouded the mountain in a drizzle of rain. If she could see twenty steps ahead, she was lucky. She took her time and found her snares. Of the twelve set, two held hares. One of them was still warm. She reset the traps, set six more, and moved to a spot further away under the canopy of trees where she gutted the two rabbits. She salted the insides of one, and kept the freshest to make stew.

While the salt did its work, Nagora sat, scratching Keng's broad head. All this suffering in the land. What can I do? I'm powerless. It's like leaning against a boulder a thousand times bigger than me, trying to prevent it from rolling down this mountain. What about The Cause? What's being done to help? How many of us are there? Something has to be done. I can't do it myself. I need help.

How many in The Cause would come to her aid? It was urgent. If she cried out for help, how many would hear? And if they heard, would they come? She shrank and shrank until she was just a speck of sand, and the boulder rolled right over her like a big wave on her beach, not even noticing her. No way could she stop it. It was too big.

What did Uncle say? Focus on the things you can control. Let the leaders worry about the big picture. Do your best to carry out your task. Nagora looked at her bow and the three arrows she had brought with her. Okay. I'll do that. Bring the chain back. It'll have important information for The Cause. I'll have done my part. Then I'll see what the next assignment is. That's all I can do.

And I can do one more thing. For the next two days, make music with Moreena. Maybe while we do, we'll forget and dream of a better future to come.

Two days later, Nagora and Moreena had played until hunger and the need to sleep stopped them. Nagora would never forget this privileged time with her new friend. Come daylight on the fourth day, Nagora didn't want to leave the tangle of Moreena's red tresses that bound their naked bodies together in a tender embrace.

Moreena's fingers caressed the features of her face again before reaching into her hair to pull Nagora to her lips. "Tars, I'll never forget you. You've won a dear place in my heart. I'll dream someday we'll meet again and play our songs. Until then I wish you safety and strength on all the roads you travel so you can come back to me."

Nagora hugged her close. "I'll never be able to play my flute without thinking of you. Never. What you've given me has no price. I'll bear you and your wishes in my heart wherever I go. The day we meet again will not come soon enough."

That morning, they left the secret cave in the rain, but by the time they reached the scree, the sky had cleared. As they walked into the village, people gave them cursory looks. Only one waved and then seemed to realize Moreena most likely had not seen her.

Bardas's hammer rang out as they walked into the forge. "Father, we're back."

Bardas turned to look at them. "Well, lass, how's your auntie doing in the Lake Country?" He had obviously asked for the benefit of a customer waiting in his shop.

"She'll be fine if she eats more cabbage. I shredded a few heads and put them in brine in a big crock for her. It'll be ready in a few days. If she eats some every day, she'll not be as blocked up as she is.

"Cousin, you'll know what to do next time. Still, you did well to come for me."

Nagora put on her best Tars voice. "Aye, well, Mum was glad to see you."

"As I was her. We'll be glad to have your company to go to Windhaven tomorrow. Those salted rabbits should fetch you a few coins at the docks."

"Sure hope they do."

"Father, we'll see you later."

Bardas held out his hammer. "Tars, you might want to freshen the salt on them rabbits."

The Prince
Okimâwikosisân

Nagora sat on the overturned handcart in the back of the wagon, just behind the bench Moreena and her da sat on as they approached Windhaven's high stone wall. Keng and Quinn and their pups had taken up the back part of the wagon bed. Bardas had placed some smoked hindquarters and shoulders of wild boar beneath the overturned cart.

Nagora had heard of Windhaven's wall and seen it from the mountain. Now she understood why it was visible up there. *It's so much bigger than I imagined. It's so high.* The guards patrolling above were visible from their shoulders up.

Bardas found a place to park the wagon among others in a nearby field marked for that purpose. They were at least a count's walk from the main gate in the wall.

Now Nagora and Bardas were loading the wolfhound pups and the pieces of smoked meat into the cart Keng and Quinn would pull for them. They covered the meat with a tarp and placed a wooden separator between it and the pups. Bardas tied the dogs to the leather harness.

"Best you carry your pack with the rabbits. Be prepared to be searched by guards at the main gate." Bardas showed Nagora a cloth wrapped package the size of his hand. "Cured strips of boar belly, a delicacy. Turn around. I'll put it in with your rabbits. If they give you rough time, offer it to them. Soon as they get a whiff of it, they'll wave you through. Just answer their questions."

Nagora shifted to offer her pack. "Do they know you?"

"Depends who's on guard. If they know me, most likely it's not by name, but by Moreena. Remember, if they ask, you're my nephew from the Lake Country, hoping to get a few coins for your rabbits at the docks."

Moreena held out her hand. "Give me your hand, Tars."

They were not the only ones going through the gate. They joined the slow-moving line. The guard had a quick look under the tarp and patted the runt before asking, "What's in yer pack?"

Nagora wiped a dirty sleeve across her nose. "Salted rabbits."

The guard waved them through and moved on to the two people who followed.

Inside Windhaven's walls, Nagora stopped to look back up at the wall. Tars, guards could walk four abreast up there. Look at the size of those beams on the gate. Can you imagine the size of the windlass up in that tower? How many do you think it takes to lower and raise it?

Nagora looked down at the cobblestones at her feet. They stretched on as far as she could see. Everything is measured and even, Tars. No rutted roads here with foul-smelling ditches.

Bardas must've been watching. He pointed to the cobblestone way. "They call this a 'way' or 'street.' Actually most say Main Gate Way for this one, Tars."

Nagora had seen covered cobblestone surfaces on some of the sizable bridges she crossed, but never a complete roadway in any of the towns she had been to.

And so many buildings, all close together, often with many doors on a single long wall. "Where does the rainwater and wash water go?"

Bardas laughed. "Stop, Keng, Quinn. Come on this side, Tars." He pointed to where the side of the street sloped to meet the edge of the building walls. "This is called a drain."

It was a round metal grate, about the diameter of one of the wheels on the cart the dogs pulled, covering a hole on that side of the street. "Rainwater that doesn't get collected in barrels for the latrines inside the houses runs along the stone ditches until it hits one of these drains. It goes down the drain to an underground waterway that brings it all the way down to the bay. Same thing for wash water and whatever gets washed out of the indoor latrines. The foul smells stay down there."

However was this all built? Someone had a master plan. Was it something the dragons had come up with?

They came to a corner where the two streets crossed. Bardas pointed up the street. "See the wagon, there? The nearest one without an animal hitched to it? A friend of mine runs the smithy there. If we end up going our separate ways, we'll meet there a count before sunset. Understood?"

"Aye. Pretty easy to find."

Bardas pointed back the way they had come. "We're on Main Gate Way." He indicated the crossing street. "This is the last street to cross it on the way out of town, known as Stables Way because it leads to the stables at the castle. So to yer right on yer way to the main gate. Six doors down. The big doors. My friend's stable."

"Tar piss! Can't miss it, can I?"

Moreena held out her hand. "Tars, soon we'll be arriving at the Temple of Fire."

When Nagora took it, Moreena's grip was stronger, tighter. I feel you. I know your pain. She placed her other hand over Moreena's for a moment. "I'm with you."

As they approached the next street, from it on to the next one in the distance, not a single building lined the right side of the street. At the corner, Nagora stopped to take in the immenseness of Temple Square.

The towering gray stone Temple of Fire stood almost two hundred strides away. From where they were, three of its eight sides were visible. The arches of the tall, empty window frames pointed skyward to the edges of the downward slanting roof that probably reached over the surrounding seating area inside, leaving the main stage area open to the sky. Beneath each window, a heavy windowless wooden door blocked the exit. No outside handle. Probably one on the inside.

"Where's the main entrance, Moreena?"

"It's on the next wall to our left. It faces the midday sun."

"So Moreena, the last remaining," Nagora paused to look around, "stained-glass window would be the next one to our right?"

"That's right, Tars. We'll go that way."

Bardas pointed in the direction they had been going. "Take your time. I'll meet you on the other side, at the corner of Castle Way."

"We'll not be long, Father."

As they made their way across Temple Square, Nagora could easily pick out the local people going about their own business in a listless way compared to most of those she had seen coming through the main gate from out of town, with determination and purpose in their step. Must be the water, Tars.

The eight tiers that rose to the temple's walls were of equal height and depth. Comfortable sets of steps up to each tier were located ten paces from one another. The tiers gave the Temple of Fire its prominence in the square.

"Tars, did you notice the tiered steps in front of the buildings surrounding the square? They're twice as high as those of the temple and not as deep." Moreena looked around before leaning closer and lowering her voice. "I remember sitting on them with my sister and my father to watch the parade of musicians and dancers go by. Those were the long ago good times."

Moreena stopped in front of the wall with the last stained-glass window. "Not much to see. Only the supporting bars and the main lead outlines of the picture. No color visible with the tapestry hanging in front of it."

Moreena looked around and pulled Nagora closer again so she could whisper. "Tars, you can't image what it was like to be in this spot at night when all the lamps and candles inside were lit. The windows were beautiful. To be inside, on a sunny winter's day after a fresh snowfall, looking around at all the windows … I can't describe the beauty of the colors, or the feeling it gave me when looking at them."

Nagora had only ever seen two pieces of colored glass in her life. Both were at Geirador's in the two loft windows that closed out the cold in winter. One was green, the other yellow. Up to now it was always the color of the pale pink filament that seemed to float within the red crystal of her amulet that held her fascination. That could change if I ever get to see this window.

"Tonight, Hag will stand at the main entrance to make her announcements. First will be the name of the virgin who died this month and whose body will be delivered in sacrifice to the flames of the temple fire."

"How does that happen, Moreena?"

"The main entrance doors will be opened. The dead girl's body will be on display from the open side of the top level of the furnace. She'll be hanging by her arms from a long metal bar that was lowered onto the top of the furnace."

"A furnace?"

"Yes, it sits on the stone floor at the center stage of the temple. You'll understand if you see it."

Nagora's eyes darted around her as she clenched her teeth. She wanted to scream, but kept her words a hissed whisper. "That's no way to treat a dead body. Is there no end to Prince Acindor's cruelty?"

Moreena shook her head. "Just before the doors are closed, the dragon oil in the cauldron, inside the base of the furnace below the dead girl, is set on fire."

"How can parents watch that?"

"If they want their daughter's bones, they have to."

If I were a parent, I would kill Hag on the spot before letting that happen.

"What about the virgins? Will we see them tonight?"

"Oh! Yes! They'll parade three times around the temple on the top tier carrying the empty trays that will hold the dead virgin's bones which they'll sell tomorrow. They have assigned windows to stand under. Erin will stand beneath this window with two other girls. One of Hag's soldiers will guard them. Hag will make her announcements at the opposite side of the temple. We'll be here with Erin."

Ka Peyakot Mahihkan saskisam ekosani pakoseyihtâkosiw. Miskam tipêyimisowin. Those words were ice water on the back of her head, sending a chill of fear through her. "Lone Wolf sets fire to it and brings hope. She finds freedom." Who are you to speak my deepest thoughts as I think them? Yes, I would like to free Erin. But I can't do that. I was not sent here to do that. Bring the chain back. Stay out of trouble. That is my task. I've already come close to failing. You warned me about the witch with a single word. Are you telling me my future? No one knows my future.

Nagora looked up at the tall window, trying to see the dragon hidden in the dark pieces of glass encased in the lines of lead. She shivered as the words of the witch came back to her. "A dragon awaits you."

Moreena gave her hand a light tug. "Tars, are you well?"

"Aye." She made her voice a whisper. "Just trying to make out the dragon in the dark shapes of the window."

"That'll only happen if ever the tapestry comes down and all the lanterns and candles are lit inside. Perhaps when you return in better times." Moreena pulled her closer and whispered, "Believe me, Tars, you'll not regret seeing the dragon then."

As they left the closed doors of the temple's main entrance behind them, questions about the virgins inside the temple bothered Nagora, especially the one who was dead. How did she die? Had her arms been tied to the bar already? Who did it? Which of the other virgins? Did they have rules to follow? Was one of them a leader? Most likely. How did she convince the others to do that? What else did she have to convince them to do? A furnace and a cauldron of dragon oil? For a sacrifice? Would that be oil rendered from the bodies of the dragons Raganora ordered slain those years ago? I'm not sure I understand the furnace. Is it like a pyre?

She didn't want to bother Moreena with her questions. Her new friend had enough on her mind already with worrying about Erin. No need to cause her more worry.

Bardas was waiting on the corner of Castle Way and Main Gate Way. His daughters must be his reason to go on living. It must break his heart when he sees Erin. Perhaps being involved in The Cause helps give him some hope for the future.

As they crossed to him, the castle rose on the hill in the distance. Long ago, Castle Way brought a good king and his queen to the Centre for the Arts. Who did it bring now? From what Moreena said, only Hag. Did Queen Raganora and her son ever attend?

How did the people feel about the castle now? Did it house hope or hatred? Nagora's answer to her own question turned her stomach. Though, if it housed hope, that would probably be enough for Raganora to have the castle torn down.

They continued on along Main Gate Way. From Castle Way on, it and all the other streets headed down to the bay on an ever-increasing slope. There seemed to be more drains as they moved down the way. Was she mistaken?

The memory of sitting in an old, unrepairable curragh with Uncle came back to Nagora. He had punched over a dozen holes in its bottom with his knife, allowing the seawater in to fill the curragh until it sank and they swam back to shore.

Wherever the runoff from a heavy rainfall goes down these drains, it better be big enough to carry it all away or these drains will be useless. It only makes sense to have a big drain beneath the way to carry all the excess rainwater down to the bay.

"Father, do you see many masts?"

"I'd say the docks are almost full. Masts aplenty all along from what I can see from here. Right, Tars?"

"Aye. Plenty of masts down there."

At the bottom of the hill, all along Harbour Way, the crowd of people slowed their progress. Nagora had never been in such a crowd before. She was vulnerable and protected at the same time. A few soldiers stood guard. Almost useless. Just a presence, not truly involved with the crowd.

Temporary stalls were set up to one side of the wide street, leaving just enough room between them for those seeking to do business on the vessels tied along the docks. Every manner of goods seemed to be offered for sale or trade. From the smells, a variety of cooked foods were also on offer.

Two young men on stilts picked their way through the crowd, pausing every ten paces to holler their message in unison. "Come to the castle gates! Witness the trial of a captured rebel! Bring a hammer! Bring a big nail! They'll win you Prince Acindor's favor—as much food as you can carry away!"

Bardas spit on the ground and muttered something under his breath.

I have to see this, witness the prince in action. Nagora let go of Moreena's hand. "Here. Bardas, take my rabbits. Sell them for what you can get. Keep the coins for Erin. If you can get me some dried meat and nuts, I'll be fine. If I don't find you down here, I'll see you at our meeting place before sunset. I have to see Acindor's justice with my own eyes."

Bardas spit again. "I warn you, lad, it'll be a sorry spectacle. Don't do anything foolish. The place'll be swarming with guards."

Moreena took her arm. "Tars, be careful."

"Don't worry about me. I'll see you later." She hugged Moreena.

Bardas grabbed her arm. "Hold on. Take these. You'll be getting hungry." It was the package of cured strips of boar belly.

She put them in her pouch. "Thanks, Bardas."

…

Nagora had made her way up the crowded street, passing many of the people who seemed to be headed in that direction. So far, she had only seen one with a hammer in his hand. She overheard two people mention the trial was to start at midday. She cut back along a side street to take the next one up in the hopes it would be quicker.

Nagora followed two men who were almost running, each carrying a hammer and a nail the length of the knife on her belt. Even as the crowd thickened on that street, she stuck close to them. Their pace had now slackened, though, even if their urgency to make it to the castle gates had not. Now they were pushing people aside and yelling: "Make way! 'Cutioners comin' through."

Their words made Nagora's stomach turn. *The rebel doesn't stand a chance. The promise of food and a spectacle are the draw. Do I truly want to be a witness to a mockery of justice? There's no justice in this land. Who is the rebel? What are the charges?*

Nagora kept pace and profited from the path the two men opened just ahead of her, uttering an occasional "Comin' through" to make sure she wasn't cut off from them. One of them looked back past her. A burn scar on one side of his face had left him with a deformed yellow ear. She looked back too. *Probably getting his bearings.* She followed them up a side street to the more crowded way ahead.

...

A gang of ruffians blocked the way not far from the corner, demanding a tribute of their own to those wanting to get by. Nagora stuck with the two. They were let through, but she was held back.

Should I try to buy my way past with the boar belly? The press of people behind her was growing and challenging the illegal blockade. The looks on the thugs' faces told her they wouldn't be able to control the crowd much longer. She added Tars' voice to the protest and, within moments, their line gave way to the mass.

Nagora couldn't spot the two she had followed. But she could see the tops of the castle gates in the distance. She hugged the building walls and moved along them to get closer, occasionally bypassing someone who seemed to have camped next to the wall to watch events unfold. Those, she moved around with a "'Cuse me. Goin' that way."

Ahead of Nagora, along the wall, a crowd of people was standing on some tall stone steps, obviously with a clear view of what was about to happen in front of the gates. Will they be able to hear what's said? Let's see if we can get a spot, Tars. Top step would be good.

Nagora leaned her left shoulder against the building wall as she stared up at a stranger's knee. It was within reach. He was standing on the sixth step, the top step. How badly does he want to see the trial?

She tapped his knee. He looked down at her.

"No more room up here. Go somewhere else."

She pulled the package from her scrip, unwrapped it, broke it in two, and put half back in her pouch. She re-wrapped the other half. She tapped the knee again. "Are you hungry?" Her words came out before he could speak. "I'll trade places with you for this." She held up the package.

He barely unwrapped it. He put his nose to it. The smile on his face told Nagora he knew what it was. He nodded, climbed down, and helped her climb to the top step.

The sun's position overhead told Nagora it was almost midday. Now she could see over the crowd to a line of guards standing shoulder to shoulder, marking off a square space about three hundred strides from the castle entrance. Two other lines of soldiers guarded the way to the castle gate.

An open wagon, with a big barrel sitting on its bed, stood in the middle of the square space. The bed of the wagon was wet and many of the surrounding crowd held bowls or cups they were sipping from. Wine from the barrel.

Ahead of that wagon, another wagon, laden with food, stood nearest to the street leading to the docks. The promised food for those who bring a hammer and a nail? Where's the prince?

Nagora didn't have long to wait. The castle gate rose and an open carriage rolled out, drawn by two black horses. The driver was dressed in black leather from head to foot. Behind him, eight people sat facing each other on benches around the insides of the carriage. The first line of guards in Castle Square moved to let the carriage enter.

...

When it came to a stop, the man seated directly behind the driver stood and moved toward the post set in the middle of the wagon's bed. His movements were slow. Is he drunk? Or just unsteady on his feet? His belly seemed to lead him as he peered over his long hooked nose, one hand reaching out to take hold of the post. Maybe he doesn't see so well.

"Thar's our Prince Acindor," the voice drew out the prince's name to make it sound like "Ass-in-door," "an' all his fine friends." It was the man standing just below her, talking aloud more to himself than anyone nearby. "Couldn't get me to sit thar for all the coins in the castle. What's he got for us today?"

Prince Acindor raised a hand and waved to the crowd on one side then the other. A few hands waved back. Then he raised both hands and the crowd seemed to know he wanted silence, for a hush fell over them. "Bring the rebels." She barely heard his command. Did he say rebels? More than one?

Six soldiers escorted a young girl dressed in a long white garment. She led a person who walked backwards behind her with hands tied to the rope the girl held. That person was dressed in white also and walked with head hung. The girl reached up with a sleeve of her garment to wipe away a tear. Oh! No! It can't be! It was Ilma, Maton's sister. That must be Maton. They've caught him.

When they reached the wagon with the barrel, guards lifted them up onto its bed. Four of the guards climbed on. Nagora caught a glimpse of Maton's swollen face. He had been beaten badly. He could barely stand.

Prince Acindor raised two hands again. "This rebel, who will go nameless, stands here before you today accused of murder and theft. He murdered the driver of a royal wagon and the wagon's single escort while they were on royal business, bringing a virgin to our Temple of Fire. He stole the wagon and its contents and hid them, hoping to gain profit.

"This rebel had an accomplice. He refuses to tell who the accomplice was.

"So as punishment for not cooperating with my investigation, I am sentencing him to judgment by the barrel.

"Rebel, you are now in the presence of your ruler and his people. You will be placed in the barrel. It will be sealed and rolled down the hill. If you come out alive at the bottom, that will mean you are innocent of the charge, and will be freed. Do you have anything to say?"

Maton lifted his battered face and looked at the prince. Did he have the strength to glare back? Maton said nothing.

"Very well. Put him in the barrel, head first."

Ilma cried out, "No! No!" One guard held her aside as the others obeyed the prince. Her screams and cries did not stop.

Prince Acindor waved a hand, and a guard slapped Ilma with all his might.

Acindor smiled. "I've had enough of her wailing. Put her in too. Seal the barrel."

Those in the prince's carriage clapped their hands.

Once the guards had hammered the barrel cover in place, Acindor raised both hands. "Those of you who came with hammers and nails, I invite you to come and drive your nails into the barrel. You will collect your reward from this food wagon when it reaches the docks."

A death sentence! I could be in that barrel too! Why did I get involved? I bear a good part of the blame in this. Nagora had been biting her fist, forcing herself to watch. Acindor, you've earned one of my arrows. If I could I'd do it now. Bardas was right. Not here. At the docks. Maybe I can get a clear shot down there and get away.

The first two people from the crowd climbed onto the wagon and began to drive in their nails. At least a dozen others waited their turn. Nagora closed her eyes and turned her head away before jumping down. She couldn't stop the tears. But she could try to find a place from where she could make her shot count.

Nagora left before the crowd around Castle Square dispersed, pushing her way through those wanting to follow the barrel.

At the docks, a contingent of guards had assembled and marked off an area near a vacant wharf spot, opposite a post with a swinging hoist used to load and unload cargo from a boat that could dock there.

Nagora looked around for a place where she could safely prepare her bow to get off a shot. She needed to be above the crowd. Where? She searched along the building fronts, looking at the hoists sticking out above the upper level windows.

Perhaps a merchant's stock window would do. But how to get inside without being stopped? She needed to be in range. Pick the best one and check it out. You'll have to be able to make your escape. You won't have much time before the crowd is upon you.

Already the crowd was gathering around the guards.

Nagora hurried to the basket merchant's storefront. He had wooden boxes of all sizes and woven baskets of branches and rushes piled out front. Some of the baskets held coils of hemp rope of various sizes and lengths.

"You see what yer lookin' for?" He must be the merchant.

"Naw, my da sent me to look for, ya know, one of them long baskets."

"For a body?"

"Yes. That's what he wants. Said if you have one the size he wants, he'll come get it."

The merchant pointed through the doorway. "Up the stairs. Go to the back. Should be one that'll do the job." He handed her a short length of black cord. "If ya find one the right size, tie this to one of the handles. I'll know it's spoken for. I'll hold it for yer da until tomorrow midday."

Nagora looked out the tall stock window beyond the pulley hanging just outside it.

Inside, at the top of the window frame, was another block and pulley tied to a rail on a beam running to the back of the stock room.

She had a diagonal view across Harbor Way to where the soldiers had assembled. It was as close as she dared get and just within the range of her bow.

The gathered crowd had become noisier with the approach of mounted soldiers making their way toward them. Behind them, she glimpsed Prince Acindor's carriage and more foot soldiers shoving the crowd aside.

A group of men followed, pushing and guiding the barrel as it rolled. If she wasn't mistaken, their hands and clothes were covered in blood, as was the barrel.

She forced herself to look away. She unclipped her quiver, pulled out her bow, and assembled it. A whistle arrow to create a distraction and a broad tipped arrow for you, Acindor. Make my shot before the whistle's scream ends? I'll see. Then duck out of sight. Take down my bow and get out of here. If I can get to Main Gate Way, I should be fine.

The mounted soldiers surrounded Prince Acindor's carriage and the food wagon, facing out and looking over the heads of the foot soldiers in front of them, into the crowd. The prince wasn't taking any chances.

Wait for the clear shot, Tars. If he stands to speak, I might just have it. Nagora had nocked her arrow and stood in the shadow of the tall window frame, watching and waiting.

The barrel rollers seemed to have brought it to a stop near the hoist post at the edge of the wharf. Maton and Ilma can't have survived that. Come on, Acindor, stand up. Say something stupid to the crowd.

The crowd laughed, but she had not heard nor seen what had caused the laughter. She could only guess it was something the prince might have said.

Now a collective gasp came from the crowd. Heads strained to see what others, closer by, had.

The arm of the hoist swung inshore and the rope on its pulley moved. They're not. They can't be. The rope on the pulley became taut and squealed under the load put on it. Why?

...

Slowly, the bloodied bodies of Maton and Ilma came into view. A noose, tied to each end of a piece of rope, had been placed around their necks to allow them to be hauled up into view of all on the dock. Many looked away. Whoever pulled the rope, attached to the hoist's arm, caused it to point into the bay so their bodies now hung over the water.

Prince Acindor stood and raised both arms.

Nagora had her shot.

"Let this be an example to those who would join the rebels. The gulls and crows will feed on the traitors until only their bones remain."

Nagora knelt and shot the whistle arrow skyward so it would come down into the bay.

She nocked the broad tipped arrow to take aim at the prince. I've got one shot today. I won't waste it on you, Acindor. I'll put an end to the indignity of my friends.

The scream of the whistle arrow had everyone on the dock searching for the origin of the sound. Some panicked and tried to leave.

Nagora took aim and released her arrow. It cut the pulley rope just above the hook. The bodies of Maton and Ilma dropped into the water of the bay before the screaming arrow struck the water.

Nagora ducked into the shadow of the window frame, took her bow apart, and stuck it into her quiver. As soon as she had it hidden beneath her shirt and vest, she took the stairs down and slipped out the shop door.

Outside, on Harbour Way, the crowd was in confusion. People were yelling and screaming, trying to understand what had happened. Nagora didn't waste a moment. She pushed her way toward the next street. She was the only one going that way through the pushing crowd headed toward Prince Acindor.

Voices hollered, "You, there! Stop! Stop him!" She didn't need to stop to look back. Those ahead of her were now looking at her.

"Comin' through. 'Cuse me. Comin' through." She pulled away from hands reaching out for her and kept pushing on.

"Hey! You! They want you. What'd you do?"

"Comin' through. Me? They want me? Pay no mind, mate, I didn't do anythin'." Don't panic, Tars. Keep going. The street corner was closer. The crowd had grown, with more onlookers trying to get closer to see what was going on.

"Stop him! Stop him!" The yells were further back now and the people in front of her didn't pay her any attention. She chanced a peek over her shoulder. A mounted soldier struggled with his horse and the crowd, trying to keep his eye on her. He could barely maneuver.

Nagora ducked her shoulder in between two people and pushed through. Maybe I'll make faster progress along the wharf.

She moved on at an angle to the crowd until she reached the side of the wharf.

Nagora stepped up onto the big wooden beam and skipped along it. The crowd was to her right and a trader's boat was tied up on her left. I'll grab onto the boat if I get pushed.

Nagora climbed over the docking lines running to the big bollards just off the wharf beam. Another boat was tied up about fifty paces away. Just about halfway on the beam she could see where a ladder top was attached to the side of the wharf. Does it lead down to where the main water drain empties?

"Stop him! Stop him!" The screams were closer by. Nagora stepped onto the ladder and climbed down. She reached the top of the big drain. Tar piss! Most of it was below the waterline and, where she was, it was covered by a grate of metal bars.

"You! Stop! Come back up! Now!" She looked up at the soldier who peered down at her.

Nagora didn't wait. She took a deep breath, pretended to slip and panic as she dropped into the water. She let herself sink part of the way before pulling herself down along the grate. Sure enough, it was as she thought. The lower she went, the more the bars had been eaten away by the saltwater of the bay. At the bottom of the pipe, several rows of bars had rusted away.

Nagora pulled herself under and swam up on the other side of the grid to catch her breath. It'll be uphill from here. Are they going to follow me? I better get moving. With just enough light to see where she had to swim to, she pushed away from the grate.

Nagora reached the slope of the main drain at the water's edge. The smell was foul, and the trickle of dirty water flowed over a slimy coating of latrine pail matter and every imaginable thing people get rid of from their kitchens. Climbing along this wouldn't be easy.

Nagora reached out beyond the edges of the trickle to find stones dry enough for her to get some purchase and pull herself out of the water. She didn't have the choice but to let her knees drag through the slime until her feet were out of the water.

Now, if I can get my feet up on each side of this, I might get somewhere. Nagora could barely see. Far ahead in the distance, dim light shone. Probably light from a street drain grate. Carefully, she moved ahead in a crouched position with one hand touching the side of the stone-lined drain at the height of her waist. Her other hand touched the other side at the height of her knee. If I can keep my boots out of the water they'll not be as slippery.

Nagora spit. Ugh. That smell. I'll never complain again to Uncle about his smell after using our latrine. She was getting cold. If I can get moving faster, I'll warm up.

As Nagora approached the light shining down from the grate, it changed. It was either someone going by or someone watching. The shaft of light slanted down. She would have to keep to the right of it with her back against the curved wall and not slip into the water. Should be easy enough.

Nagora kept her eyes on the grate above and listened for anything to warn her someone was watching. They could send soldiers down here. Maybe they have, further up. I'll take out my blade if I see or hear someone. Do they truly think I might've drowned? Did they even know I shot the arrows? Why else would they chase me? Just because I was going in the opposite direction of everyone else? She put her questions aside and kept moving toward the next shaft of light.

Edana
Onâpehkâsoweyinis

Nagora had made it up the Main Gate Way underground drain system. She had passed the side street drains with her big blade in hand, expecting to be trapped at one of those drain crossings.

Now, if I guessed right, from the time I dropped into the water at the wharf opposite Main Gate Way, I've climbed the drain uphill to where it almost levels off. Main Gate Way began to slope down at Castle Way. So Tars, if we're facing the main gate, the drains to our left and right are under Castle Way. If we keep going right, we should come to a drain below Stables Way. But we have this extra drain here on the corner to our left, between Main Gate Way and Castle Way. That's right, Tars. It most likely goes to the temple. Let's go see.

Nagora followed the drain coming from the Temple of Fire. The first rectangular grate she came to was near the inside of the main entrance of the temple at the edge of the stage. From this one she had a view of a portion of the temple roof high above. It hung over the seating area with its opening to the sky. Ropes hung from pulleys on the opposite edges of the roof opening. Lower down, she saw part of the embroidered tapestry, the seating levels around the center stage, and a good portion of what must be the furnace Moreena spoke of.

It was a metal cage structure of three levels that held in place stacked spruce and birch logs and straw, stuffed into the spaces among the corded logs at each level. The top cage was the smallest, the bottom the largest, and almost four strides across on the side she could see.

Tars, that furnace will burn hot and fast when lit. There'll be sparks flying to the sky above the temple for sure. If the virgins stay inside once the fire is lit, they'll have to sit as far away as possible, most likely along the top tier seating level.

On the bottom level of the furnace, Nagora could make out the top of what must be an opening in its middle at floor level, most likely for access to the cauldron of dragon oil.

And she heard occasional voices to her right, probably from near the main entrance.

Nagora moved on to the next grate and got confirmation of where the whispers were coming from. Groups of girls huddled on two of the seating levels to the right of the closed doors of the entrance. Some were looking toward the tapestry. Or were they looking at the dead girl's body? How long has she been dead? Some rested their heads on folded arms on their drawn-up knees. Three were huddled in animated discussion.

She couldn't see the victim's body from this grate either.

...

Now Nagora crouched beneath the drain grate she was sure was near the dragon window opposite to the temple entrance. She listened carefully. The voices seemed to come from above her. Are they behind the tapestry? Nagora cocked her ear to better catch their words.

" ... but aren't you afraid to go to Prince Acindor?" said a first voice.

"Why should I be? I've fought these past months to get chosen. It'll be better than living in here. Going to his bed is a small price to pay to get out of here. You better start thinking that way too. You've been my best. You know how much I love you. You've earned the right to replace me. I don't think anyone else'll challenge you." The second voice paused.

"And I'll recommend you to Prince Acindor, but only if you promise you'll do everything to please him. Everything I've taught you. You have to be ready to do it all because that's how I'll sell him on you."

"But I've never done any of those things. Some I can see myself doing, but the thought of doing some of those other things makes me sick to think about it," said the first voice. She's afraid, Tars. I'd be scared too.

"You've got a month to get over it. I haven't done most of those things myself, but I will because I know what it'll get me. And if Prince Acindor gets me with child, he'll marry me. I'll be his princess," the second voice said. She sounds so sure of herself. If she truly knew what she's in for ...

"I don't know. So many have gone before us. It doesn't seem right," said the worried first voice.

"If you're unsure, I won't try to sell you on what you won't give. You've heard what Hag's told us again and again. What he needs to be able to do, you know. Sooner or later it's going to work with one of us. You want out of here, don't you? This isn't a fairy tale you know." Did I hear her spit?

"Okay, Myra. If you're able to, so can I."

"I know you can do it. That's why I love you, why I chose you. Give me a kiss, Bess, and promise not to make me look bad when you get chosen." Myra's voice was honey.

"I promise. I'll do it all. Myra?"

"What is it?"

"Who dies next? You have to help me with that before you go." Tars, I don't think she's as strong as Myra makes her out to be.

"I knew you'd ask. It's not easy. That's why you have to be careful about who you get close to. You have to stick with the strong. And sometimes you have to make the weak appear weaker."

"Like you did to Erin, last week?"

Erin! What had she done to Erin? Did I hear a sigh of regret?

"Aye, well, sometimes that's what you have to do. We never know about the new girl coming in, do we? How strong she'll be. How old she truly is. What support she'll be getting to buy food. We don't know those things. So you have to prepare in case the new girl comes in strong," said Myra.

"But Erin only complained once about her food portion not being weighed fairly. It was the only time I ever heard her speak. I thought she was a mute until then," said Bess.

"So did I."

"But you lashed out at her. You beat her, kicked her. Myra, you scared us all."

"Don't get me going on this. You don't realize how hard it is to take control and keep everyone in line. Wait 'til you try to use rations to bribe those willing to sell their favors in the middle of the night to the drunkards who come knocking. Don't forget, the night guard takes a cut of that." Myra paused. She's trying to control her temper.

"Most often it's the only way to ensure we have enough coins to buy wood to rebuild the furnace each month. I did what I had to do. Erin challenged my use of the scales. And besides, I set things up for you." Myra's voice was pleading.

"But—"

"Listen, Bess. If the new girl comes in weak, then it's easy for you. Make sure she only gets half portions. Work her hard on one of the tapestry ladders. You know. Keep her polishing the threads. She'll never be able to keep the silver ones shiny. On day 25 or 26, cut her water ration. If she doesn't throw herself off the ladder or fall off it, she'll die in her sleep, on time for the next sacrifice." Her heart is cruel, Tars. Was it always like that or has survival in the Temple of Fire made it so?

"Myra—"

"That's how it works! You know that! But if the new girl comes in strong, well, you've got Erin to work on." Myra paused.

Tar piss! I have to get Erin out of here.

"Keep her weak. Beat her if you have to. There's never been a month. Not a single month without a sacrifice to the fire. No sacrifice, no bones. No bones, no food. No food, we all die. That's how it works, Bess. You're going to make it work for the next month or more if you have to."

Was Bess crying?

"You can cry about it. That won't change anything. If you don't want to take control, just say so. You'll see what happens when the others fight for it. It won't be a pretty sight and you just might end up tied to the bar ready to become cooked bones, just like what happened to Edana."

Bess sniffled and then coughed. "But we're not sure she's dead."

"Don't worry, she will be as soon as the furnace flames set her on fire."

Is Edana alive, Tars? If she is, perhaps we can save her.

"Okay. Tonight, together, we'll raise Edana's body and lower her onto the furnace," said Bess.

"And then, when we come back in from our parade, I'll hand you the torch. You'll set fire to the dragon oil in the cauldron. The straw and the kindling above will catch fire and the furnace will roar to life." Myra's voice was proud. "Edana will become the temple fire's brightest flame." Myra paused.

"And tomorrow you'll collect Edana's bones that fell inside the cage of the furnace chimney and those that ended up in the cauldron. You'll divide them up among the virgins so they can sell them. Control will be yours until you hand it on to someone you trust. You see, Bess, it's that simple."

"No! It's never that simple."

Myra laughed. "Come. Wipe away those tears. Let's go prepare the portions for our meal. The others are surely as hungry as we are."

It became quiet.

So this is the perverted game of survival Acindor and Hag force these girls to play. It brings out the worst in the strong who pick on the weak. Tars, this has to end.

Nagora continued along the drain past two more grates. The closer she came to the next one, the stronger was the smell of the latrine, stronger than the smell coming from her damp clothes and hair. As she peered through the grate to look to the other side of the temple's seating area, she saw where the girls had set up their sleeping area. Bedrolls and clothes were mostly piled in an orderly fashion. Where do Myra and Bess sleep? On the upper level?

One girl came down from where she sat to take the nearest passage separating each of the temple's sitting areas. Other girls moved closer to the passageway. When the girl came back out with a steaming bowl, another went in. Ah! Tars, the kitchen must be set up in the latrines on that side of the temple. That's why there was no foul smell over there.

Nagora turned the other way in the dark. She moved along the wall to find the latrine drain where a bit of light might shine down. No mistaking it. I could fit in there on my belly. Can I climb up it? Not in this mess. Phew. She moved on and found the other pipe coming from the latrines above. It was just as foul smelling.

So they use the latrines on the other side as a cooking space. They probably don't waste anything. They probably empty any scraps over here. Cook and store their food over there.

···

Nagora returned to the grate to watch the girls eat. Whatever it was they were eating, they weren't turning their noses up at it. Their spoons weren't missing a thing. They were hungry. Probably at the end of their supplies for the month. They were just surviving. It would be easy to weaken a girl for sacrifice. Only people could be made to do this to others. I would rather live as an animal in the forest.

Damn you, Queen Raganora! Damn you, Prince Acindor! Damn you, Hag! This has gone on far too long.

Now Nagora stood below a drain grate on Stables Way. Was it the one near the meeting place Bardas had given her? I hope so, Tars. The wagon was still in place, right above Nagora. Would she be able to climb up and actually move the grate to get out? Or would she have to wait until she heard Moreena and her da arrive and get their attention somehow?

I'm hungry, but I want to clean my hands before eating. Are the rations in my scrip safe to eat? I doubt it. She squirted some water into her mouth from her waterskin to slack her thirst. Think. Uncle would ask, "How're you going to climb up to that drain grate and move it out of the way?"

Nagora unclipped her quiver and removed its strap, then unfastened the belt at her waist. Finally, she lifted the strap of her scrip over her head. I'll tie these three together and get the belt buckle up to the grate.

She assembled her bow, but did not string it. She used her bow string to lash a blunt tipped arrow to one of the bow limbs, making a long pole. I can probably squeeze a hand through one of the grate openings. No way I can thread these straps back through the buckle. I know!

Nagora pulled her flute from the pocket on her quiver and tied her belt to its middle with a double hitch, setting the buckle close to the instrument. Tars, this part of the buckle is thin enough to just rest in the nock of the arrow. She tested it. It did. See, Tars? I'll be able to lift my flute up through the grate bars and let it fall over across them.

She tied the pouch strap to the quiver strap, and that one to her belt. Now Tars, line up the flute, set the buckle on the nock, and up goes the flute, slow and easy.

Once the flute went through the opening, Nagora let it fall over across the top of the grate bars. She brought her bow down, took it apart, and fastened her quiver to the pouch that now hung before her eyes. These straps better hold. Ready to climb up, Tars? Go.

Nagora shinnied up the straps until she could grab onto the grate. Okay Tars, can I get my feet up to brace myself on the pipe sides so I don't slip? Okay, this seems good. I've got some flex. Will the grate move? Without letting go of her grip on the bars, she bent her head forward and brought her shoulder up against the grate. She let her legs carry her weight and pushed up with them. The grate barely moved.

Nagora transferred her weight back to her hands and repositioned her legs, raising her footholds a little higher. This time, the grate lifted, and she moved it the width of a hand away from the side of the building onto the cobblestones of the street. Okay, good, Tars. Rest a bit. Change your position so you can push on it and keep your hands on it. Listen first. Make sure you don't hear someone passing by.

With her feet and legs bracing her, and her back against the pipe, Nagora pushed with all her strength to move the grate another hand's width. *Not quite enough to stick my head out.* She held on as she caught her breath before readying herself for another push. *This should do it, Tars.* She pushed, and the grate moved again, almost off the hole.

Good, Tars. Nagora caught her breath, listened first, popped her head up, took a quick peek in one direction, and brought her head back down. She stuck her head up, looked toward the castle. *People in the distance were going that way. We're good, Tars.* The sound of voices rolled in the distance behind her. *Do I look there now?* She listened and waited. *Now Tars.*

People were going by on Main Gate Way. *See Tars, that's where the sounds came from. I'll keep my eyes in that direction when I climb out.* Nagora looked back in the other direction again before making her move. She pulled herself up over the grate, pushing, and wiggling her hips up until only her legs hung in the drainpipe.

Nagora lifted one leg up until her knee rested next to the grate. She brought her rear end up, and then her other leg. She let herself fall on her side, curling up near the drain to hide it should someone come by. She looked in both directions before pulling up her quiver and pouch.

Once Nagora had untied her flute, belt, and straps, she hid her quiver beneath her clothes and slipped the strap of her pouch over her shoulder again. *Okay, Tars. Now push the grate back in place.* Still lying on her side, she set both feet against the edge of the grate. She looked in both directions. All clear. Push, Tars. It slid into place.

I wish Bardas had told me the smith's name. And I wish he were here now to introduce me. Tars, are you ready for introductions? This smithy isn't on our map, but he's most likely our best chance to not be found.

Nagora rolled out from under the big wagon, stood, and walked to the front of it, past its tongue and the neck yoke resting on the ground, waiting for a team of harnessed horses or mules to be attached.

The shop's wide doors were open, but its adjoining stable doors were closed. The blacksmith couldn't be far. Nagora looked in, but couldn't see him. Maybe he was in the stable.

Nagora stepped in with a hand on her pouch, feeling the broken shoe it carried. No fire in the hearth. All the tools were in place. She could've struck the triangle with the nail to summon the smith, but didn't. I want to be able to watch him before I talk to him, Tars. The inside door to the stable side was open.

Nagora stepped through it into the stable. I didn't expect it to be this big, Tars. The two rows of stalls stretched away to her left. She counted twelve stalls in all. Most appeared to be empty. Someone was humming down at the end where double doors stood open onto what must be an inner yard. She walked along the cobblestone floor toward the humming. What looked like a sack of oats, sat next to the pile of fresh straw on the floor near the last stall.

...

The smith was in the last stall, his back to Nagora. He was brushing a horse and whistling a tune. His big free hand moving over the horse's neck reminded her of Geirador. This man too loved animals. I know that tune! Moreena taught it to me. Softly, she whistled it to accompany him. The horse's ears twitched. The smith paused for a moment, and then continued to whistle as he slowly turned to look in her direction.

The blacksmith stepped from the stall, brush still in hand. "Not many people know that one." His eyes took her in from head to toe. "Where'd you learn it?"

"Bardas's daughter taught it to me."

He crossed his big arms. "You know her?"

"Yes, Moreena. She's my cousin. I come from the Lake Country. My mum was ill and sent me to fetch Moreena last week. Today I came here with them to sell some salted rabbits. Uncle Bardas said if we were to get separated, we were to meet here."

The smith nodded. "You like horses?"

"Sure do. My dream's to have one of my own someday."

He waved to her. "Come, have a look at this one."

Nagora had just stepped into the stall when it happened. Now stars circled before her eyes. Her feet did not touch the ground. One big hand held her by the throat against the wall of the stall and the other pinned her two wrists together above her head. She struggled to breathe and speak at the same time as she blinked tears from her eyes, to get a clear view of the smith's face, a finger's width from hers.

"You better have a damn good explanation of why you smell like you just crawled out of a latrine drain." He loosened his grip at her throat.

She tried to nod, but couldn't, and could only barely speak. She coughed and managed to utter something between clenched teeth. She hoped he understood it.

He brought her down until her feet touched the floor. He relaxed the grip on her throat, but left his hand on it. He kept his other hand clamped to her wrists.

Nagora coughed again and took a few breaths as the stars disappeared. The back of her head hurt. "I did—crawl out of a drain. I moved the grate under the wagon outside."

His big face moved back from hers and he cocked his head to one side as he looked deep into her eyes. He looked over his shoulder, then back at her. He removed his hand from her throat and let go of her wrists. "You the one caused all the commotion down at the docks?"

Nagora rubbed her neck. The smith wore the four eights at his neck. "Y—yes. That was me. How'd you know about that?"

"News like that travels fast to those who should know of such things." He looked behind him again, stepping out of the stall and gazing toward the street door, then came back. He grabbed her arm. "Come with me."

He led her out of the stable, across the interior yard, where two mules chewed on hay, and over to a small shed attached to the building right next to one of its doors. He opened the shed door and showed her in. It was a latrine. "I'll bring what you need to wash up and a change of clothes. I should be able to find something that'll fit you. Listen. Whatever you do, don't leave this place until I come back to get you. And keep quiet.

"You're damn lucky. The castle stables are full. Ten of the queen's mounts use mine. Her horse guards left with them this morning. I'm expecting them back at any moment. They usually bring their mounts back well before the evening meal so they can stop at the alehouse for a few mugs."

She held out a hand. "My name's Tars."

He hesitated. "Olen."

Nagora sat in Olen's kitchen near the fire where she had hung her own clothes to dry. She had done as good a job with them as she had washing her hair, given she only had three buckets of clean water. She counted herself lucky to be clean again and now sipping some hot soup.

"You're not from the Lake Country, are you?"

Nagora hung her head for a moment. How did Olen know? "No."

"I figured as much. Not with weapons like those. I watched you clean them. I think I can guess who made that big blade."

Nagora looked him in the eye. "Then you must be a friend of that man."

"Fought alongside him for a year. He gave up his weapons to be a medic. Figured what he knew about healing would be put to better use than all the killing he could do. Geirador works magic at his forge. Any decent smith in the land wishes he had half the knowledge of working metal as he has."

She smiled at Olen. "He's the one."

"If he gifted you with those, you must've earned them."

She sighed and sipped some more soup from the bowl in her hands. "That's what I've been told."

"Now I don't doubt you're the one they're after. From what the mounted soldiers said, you did more than kick a hornets' nest today."

She looked at her spoon, squeezed its handle almost bending it. I wish I had been able to take out Prince Acindor. Someday he'll get his turn.

"Bardas could show up any moment now. He'll have more news."

And I'll have news for him and Moreena.

Nagora held Moreena in her arms. She hadn't stopped crying since Nagora told them what she had learned about Erin and how she learned it. Then she told them of her plan. Bardas told her it was bold and she was risking her life.

"I know. If I'm to call myself a warrior, I better act like one. If I can give you back Erin, I'll have succeeded. If I make it back here to get my stuff, and you can get us out of Windhaven, I'll be on my way. If I don't make it, can I count on you to get the chain to Geirador?"

Bardas placed a hand on her shoulder. "Aye, you can."

That evening Nagora had left first. She was ready. She wore an old coat Olen had given her. It was too big for her, but long enough to hide her strung bow under it along with three fire arrows and three broad-tipped arrows. She had a coil of rope wrapped around her waist and she wore her blades under her hooded shirt. She had tested the access to her big blade. By shrugging back the coat and pushing her hood back, she could easily grab the handle of her blade. The sun would set soon.

Nagora walked down Main Gate Way to Temple Square. All the torches on the posts along the building walls surrounding the square had already been lit. She moved on to take up position on the top step of the corner building. It gave her a view of Castle Way to her right just on the other side of Main Gate Way. And straight across from her was the temple's main entrance.

If she stood on tiptoe, holding the feather end of a fire arrow, she could reach it to the lit torch set on the post just above her. Depending on people's reaction to the arrows she planned to shoot, she could jump down onto Main Gate Way and run from pursuit. But that wasn't her plan. I'm going to attack. They won't be expecting that, will they Tars?

People were assembling around the temple tiers. Relatives of the virgins were taking up the places closest to the top tier beneath the windows where their daughters would stand with Hag's guards.

People below Nagora were casting glances up Castle Way. The sun had set and the murmuring in the crowd was taking on an angry tone. Could Hag being late not be a good sign? Most likely. We can guess why, can't we, Tars?

A young man bounded up the steps toward Nagora, looking up Castle Way as he did. He stopped on the step below her and squinted as he searched in the distance. He pointed and yelled to the people below. "I see it. The carriage. It's coming."

His words spread among the crowd and, though she couldn't hear what they were saying, they seemed to be speculating what bad news Hag would bring. Not one of them smiled.

Nagora kept her back against the wall, her right shoulder against the wooden post to which the torch was attached. She kept her eye on the crowd and, when they moved out of the way to let the horse-drawn carriage pass, she peeked past the post to watch. See the red scarf at her hands and neck? It's her, Tars. This time it's my turn. I'll use arrows, not apples.

The carriage went by, all the way to the other side of Temple Square, and then turned and came back to stop across from the temple wall to her left. It looked like the prince's carriage. Hag sat where Prince Acindor had previously, behind the driver. Nine guards occupied the other seats. The guard opposite Hag stood, lifted the seat, and pushed it over the back. Steps under the seat unfolded to the ground.

Eight guards stepped down and lined up. The ninth guard helped Hag down the steps. Too many people nearby to risk a shot. Hag made her way to the side steps leading up to the temple tiers. Eight guards flanked her. One led the way. The people nearby moved aside to let them pass.

Hag has her staff today, Tars. Look at the people. They're staring at the amber eye the silver snakes hold. They must know the evil the witch has done with it.

When Hag reached the top tier, the small exit door opened to darkness within the temple. When the door closed, light from inside appeared in the empty frames of the windows. Hag must be speaking to the girls.

Seven guards spread out around the temple. Most likely to keep watch on the virgins at their stations. Two guards took up position at the main entrance, one on each side. Tars, they'll watch over Hag when she comes out to make her announcements.

The lights inside the Temple of Fire went out. A hush came over the crowd. They were listening. Nagora heard it too, the squeak of the pulleys under strain. Tars, they're raising Edana's body for display. The light from inside returned, brighter this time. I had seen torches, but didn't count how many. Perhaps there were candle lanterns too.

The crowd below the main entrance pressed together as the big wooden doors opened inward and the virgins came out in procession, two by two, each carrying an empty tray and a lantern, except for the one who led them with a torch on a long handle. She must be Myra. One line of girls went to the left on the top tier, the other to the right with Myra. Twenty-one girls, seven windows, three girls per window. Hag's guards will be busy, Tars.

Most of Edana's body hung inside the top cage of the furnace. Her arms were spread and tied to a long metal bar which rested on the top of the cage. Except for her head and shoulders, the rest of Edana's body was surrounded on three sides by straw tightly packed into the spaces left by the wood corded inside the cage. The fourth open side of the cage displayed Edana's body draped in white gauze.

Look, Tars. Four ropes tied to the bar, two at each end. Two are anchored somewhere at the back of the stage. They pulled the bar back so the two front ropes connected to those pulleys above could lower Edana into the open chimney. Those same two forward ropes raised her up from the floor in front of the furnace. We have to get her down.

The virgins paraded around the Temple of Fire three times. See, Tars. Along those two walls, they're stopping at their assigned windows, next to Hag's soldiers.

Hag stepped out of the temple. She raised her staff with both hands. "I offer you Edana, the twenty-ninth virgin to be offered in sacrifice at the Temple of Fire." The witch turned to point the amber eye at Edana.

Nagora held a fire arrow by its feathers. She stood on tip-toe and reached the tar-soaked cloth strips of the arrow's tip up to the flame of the torch. The arrow tip caught fire instant-ly. Nagora brought the arrow down, and in one motion nocked, pulled, aimed, and released it.

The flaming arrow flew over Hag's head, over Edana's head, and struck the black Tapestry of Fire. Hag froze, as did all who had their eyes on the growing flame the arrow had lit in the tapestry at the back of the temple.

Already, Nagora had touched a second fire arrow to the torch's flame and nocked it.

This one's for you, Hag.

She pulled, aimed, and released just as Hag turned to face the crowd.

Hag knocked the arrow aside with her staff, sending it to stick in the door frame.

Hag ran inside. The two guards following her pulled on the big doors to close them.

Nagora loosed a broad-tipped arrow and brought down one guard. Before he fell, she had the next arrow nocked and the second guard in her sights. He too fell out onto the top tier of the temple.

Hag came out, waving her staff and yelling for the other guards to come to her.

Nagora pulled, aimed, and released her last fire arrow.

Hag moved to run for the approaching guards, but the arrow struck the wide sleeve of her black cloak, pinning it to the door. The witch screamed and struggled to pull herself from her flaming mantle.

Nagora nocked her last broad-tipped arrow, but because the three guards covered Hag as they helped her out of her cloak, she did not have a clear shot.

Nagora jumped down from the step and rushed through the stunned crowd toward the temple entrance.

Hag and the soldiers were running for the carriage.

Nagora couldn't get to them for a clear shot, but if she could make it to the top tier of the temple, she just might have a shot. As she fought her way through the crowd, the carriage driver tried to maneuver the carriage closer to Hag. Three other guards joined the three with Hag to shield her.

...

A last guard came around the corner to see what the commotion was about. He looked from his fellow soldiers with Hag near the carriage to the witch's flaming cloak on the door. He did a quick scan of the crowd.

Now you see me. This arrow can be yours. Smart choice. Go protect your witch.

The crowd at the bottom of the main temple steps made way for Nagora. Some were cheering her on as she bounded up the steps.

People at the side of the temple nearest her were climbing the side steps to meet their unguarded daughters. Don't miss this chance. Take them away. Run for it.

Nagora stood before the main entrance just as the carriage driver whipped the horse to urge it forward. She raised her bow in the air and looked out over the people.

She raised her right hand, her fingers splayed as they would be if they were to play the dragon chord. Finally, the carriage lurched across Main Gate Way onto Castle Way. Hag, we'll meet again, someday.

The crowd became quiet. They were waiting. Some raised their hands like hers.

"Who are you?" It was a lone voice from the crowd.

Nagora placed her splayed-fingered hand over her heart. "I have a message for you." Then she raised her hand high in the air. "Dragons will fly here again! Edana will return. Believe me! Dragons will fly again! Edana will return!"

"Soldiers!" someone yelled.

She pulled her flaming arrow from the door frame and tossed it inside the temple. She ran inside, then closed and barred the doors.

Nagora looked up at the ropes attached to the pulleys and followed them back down to where hooks anchored them to drain grates on each side of the stage. Better than I thought, Tars.

Nagora ran around to the back of the stage where the wire embroidery of the tapestry now lay crumpled in the smoldering ash on the tiered stone seats. She pulled her big blade from its sheath and slashed the ropes that had pulled the bar back so Edana could be lowered to the top cage.

See, Tars! Now we just have to pull the bar up with the other ropes. Edana will swing forward and we'll lower her.

Back at the front of the stage, Nagora unhooked one anchor rope, then the other. She crossed the hooks together behind her back, grabbed onto the ropes, and pushed back with her legs.

The bar rose and cleared the top of the top cage of the furnace. Edana swung forward out of its open front side, and at the same time, Nagora stepped forward to bring her down.

"Are you alive?" Nagora rushed to Edana and placed four fingers beneath the girl's breast. The heartbeat was weak. "You're alive! Edana, hold on. You can make it." She released the cap on her waterskin and dribbled water onto Edana's lips. They parted, and Nagora dribbled a little more water into her mouth. Edana coughed. Nagora lifted the girl's head and poured just a little more water. Edana drank it in.

Pounding on the doors brought Nagora to her feet. She ran up the steps to the tiers where the virgins' bedrolls were located. She grabbed two, ran to the opening at the front of the furnace, crawled in to the cauldron, and dipped the bedrolls in.

Then Nagora ran to the doors with the oil-soaked bedrolls, threw them against the doors, and picked up her fire arrow to set the pile on fire.

Nagora ran back to Edana, cut her free from the bar, and lifted her up. She bent to one knee and was able to lift the girl onto her shoulder. Nagora pushed up and staggered for a moment as she got her bearings.

Nagora headed for the latrine used as a kitchen area, pausing at the tiered seat steps to peer through the glass panes of the lit candle lanterns. She grabbed the one with the biggest candle.

Nagora set Edana down on the boards covering some of the latrine holes. She went to the hole at the far end with the candle lantern, stuck the lantern in, leaned in after it, and peered down the drain.

She would have to remove her weapons and even her clothes to squeeze down that curved pipe to the sewer. No way I'll be able to get Edana down through there. Trying would probably kill her. Nagora pulled herself back up.

...

Nagora looked around at the setup for the cooking area. She went over to a long wooden box and lifted its cover. It was empty. Something wasn't right. She looked back at the outside of the box and back in again. Of course!

She reached a finger into the knot hole of one of the bottom boards of the box and lifted it. She lifted all the boards out. A secret food stash! For whose benefit? She found three hemp bags. A quick sniff at each revealed barley in one, buckwheat flour in another, and dried berries in the last bag.

Nagora bent to the girl's face. She's still breathing, Tars. Nagora took the girl's hand. "Edana, if you hear me, squeeze my hand." Nothing. She's unconscious. "Edana, just in case you hear me, I want you to know, I'll hide you in this food locker. I'll tell Olen. He'll get word to your parents. They'll come to get you. Hang on Edana. You're strong. You can make it." She made Edana drink another sip before placing her into the bottom of the box and covering her with the boards.

Nagora ran back to the main stage. The noise from outside told her confusion now reigned in Temple Square. That's a good thing, Tars. Let's hope the virgins have chanced their escape. She hauled a pile of bedclothes over to the furnace cauldron and stuffed them into the dragon oil.

She set an oil-soaked shirt aside on the floor before running to her fire arrow. It was in its last moments, but would have enough life left to set fire to the dragon oil in the cauldron. We'll let the people outside see their stained-glass drag-on window. Right, Tars?

Nagora touched the arrow to the lip of the cauldron, wet with dragon oil. The bedclothes caught fire, the flames grew, and she let her arrow tip into the cauldron. As she backed away, the flames burst up high and the whole furnace roared. She scooped up the oily shirt, rolled it into a ball, and ran to the kitchen area.

Nagora paused for a moment to look at the cover of the box. "Goodbye, Edana. Hold on. Your father will come for you. You can make it. Maybe someday we'll meet again in better times."

Nagora stripped and pushed her weapons and clothes down the hole. She leaned into the hole as far as she could and wrung as much oil out of the shirt as she could. Tars, this bet-ter work or else I'll be in a real jam. She climbed into the hole feet first with the shirt in one hand and the candle lantern in her other.

Nagora stood in the sewer, pulling on her clothes. Some-how, she had been able to wiggle and squeeze down that hole. If she hadn't oiled the way and stripped off her clothes, she would still be stuck in there. The scrapes and scratches along her ribs, hips, elbows, and knees would testify to her painful escape.

Now to Olen's. Not as easy at night without shafts of light to guide us, aye, Tars? If the lantern didn't last, Nagora had the oily shirt. Strips of it tied to her big blade and lit could give her enough light to find her way.

Noise from Temple Square above found its way down into the sewer each time she passed a drain grate overhead. Only once did she see flickers of light from above. Had a building been set on fire? Is Erin with Moreena and her da? We'll find out soon, Tars.

Nagora came to the knotted rope hanging down the drain. Olen had tied it to his wagon above, so climbing it was all she had to do this time.

When Nagora reached the street above, she untied the rope and pushed the grate back in place. Olen must've been waiting and listening for as soon as she came alongside the shop door, it opened before she could knock.

"Damn! Tars! You made it! Bardas says the place is in an uproar."

Nagora grabbed Olen's arm. "He's got Erin?"

"Aye." Olen pointed over his shoulder with his thumb. "They're inside. They made it. Like you said it would happen. Hag's temple guards weren't expecting to be caught in a skirmish. Good that Bardas was prepared and had those clothes for Erin. Made getting her away easier before more soldiers showed up."

"Olen, I need your help. The virgin who was to be sacrificed tonight is not dead."

He looked at Nagora in disbelief. "What? How can that be?"

"She's been injured. I don't know how. She's not awake. But I was able to make her drink some water. Listen, Olen. You have to find her parents. Tell them she's alive."

"Is she still in the Temple of Fire?"

"Yes. If I could've gotten her out, she'd be with me now. If they can get into the temple, they'll find her in the latrine area where the virgins cooked their food. I put her in the long food storage box. It has a false bottom. She's under the boards of the false bottom."

"What's her name?"

"Edana." The look on Olen's face became somber. "Do you know her parents, Olen?"

"Aye. This is not going to be easy. It could put The Cause in jeopardy. Then again, it could be a boon for The Cause."

"What do you mean? How can that be?"

"Edana's father is the captain of The Guard."

"Queen Raganora's guards?" That wouldn't make sense.

He placed a big hand on her shoulder. "No. Oh no." Olen paused, bared his teeth, and shook his head. "The Guard." He paused again. "Good King Bernhard's King's Guard—his personal guards. They're an outlaw group now, living on the limits of Raganora's law. Loyal to no one but themselves. They'll track thieves and murderers and hand them over to Raganora or Acindor for a price. Or, if no gold is forthcoming, they'll carry out justice on their own."

Nagora shook her head. "But Olen, how would the daughter of the captain of The Guard end up in the Temple of Fire?"

Olen rolled his eyes. "That's Prince Acindor's doing. His way of putting pressure on The Guard. Now he wants them to start rooting out rebels. The captain'll get his daughter back if they do. All this because Raganora's mercenaries have been slacking off. They want more pay to quell the growing whispers of a rebellion."

"So Acindor is trying to get The Guard to do what the mercenaries were doing?"

"Aye. If the rebel who kicked this hornet's nest, twice today," he shook her shoulder, "is not caught in Windhaven by tomorrow, he'll have a price on his head for sure. And you can bet The Guard will be called upon to find him outside the walls of Windhaven. The Guard always finds the one it goes after."

Nagora shook her head. "My lucky day. Should I just give myself up?"

"No, Tars. Best we get you out of Windhaven as soon as possible. Put some distance between you and Prince Acindor and his witch. Let me worry about contacting Edana's father. If you get caught by The Guard, be sure to insist they let you speak to their captain before they turn you in." He patted her shoulder and gave her a warm smile.

"Thanks for your advice. I hope Edana survives."

"If she does, The Guard'll be with us for sure.

"Come, Tars, let's get you ready for a ride in a cart full of manure."

Nagora found Moreena in Olen's kitchen, holding Erin in her arms. Bardas stood with them, his big hands to their backs. He wore a teary smile as he nodded to Nagora.

"Tars, is that you?" said Moreena.

"Aye, Moreena. I've come to meet your sister."

Erin clung to Moreena as they stepped closer. "Erin, this is my friend, Tars. We owe your freedom to him. Say thank you to Tars." Erin stared at Nagora, but did not speak. She looked younger than her age. She was weak and probably had lost weight.

"No need to say anything, Erin. To see Moreena's smile and your da's as they hold you is thanks enough. We have to get ready now to take you home. Best we not waste any time."

With a hesitant motion, Erin splayed her fingers in the dragon chord over her heart, brought the head to her lips, kissed it, and with a timid smile on her face, stretched her arm out to Nagora.

Nagora smiled back. "Thank you, Erin."

Erin let go of her hold on Moreena and took two quick steps to throw her arms around her new friend.

Bardas held a hand over his heart, as his tears ran into his beard.

Nagora and Erin climbed into the cart that Keng and Quinn would pull. Bardas had hacked two holes in the boards of the cart bed so she and Erin could stick their faces out to breathe. Olen covered them with an old blanket. Bardas placed the cart's separator board over Nagora and another piece of board over Erin. Nagora held Erin's hand.

Olen piled the horse manure on top of them. He had shown Nagora an old pitchfork with a broken handle which he would leave on top of the pile, making sure it was coated in manure. *I hope this works, Tars.*

Finally, Nagora heard what she had been waiting for. Before that, the mounted soldiers had caused a lot of commotion when they came by the main gate with their commander to issue orders to the guards on duty. Extra guards were on their way. Everyone leaving Windhaven, without exception, was to be searched. The officer described the bow and the clothes the rebel wore. She wasn't wearing those now. Her bow was safely packed away in her quiver which lay at her side.

She lost count of the time it took for the line to move forward.

When at last Bardas spoke, Nagora was almost relieved. She squeezed Erin's hand and braced herself.

"Want to poke this in the horse shit?"

Nagora didn't hear the reply.

"Sorry, I can do it for you. Keep yer hands clean."

She took a breath and clenched her teeth. Tars, he better remember where to poke.

"Sure you want to stick your sword in there? Horse shit'll cost you a new blade. That's what? A sword like that—at least two months' pay. Look at what it does to the tines on the pitchfork. I can empty the cart right here if you want. Don't have a shovel, though, to load it up again."

"On your way. Take your horse shit with you."

Those words were sweet to Nagora's ears. Erin gave her hand a long squeeze.

The Guard
Okanaweyihcikew

Once they arrived at the wagon, Bardas unhitched the dogs. "Brace yourselves. I'm going to spill the manure."

Nagora pulled the blanket off as Bardas took away the separator and the board that covered them. She grabbed her quiver and Erin's hand before stepping off the cart.

"Enjoy the smell of freedom," said Moreena. She and her da hugged Erin.

After helping Bardas load the empty cart and the dogs into the wagon, Nagora sat behind the bench in the wagon, Keng at her side, his big head resting on her knee. Erin sat just above her, huddled between Moreena and her da.

As the wagon climbed the road, Nagora scratched the back of Keng's neck. Windhaven receded into the distance. Only the distinctive flames of the big fire, which licked at the night sky, hinted at the events that had taken place within its walls this day. She reached for her amulet and brought it to her lips.

What have I done? I set a fire. I freed Erin. Perhaps Edana too. At what cost to The Cause? Will I be able to get away from The Guard? Will I make it home? It feels so far away right now. Why does this feel like the beginning of my journey and not its end?

Nagora searched the sky for her mum's star. Mum, if you've been looking down and watching me, I hope you're proud. That I've made it this far, it's probably because you've been watching over me. If it's not you, it's someone else. I hear a voice speak in a language I seem to know. Today, it guided me. Now when I think about what I did, I feel scared. But I wasn't scared when I did those things. Now I am. Mum, continue to watch over me.

Moreena touched Nagora's shoulder. "Erin, best you get under that blanket next to Tars. We want no one to see you when we arrive home. Remember. We'll carry you in like a sack of vegetables."

Nagora helped Erin climb down from the bench and covered her with the blanket. She held Erin's hand until the wagon stopped.

Nagora returned with Bardas to his forge. He fished the chain from the ashes of his hearth with a poker and placed it on his anvil before stepping over to a shelf to take down a box containing a set of steel punches. He scratched some figures on the wooden workbench surface. Four rows of figures and a line beneath them. He closed his eyes for a moment. He must be making a tally.

He ran his finger over the fifth row and nodded to himself before setting aside three punches. He double-checked them, wrapped his fingers around them, then picked up a hammer and returned to the chain. He placed the tip of one punch on his link and struck its head once. Two more strikes of the hammer and he was done.

He handed the chain to Nagora. "Good luck with this. I hope you make it home safely. I wish I could guarantee your safety."

Two came before me but didn't make it back. Will I? "Say, Bardas, did you meet either of the two who came before me to collect the information you've put on this chain?"

Bardas cocked his head and gave her a bewildered look. "What two others? I've not given this information to anyone else, ever."

Could it be they were captured before reaching Bardas? Or did Uncle lie to me? "I must've misunderstood. I was led to believe the information on the chain would confirm what had been told to the two who came before me."

Bardas shook his head. "No. When we met to discuss how we'd relay this information, we agreed to use our own separate codes and only one person would have the keys to read those secret codes. No way we'd give this information by word of mouth. Not a risk we'd take."

So Uncle did lie to me. Why? The person I trust the most. What was his lie hiding? Or what … is his lie hiding?

"Maybe two others had been considered before they chose you and somehow in explaining they led you to believe two had come before you," said Bardas.

Nagora pretended to consider Bardas's words. Then she nodded. "You're right, Bardas. Now that you mention it, there was talk of why I was chosen instead of others. And it all happened so suddenly. Of course it makes sense to use a code.

That way the information is truly kept secret." She smiled at him.

Bardas returned Nagora's smile. "Tars, I owe you more than you'll ever know. Erin'll thank you someday."

"She already has." She would never forget Erin's hug.

Bardas placed a hand on Nagora's shoulder. "Come, Tars. We'll eat and then plan your next move." He guided her to the yard door. "I wish you'd been there to see the dragon window light up. And I wish I'd been there to see you set the tapestry on fire. You should've seen the faces of those who witnessed the window light up."

"Someday, I'll come back to see it. Right now I have to run for my life."

Early the next day, the dark before dawn's light found Nagora and Bardas loading two sacks of something into the wagon while Moreena climbed up onto the seat. Keng and Quinn jumped up on the wagon bed. Keng took his place next to Nagora and Quinn lay next to Erin. Nagora held her hand.

Bardas took the road to the Lake Country. The idea was to give the curious locals the impression that Moreena was returning there with her cousin to care for her ailing aunt. In fact, he would be bringing Moreena and Erin to a trailhead from where they would hike to the mountain trail leading to their secret cave. They each had a pack of provisions. Erin would be Moreena's eyes. Quinn would go with them.

The night before Bardas's words were firm. "I insist, Tars. You take Keng with you. He'll find his way back to Quinn." Then he showed Nagora the simple hand commands Keng would obey to defend her from an attacker.

He showed Nagora, on the map painted on her vest, why her chances of getting home safely would be greater by taking an alternate way. "Word will be out to all towns within three days' travel. Checkpoint guards will be doubled, and they'll search everyone tight. Anyone close to matching your description will be held for questions. Trying to go back the way you came to get to the coast takes you through all these checkpoints. You can't avoid them because of the rivers you have to cross." He pointed to all of them.

"And with the price that'll be on your head, your chances of getting through and avoiding patrols will decrease tenfold. So here's what I suggest." Bardas pointed to the Lake Country on her map. "The people who live in what we call the Lake Country live around Feather Lake." I see why it's called that, because of its shape.

"The river that empties into Feather Lake is called the Great Snake River. It brings water from Great Snake Lake."

"Bardas, it's a big lake but doesn't look like a snake, more like a giant running with arms outstretched."

"Aye, true. It's called that because of the size of the waves on it when the wind blows." He made long rolling waves with his hand as he said, "Like this when the wind blows up the giant's straight leg to his head, carrying you in the direction you'll be going." He made short, high, choppy waves with his hand. "Like this when it blows down from his head to his foot, slowing your progress to the direction you'll be going."

She pointed to the map. "Because of the mountains on both sides, right?"

"Aye, to your left here," Bardas ran a finger along the side of Great Snake Lake, "it's all high cliffs, all the way up the leg and body to the arm, hardly a single place to put ashore until you get to the top, here at the arm, your destination, the mouth of Small Snake River."

His finger ran down the other side of Great Snake Lake. "The other side is mountains, so wherever a valley comes down to the water, you stand a chance to make it to shore in a blow. Trouble is, favorable wind doesn't hold for long. Sometimes it changes in the same day."

"So you're suggesting I travel by water on Great Snake Lake?"

"You know curraghs, Tars. You've used them on the sea. You can swim."

"Do no bigger craft travel the lake?"

"Not its whole length. Fishers, who know the weather and winds well, might take their curraghs halfway up at the most."

"So you think no one would suspect I might run that way?"

"Almost no one. To get to Great Snake Lake, you'll be going through the domain of The Guard. No one ventures there without cause."

Nagora shifted on her chair. What he'd said made her feel uneasy. "From what Olen told me, they'll be called upon to look for me. The price on my head'll surely incite them to do so."

"Aye. True that. You'll be alone with Keng, on foot, heading into their country through the forest, taking your time, scouting your way ahead. They won't be expecting you to be going in that direction."

"So if I make it to the lake, where do I get a boat?"

"Where do fishers in your parts get theirs?"

Of course! Wake up! "From a maker of curraghs. Or perhaps a fisher might have an old one that'll last the trip. I'll need to pay for it. I don't have a coin on me."

Bardas set a small pouch on the table in front of Nagora. "It's the least I can do. Buy a good one. Send Keng back before you put your oars in the water. Say, 'Keng, find Quinn.'"

Bardas put his thumb on her first destination on the lower shore of Great Snake Lake. "Three, four days at most to hike here."

His thumb traveled up the lake to its head. "You're a good rower. With the winds at your back, five days. Wind on your nose maybe nine or more if you have to hold over to wait for better conditions.

"When you land here," Bardas pointed to the mouth of Small Snake River, "follow it. Soon enough you'll be in familiar country, almost home. Yhorgal's just over here. Four days, five at the most, to hike there."

What do you think, Tars? He makes it sound like we're almost home. In the best conditions, I'll be home on the day my banishment ends.

"Bardas, you make it sound so easy." She placed the pouch in her scrip.

Nagora stared at the map for a long moment. "Bardas, you're right. It'll be my best chance to make it home. Thanks for your advice."

They pulled off the main road just as the sun came up. The track they had turned onto was overgrown with brush. I would've missed this. Lots to be said about local knowledge, Tars. The going was slower.

Erin peeked out from beneath the blanket to smile at Nagora when Moreena's hand tentatively tried to find her little sister's shoulder. "Erin, you can come up or stay with Tars."

Erin held a finger to her lips before reaching up to touch her sister's hand and sit up.

Nagora winked at Erin. Erin grabbed Nagora's arm and pulled herself close and leaned against her. I hardly know you and already I know I'll miss you. She kissed the top of Erin's head and placed a hand over hers as she hugged her. Erin took hold of Nagora's thumb and smiled up at her as she leaned even closer.

A full three counts later, they entered a clearing and Bardas brought the wagon to a stop.

Nagora put her arms around Erin and held her for a long moment before getting up.

Nagora jumped down next to the dogs as Bardas helped Erin from the wagon. Moreena made her way toward her. "I'm right here, Moreena. This is where we go our separate ways. I wish you a happy time with Erin."

Moreena held out her arms. "Tars, I owe you so much. I'll never forget you. I so want to know if you make it home safely. If ever there's a way to send news by someone coming our way, please give me news."

For what she hoped would not be the last time, she breathed in the smell of Moreena's hair. "I'll not forget you either."

Bardas and Erin came around to them. He pulled the blanket off the three packs and pulled them closer to the back of the wagon.

Before reaching for her pack, Nagora unclipped her quiver and slipped it out from under her hooded shirt to take out her bow and assemble it. After she did, she pulled her flute from its pocket and stood before Moreena's sister. "Erin, my friend,

I want you to have this. It'll make your time with Moreena a happy time. Maybe you'll even forget some of the bad times."

Erin threw Nagora a dragon chord kiss before accepting the flute. She held it in her hands and examined it. She looked up with a tear on her cheek and a smile on her face. "Thank you, Tars. I love you too." Three faces had a look of relief as they stared at Erin.

Nagora slipped her quiver over her sheepskin vest, clipped it, and grabbed her pack from the wagon and fitted it to her shoulders. "Bardas, Moreena, Erin. Best of luck to you, my friends."

Bardas shook her hand. "Good speed to you. Straight ahead with my girls. You'll come to the lower woodland trail, to your left. It'll take you along this side of Feather Lake. You can't miss it. If all goes well, you should be at the lake before nightfall. Go with care. Don't rush ahead.

"Follow Keng. Trust he'll spot danger before you do. If he looks back at you and lies down, find cover. Keng'll follow you and won't bark unless you order him to. Keng, go with Tars."

Nagora and the sisters watched Bardas turn the wagon around and leave before they set off into the forest.

At the woodland trail, Nagora held the two sisters close, kissed each of their cheeks, said goodbye, and was on her way. Am I out of sight? She turned to look back. The sisters waved in the distance. She waved back. They must've followed me.

As Bardas had predicted, Nagora made Feather Lake before nightfall. She set up camp well above the lake with a good view of the other side where most of the farmland of the Lake Country lay.

Nagora's campsite on the hillside had a big rock behind which she could safely build a small fire out of sight. The land on this side of the lake was rockier with rougher terrain. Bardas had done well to send her this way.

She had killed a partridge and looked forward to having it for her evening meal. No harm in making our provisions last, Tars. She readied her fire pit and her tarp.

A crack of thunder in the dark woke Nagora. Rain came down in torrents, pushed by a wild wind. Keng lay at her side and did not move. She scratched his head just above his eyes. At least we're dry and we ate well. Let's hope this blows over.

Nagora awoke just before dawn. It was quiet except for the occasional heavy drop of rain falling from one leaf to another. Mist covered the hillside she was on. She couldn't see the lake below. She set water to boil for tea to wash down the biscuits she had made the night before while the partridge cooked. The water would also help soften the strip of cured boar meat she planned to eat.

She packed away her bedroll in the tarp before pouring tea into her bowl and dropping the meat into the pot.

She gave Keng a biscuit and half the strip of meat. While she ate, she tried to see the lake below. To go for a quick swim while the mist holds would be nice, aye, Tars? Some other time. We've got a lot of ground to cover.

Nagora was on one knee scratching Keng's chest after tying her boot. Keng, today we enter The Guard's domain.

Bardas said we would have to be extra vigilant. We'll do that, you and I. "Good dog." She stood and heaved her pack onto her shoulders. "Let's go."

It was near midday when Nagora looked down to where the Big Snake River emptied into Feather Lake. She had spotted fishers on the lake earlier. They had most likely come from the village at the river's mouth. For so many to be on the water, the weather would most likely clear. Though, the sun seemed to be fighting a losing battle.

Okay, Keng, we stay high on this side, keep the river in view, and our eyes and ears peeled. We'll have some rations when we're well past the village.

Bardas had told her that after the village, two other bridges crossed Big Snake River, one at about the halfway point and the other at the village at the other end of the river. And he said he had heard the river could be crossed at some shallower sections. Most of the hamlets were on the other side of the river, so her chances of being seen should be slim if she kept to this side.

Nagora had just finished eating a handful of shelled hazelnuts and was about to pick up her bow when she heard the beat of grouse wings in the distance. Keng's ears had caught the sound too, and it brought him to his feet, nose toward the sound. We're upwind, Keng. Likely your nose won't be of much use to you. Your ears might though. Was it a two-legged animal that flushed that bird? Or a four-legged predator?

Nagora crouched and drew an arrow from her quiver as she scanned ahead amongst the trees for any kind of movement. Nothing. Though a hunter, if they had spotted her, would hold their position too. *Who'll move first, Keng? Let's see what happens if we backtrack.*

Nagora checked behind her and crept backward, watching where she stepped. She stopped to scan ahead. About a hundred paces back, she moved to higher ground. *I'm glad you were trained to hunt, Keng. And you're so quiet.* She aimed for a stand of boulders higher up among the trees. It would possibly give her a better view of what was ahead and she would be in a position she could defend.

Nagora couldn't see anyone from her new vantage point. No movement. *Perhaps they had backtracked too, to a better position to ambush me. Keng too watched and waited.* A crow cawed in the far distance, and then another. She waited, expecting more cawing from these territorial birds. It didn't come. *Possibly just a companion call, Tars.*

Okay, Keng, we'll go up higher and then move ahead. Nagora took her time and paused often to search the way ahead, down, and behind her. She crept forward. Still no movement nor sound.

Let's pick up the pace and see what happens. She covered between ten and twenty paces with each burst, rushing ahead in a crouched position, stopping to do a quick scan, and then rushing ahead again.

The spot where they had stopped to eat was now below and slightly behind them. Nagora let her eyes search ahead. Still no movement. *Maybe it was a four-legged hunter after all.* She ran ahead for fifty more paces. Keng kept up with her and stopped when she did. Keng, am I just being over-cautious?

She looked to the slope ahead, above, and below. Okay, Keng. Steady ahead.

Three counts later the river was no longer visible below her to her left. Time to angle down, Keng, until we find the river again.

Nagora came to a stand of tall pines on a plateau with no sight of the river yet. The voice she hated inside her, the one that made her hesitate, told her to go around it. Do I trust it? Or do I trust Keng? She looked at the pine needles at her feet. It all came back as if it had happened yesterday. She clenched her teeth and blinked away the tears.

Come, Keng. We're going around.

Nagora's decision took her back along the sandy plateau's edge to where the pines ended at the rocky slope. She headed down and traveled just below the plateau for a short ways before angling down further toward the river, visible through the trees. She stopped to listen. Yes, I hear it too, Keng, gentle rapids on the river. Let's keep it in sight.

Nagora had not walked another hundred paces when Keng turned to look at her and lay down. Before she could move to take cover, a voice from above her ordered, "Halt where you are." The same command came from below her, and again in front of her. The three men had their arrows drawn on their bows. She was dead in their sights. She froze.

"Put your bow down. If you tell your dog to attack, both of you'll be dead."

Nagora set her bow on the ground and raised her hands. "Stay, Keng."

"Would you be lost, by any chance?" The question came from the man on the slope above her. He had lowered his bow to his side. The other two kept their sights on her.

"I … don't think so." They were dressed in what must've been handsome uniforms long ago, but now they were tattered and patched. One wore pants that were obviously not part of the original uniform.

"Would you be hunting in our domain without our permission?"

"Only if it'll help me stretch my provisions so I can get home."

"Almost no one comes this way to go home. Those who do don't hide like you've been doing. And we know the ones going home. We don't know you. Would you have a name by any chance?"

"Aye. Tars is my name." Only answer his questions.

"Well, young Tars, do you know where you are?"

"Aye, I do. This is the domain of The Guard."

"You say you're going home. Where's that?"

"Near Yhorgal."

"And you've chosen to go home this way? Are you seeking adventure, lad?"

"You could say that."

"Or are you running?"

"You could say that too."

"You have a price on your head?"

"Could be. I don't know that."

"If you do, that means you've done something to put a price on your head. And you must be wanted badly. That's why you've run this way. Well Tars, what did you do?"

"If you don't know yet, you will soon enough. I'll be glad to tell you what I did, but only before the captain of The Guard."

"Well, Tars. This is your lucky day. I am the one you're looking for."

"You very well could be. But you'll pardon me if I say I doubt you are. If you were, you'd know what I did and probably be thanking me right now."

"Men, I'm the captain, aren't I?"

"Aye, sir. That you are, Captain Coyle," said one of them. The other seemed to be biting back a smile.

"What should I be thanking you for?" asked Captain Coyle.

"For my honesty with you so far. Truly, I don't believe you're the captain. If you are, you have a horse that travels mighty fast. Yet, you don't show any signs of having ridden a horse that hard. And you aren't showing any signs of bearing news destined for your ears."

He looked to his men and back at her. "Are you carrying other weapons?"

"I am. I'll gladly surrender them if you return them for my journey home."

"Do so."

Nagora set her pack down, unclipped her quiver, and placed it on the ground next to her bow. Reaching into the collar of her shirt at the back of her neck, she unfastened the sheath of her big blade and placed her blades on top of her quiver. Finally, she pulled the knife from the sheath on the belt at her waist and let it drop, to stick in the ground. Nagora then stepped away from the pile and raised her hands.

Coyle came down. He reached for her blades, pulled a small one from its holster, and gauged its heft. He pushed it back in and flipped the retaining clip at the mouth of the big blade's sheath. He grasped the handle and looked at her for a moment before he pulled it out.

His face showed immediate appreciation.

Coyle held it up so the other two could see. One of them whistled. He took the time to examine the handle, the cross guard, and both sides of the big leaf blade. He pointed to the grip of the handle. "Do you know what this is?"

"Walrus hide."

He frowned as he looked at it again.

"It's a big sea animal, weighs more than the four of us combined. Big tusks at its mouth. We sometimes see them in winter, on the ice. Or lying on the beach in the sun." Nagora held up three fingers together. "Hide's about this thick. Three layers of it compressed on that handle. It'll never get wet or soak up water."

"So you stole this treasure?"

You're not the captain. "No."

"I've never seen a metal like this. Why would you have it in your possession?"

"It was made for me." Nagora read the surprise and disbelief on his face.

"Then you know what metal this is."

"I don't know the name of the metal, but I know what it's made from. You'll not believe me when I tell you."

Coyle sneered. "Try me."

"Skystone."

He let the big blade slip back into its sheath. "I wasn't born yesterday, young Tars." He placed it back on the quiver and picked up her bow. "And this was made for you too?"

Be patient. She took a breath. "It was."

Coyle examined the handle. "Made to be taken apart?"

"Yes."

He looked to his men and then back at her. He handed her the bow and waved his hand. "Do it."

Nagora didn't waste a moment. It was the fastest she had ever taken it down and returned it to her quiver. His two men were slack-jawed. She stepped back from her weapons. "Please, tell your men to relax. I don't want to get killed because one of them gets a cramp on his draw and releases unintentionally."

Coyle waved them down. They lowered their bows, but kept their arrows nocked.

He bent to one knee and rummaged through her pack. He seemed satisfied and placed it at her feet. "Open your pouch."

Nagora unbuckled the flap of her scrip and held it open so he could look through it.

He reached in and felt around. "Good. Pick up your pack."

Hmm, he ignored the broken shoe. "Can I stick my blades in the quiver too? It'll be easier for whoever carries it."

Coyle looked from her to the weapons. "Do it."

Nagora did and clipped the carry strap in place. She lifted the quiver by a single finger and held it out.

He motioned one of his men forward to take it and pointed at her, and then to Keng. "Sit next to your dog."

...

Coyle took about twenty steps away from her and called his men to him. He spoke to them in a hushed voice. Whatever he was telling them, it seemed serious. It was being said with urgency. One of his men glanced over at her several times and nodded each time, and seemed to be repeating the orders he had been given. Coyle placed a hand on his shoulder and sent him away, running.

Going to find the captain? Likely.

Coyle looked over at her. "Come with us."

Nagora followed the one who carried her quiver. Keng walked at her side. Coyle followed. Their pace was slow and they were quiet, even careful, stopping often to survey the way ahead. They were getting closer to the river. No signs of a road on the other side nor of any farm or settlement nearby. Which way had the other man gone? Perhaps to the bridge. How far are we from it?

The next time they stopped, Coyle put a finger to his mouth and motioned Nagora to crouch. His man put her quiver down and crept ahead, his bow at the ready. When he was out of sight, Coyle retrieved her quiver and moved behind a tree. He signaled to her to do the same.

Keng listened and watched, and so did Nagora. When her eyes returned to Coyle, he looked at her. He held his finger across his lips again. Nagora looked around, up the slope, ahead, and down the slope to the river. She saw nothing and heard nothing. What are they worried about?

A crow cawed in the distance ahead. Coyle cawed and waved her over to him as he slung her quiver strap over his shoulder. "Can you track my man's steps?"

"I can. My dog too."

He smiled for the briefest moment. "Take your time. Stay quiet."

They had angled down the slope until they came to a tall wall of rock to their right. Nagora kept moving along it. She could hear the river to her left, but not see it. The further on they went, the thicker the brush grew along the wall. Keng led the way around a stand of hawthorn trees. Pare, we pick these berries every year so you can make jam, and Geirador medicine. But not this year, unless I get home in time. Those thorns can be wicked.

Keng stopped on the other side where a bunch of young alders grew, concealing the seam in the stone wall behind.

"In there. Watch your head."

It was dark. Nagora crouched and kept a hand on Keng. Coyle took her around a bend to a lit chamber where the other man was waiting. He was sitting on the dirt floor of the cave with three candle lanterns at his feet.

Coyle followed right behind her. "Make yourself comfortable. We'll be here until dark. Brin and I'll keep watch."

She shrugged off her pack and sat. "Can you tell me what's going on?"

"You've become a prize. The price on your head must be unheard of."

"Why do you say that?"

Coyle and Brin smiled. "Sixty mounted mercenaries came through in the night, just as we were headed this way to find you. Looks like they're thinking like you. Take the unthinkable way home. They'll do anything to find you to get the reward. Never have that many come this far. They're at the lake by now, searching, questioning, warning, offering a share in the reward."

Brin snickered. "Go that way, you'll have to swim home."

"How'd you know I was coming this way?"

Coyle smiled. "We're The Guard. It's our business to know who comes into our domain. We've got eyes in the Lake Country, and all along our border. Anyone coming our way gets reported to us. Especially those sneaking through."

"So I'm lucky you found me first."

"Lucky for us." Coyle nudged Brin. "We have to keep you out of mercenary hands so we get the reward and not them."

"What if I could match the reward? Would you help me get home?"

He waved his hand. "Your weapons aren't worth that much."

"No, but I have someone at home who'll pay for my safe return."

Coyle laughed. "I doubt that. Not my call anyway."

"What if the mercenaries find me here with you? What if those who warned you sell that information to them?"

"Only you and three others know of this place. We'll be gone come nightfall. Take you to a safe place The Guard defends. We'll learn more about you and why you're running, what the reward is."

"So we're not far from the bridge?"

"We won't be crossing on the bridge."

...

Nagora had tried to sleep while Coyle and Brin took turns at the cave entrance.

She awoke to a boot tapping hers. Coyle stood above her. "We go now."

She packed her bedroll away before getting on her feet to pull her pack onto her shoulders. She held onto Keng's collar as they crept out.

Nagora followed Brin down to the river's edge. Her eyes adjusted to the dark. The river appeared to be a dancing carpet of stars. She didn't like the sound of the rushing water. This will be dangerous, Keng.

Coyle placed a hand on her shoulder. "Wait."

Brin was bent over, his arms in the water up to his elbows. When he stood, he returned holding three loops of rope in one hand. The other ends of those ropes seemed to be anchored in the water.

Coyle pointed to the loop Brin held out to Nagora. "A long rope crosses the river. Thread your belt through the loop of the short rope. It'll follow you as you cross. Go slow. The stones are slippery. The deepest part will be up to your waist. Don't let go of the dog."

The water was cold and when it reached Nagora's waist, she relieved herself. You had your turn, Keng. Feels good, aye? Tavi, the third man Coyle had sent ahead, now waited for them on the other side. When they came ashore, he huddled with Coyle and Brin.

Nagora waited while Keng shook his coat. Soon the four were on their way through the trees. Again, Coyle kept right behind her.

The group stopped at the edge of a road. Coyle placed a hand on her shoulder. "We cross one at a time. Wait for Brin to be in the trees."

Nagora ran across like Tavi and Brin before her. It was a short sprint and as soon as Coyle followed, they moved on into the forest. They obviously knew their way, like she did around her home when out at night. Even with a starlit sky, it wasn't something she would try in unfamiliar territory. With moonlight she might.

Almost a full count later, the four began to climb, still mostly under the cover of trees. They stopped for a breather. Coyle came alongside Nagora. "We'll reach our destination soon."

They kept climbing, and the terrain became rockier. The lead man, Tavi, slowed his pace to get his bearings. He seemed to move from one big boulder to another up the mountainside. They had not crossed another road since the first one below. If there was a road or a trail to where they were headed, it was obvious they weren't on it. Were they just being careful, or avoiding a specific area? Would their captain be at their destination?

They came to an open plateau and ran across it, stopping on the other side to catch their breath before climbing again. More brush and bushes covered this slope. They climbed higher, and the slope broke in two onto a narrow valley that rose higher on the mountain. This part seemed like a trail.

At last they came to a cave entrance. They had to climb up and over the lip of the entrance. Four shapes emerged from the deeper darkness, and Nagora could make out the bows they held. They greeted the other three with raised fists and almost ignored her. As soon as the silent greetings ended, Brin and the lead man melted back into the dark.

Nagora held on to Keng in the blackness. Coyle was at her back. How did Brin and Tavi know where they were going? Then she touched it with the side of her foot, a stone or wooden rail of some kind set in the floor of the cave, raised just enough to be found. Clever.

Finally, the dull glow of candlelight lit the way ahead. The group walked into a vaulted chamber. The candle lanterns were at the far side of the chamber, one on each side of the two big sturdy timber doors that stopped their progress. It was quiet. There was no handle or knocker on either door, though high on one door, the tiny window with four metal bars crossing in front of it seemed out of place.

None of them moved. They stood, waiting for the doors to open. Only one did, inward, slowly, and only enough for a person to squeeze through to the light on the other side.

It was quiet on that side too, and Nagora could not see who had opened the door. She looked back at it and up to its window. She almost laughed at the thought that came to mind. An invisible doorkeep, Tars, a giant no less.

Onward the corridor was lit by candle lanterns hung on metal brackets at regular intervals, alternating from one side to the other. They came to three sets of doors, one directly ahead of them, a set to their right, and a set to their left. What was this place? This was no hideout.

Something smelled familiar, an odor that seemed to linger, behind the scent of the melting beeswax candles. So familiar now. It was the smell of grains—wheat, oats, and barley. Was this a secret granary? But why in such an out-of-the-way place?

Again, a single door opened, and they squeezed through onto another long passageway leading to another door. Coyle leaned over Nagora's shoulder and whispered, "It's the last door."

The door opened to the sound of voices. They grew louder as she slipped through and then the people, about twenty of them sitting at a long table, fell silent. The room was round like an upside-down bowl, except for the floor, which was of flat, polished rock. She counted six other small closed doors spread out evenly on the circular wall.

Tar piss! It's huge! Who built this place, Tars? The corridors we walked through, the big doors we passed, and now this chamber. If I ever make it home, no one will believe me when I tell them. She signaled Keng to stay at her side.

Mostly men sat at the table. Nagora looked at each of them. Who was the captain? No one moved. He isn't here, Tars. If he were, he would come to me. Or would he?

Coyle approached the table, placed Nagora's quiver before one of the men, and stepped back to his men. That old man stood and wasted no time emptying her quiver and spreading her weapons on the table. He set all the arrows to one side and pulled all the knives from their holsters and her big blade from its sheath. He assembled and strung her bow and set it back on the table.

When he was done, he turned to look at Nagora. He was probably the oldest person at the table, older than anyone she had ever met. He turned back to the table. All the others stood and slowly they circled the table. Each of them stopped to examine her weapons.

When they had returned to their places, the old man looked at each of them. A woman stood. She too was old, possibly older than the man. With people of that age it was often hard to tell. Her hair was silver as was the man's hair and beard. Her garments, like the man's, were green. "I will speak for all of us. If any of you disagree with my words, you will have your turn to voice your opinion.

"We have before us this warrior's weapons. We have heard of this warrior's deeds, yet to be confirmed by witnesses. If confirmed, they will be signs. And we have before us the warrior." The woman's eyes held Nagora's for a long moment before she continued. "Not the sign to complete the three. For in the three, we will know we have the one. I posit the warrior is not what he appears to be."

The old woman pointed at Nagora. "Am I not right, warrior?"

She knows I'm not you, Tars. What do I do?

"Warrior, before midday tomorrow, we at this table will vote. That vote will decide your future. If you are who I think you are, your future could very well be key to our future."

"A dragon awaits you." Those words. And now this woman's words. Why do they fill me with fear? I best speak my mind. "We cannot know the future. Who are you to decide my future when you cannot know it?"

The old woman smiled at her. "The words you speak are true. We cannot know ... the future. We can know ... the one who will influence our future. We can know this by the signs."

Be careful, Tars. Watch your words. "So if I understand, my weapons and my deeds are signs I will somehow influence your future?"

The old woman held up her hand. "And your own future."

Nagora pointed to herself. "So I have two of three signs? And you say I'm not who I appear to be. What do you want me to do?" Nagora's hand signaled Keng to sit.

"Reveal yourself," the old woman pointed to the others around the table, "so they may see you as the sign you are."

If this'll keep me alive ... She slipped her pack from her shoulders, stripped off her vest, hooded shirt, undershirt, and unfastened the front drawstring of her undergarment, and pulled it down, leaving the side strings tied to her leggings, yet revealing her womanhood.

All around the table looked. The old woman waved Nagora to dress.

Now you know. But you won't get my name.

As Nagora dressed, she glared at the old woman who had remained standing, watching her. When she finished pulling on her vest, she crossed her arms.

Now what?

The old woman looked down at the table for a moment, then back to her. "Thank you. It was necessary. We are awaiting a witness to your actions. Until then, you and your dog will be given food and drink and a comfortable place to rest."

Nagora scratched Keng's head and patted his neck.

Is the captain to be my witness? I hope so.

"Do you have any questions?"

You know damn well I have a hundred questions or more. You probably won't answer them until after you vote anyway. Calm down. Be polite. "What is this place? Who built it?"

Now all the people around the table were smiling.

The old woman looked around at them. She seemed to be getting their consent to answer the questions. Each gave a small nod. "What do you think this place is?"

Why did old people do that? Uncle did it all the time. Did I ask the obvious? It's an ale house, isn't it? Don't be brash. Uncle would lace me one if he ever found out.

"A granary?"

The smile on the old woman's face broadened as did those on the faces around the table. "It is. Stone Standers, with the help of dragons, built it long ago on the orders of a good king. On first look, one would ask why in such a remote place. The answer is twofold.

"First, the location. The rock in this mountain is solid through and through. Good protection from the elements and vermin.

"Second, also related to location, the granary is close to being at the center of our land. Ideal for delivery by dragons flying surpluses to areas of the land in need."

"Those must've been the good days, long ago?" said Nagora.

The old woman's face became solemn as if in recollection. "They were, as you say, the good days of our land when a just king, with a heart that cared for all his people, ruled the land. None lacked for a good roof to live under, a secure place to raise a family. None went to bed hungry. None went without good and warm clothing. None lacked opportunities to choose how to contribute to the wellness of all in the land. We were the people of the dragon living in the Land of the Dragon. The Land of the Danu was, and is, our land. The dragons shared the land with us. They and we benefitted."

The old woman bowed her head and placed a hand over her heart.

Did the others notice how she held her fingers, Tars? Or did she do so for my benefit?

"Perhaps those good days will return. If they do, the journey back will be a long one. But in the end, well worth it."

The old woman placed a hand on the table. "We too will rest while we wait for the witness to arrive. You'll be shown to a safe room. Rest. You'll need all your strength."

The people rose from the table and began conversations in small groups as they headed toward the smaller doors around the room. One woman from the table approached Nagora as she watched Coyle put her weapons back into the quiver.

The woman touched her sleeve and smiled. "Please, come with me. I'll show you where."

The woman led Nagora to one of the doors, one she had not seen anyone move toward. It opened onto a narrow corridor. They passed two doors. Each had a candle lantern on a hook next its wooden frame.

When they came to the last door, the woman took the candle lantern, opened the door, and waved Nagora in, handing her the lantern. "You and your dog will be comfortable here. In a short while someone will knock on your door. You'll find food on a tray next to your door. I'll be the one returning for you after the vote. Rest well."

"Thank you."

The woman paused before leaving. "Oh, the doors won't be locked."

Nagora smiled at the woman. Anyway, I don't think I'll be going anywhere on my own.

The room was a simple cell carved out of the rock. It had a small table, a single chair, and a hammock strung from hooks in opposite corners. There was also a bucket with a cover. "That's thoughtful. Looks like this is home, Keng. I hope you can hold it until we get out of here. Might as well get comfortable." She set the lantern on the table.

Keng did a quick inspection of the room and curled up under the table, facing the door.

Nagora had just settled in the hammock when someone knocked. By the time she reached the door, the person was gone. The tray on the floor held two big bowls of stew, a piece of bread, a pitcher of water, a spoon, and a folded piece of cloth. Next to the tray she found a folded blanket.

A firm knock on the door awoke Nagora. She blinked and rubbed sleep from her eyes. Her last memory was of her thinking she would never fall asleep. She had gotten out of the hammock and sat next to Keng to pet him and talk to him. When she returned to the hammock, she lay in it, swinging with eyes wide open. Its motion must have put her to sleep. How long have I slept?

She made her way to the door. The woman smiled. "It is time. Take a few moments to ready yourself. You know the way. Bring your pack and the dog."

Nagora kept wiping sleep from her eyes. "What time of day is it?"

"Early morning, about three counts after sunrise."

"Thank you." The captain must've made good time. Perhaps he also wanted to avoid the mercenaries. Did they vote yet? "Well, Keng, I guess we'll find out what happens to us soon enough." She went over to the pail, set the cover on the floor, and crouched over it. "Best way to start the day, aye, Keng? Poor you, I hope you won't have long to wait."

She poured water on the cloth and wiped her face before picking up her pack.

Nagora stepped into the round room. Coyle and his men stood next to the table on one side. The old woman and a man stood on the other side of the table. Could he be the captain of The Guard? Both of them were smiling. None of the other elders were in the room.

So far so good, Tars.

"Come to this side of the table. Our captain is waiting to meet you."

As Nagora moved to that side of the table, the captain moved in her direction and looked her up and down. Did he like what he saw? Or was he confirming she was the one he had seen at the Temple of Fire? Or had her bow already confirmed that?

He stopped a few paces from her and motioned her to come closer. He pursed his lips as he swallowed. His eyes filled with tears. He held open his arms. "Thank you. Thank you for giving me back my daughter."

His embrace was warm.

"I couldn't believe it. I thought she was lost to me forever." He stepped back and smiled through tears as he looked into Nagora's eyes.

"How is Edana? I did what I could for her. Made her drink. Told her to hang on, that you'd come for her, that she could make it."

"Edana has made it. Thanks to you. When she came to, she said she'd dreamt a warrior from the stars had come to free her.

"And now Edana's name is on everyone's lips in Windhaven."

Nagora touched his sleeve. "I know you only as the captain of The Guard. Please, tell me your name."

"My name is Ardal. You can call me that."

Nagora smiled at him. "Ardal, how were you able to get to her?"

"Her mother and I were late. We arrived in time to see the virgins parade with their trays and lanterns. When we didn't see Edana, we knew what it meant. My wife couldn't bear to go see her hanging inside the temple. She wanted to send me back to buy the ... bones the next day. We were just leaving Temple Square when we heard the uproar from the crowd. We looked back and saw the dragon window was lit up." Ardal's face too seemed to light up at this moment.

"I knew something unusual had just happened. I told my wife to wait for me at the main gate. I fought my way through the crowd. From the other side of the square, I saw you draw and loose a fire arrow. The crowd was pushing away, trying to get away from Hag's carriage because the driver was whipping the horse to get it to move. I saw Hag and her soldiers take to the carriage and leave."

The old woman standing next to Ardal had her eyes on him. She smiled and nodded as he recounted the events.

"By the time, I made it to the main doors, one was on fire. The burning arrow in the door gave me part of the picture. It was impossible to get an answer that made sense from those I questioned. It was too noisy."

He's right it was noisy. I remember all the pounding on the doors and the commotion beyond them.

"I thought for a moment maybe, just maybe, somehow Edana had set the fire, that the girls had planned it with outside help from the one who'd loosed the arrow. I didn't know you'd made it inside. I joined in with the soldiers pounding on the main door. When I realized it was burning from the inside too, I moved to the side door Hag habitually uses to enter the temple."

Ardal paused, but his hands became pumping fists. "I tried to smash it in. I asked for help. Three of us took turns throwing ourselves against it.

"Then someone pulled me aside, opened his coat to show me the axe he carried, and told me to trust what he was about to tell me. He had to scream into my ear for me to understand. With that axe, it didn't take me long to get through the door."

The old woman placed a hand on Ardal's arm.

"I found Edana where he told me. My only thought was to get her out. A soldier stopped me on the temple steps. I asked him if he wanted to take care of a corpse. He let me go. I joined the line at the Main Gate. My wife found me."

Ardal took a breath and blinked. "She couldn't believe her eyes, nor her ears. She said people kept talking about the warrior, Edana, who said she'd return and dragons would fly over Windhaven again. She showed me the salute they made when talking of Edana." From his heart, he extended his hand in the dragon-chord salute. Now Ardal was blinking back tears.

"And everyone kept talking about how the dragon window made them remember how beautiful their town once was, when the times were good.

"When our turn came, we begged the guards to let us take our only daughter home for burial."

Tar piss! What've I done? Created a warrior called Edana? That's not what I set out to do.

Now the old woman saluted Nagora as the captain had and placed a hand on her shoulder. "You don't yet realize the greater import of your actions."

Nagora took a deep breath. "You're right. I don't."

"Allow me to thank you for the gift you've given the people of the Land of the Danu. It is spreading throughout the land at this moment. They can't stop it. They can't arrest it. No dungeon can ever hold it. No sword can ever kill it. The hope that Edana will return with the dragons is the gift our people have been waiting for. Thank you, Edana."

Nagora looked down at her feet, and over at Coyle and his men. They were smiling at her. She looked back at the captain and the old woman. "I don't know what to say to that. I must give it some thought on my way home. It's not what I had set out to do."

"Three signs: your weapons, your deeds witnessed, and you, Edana. You are … the one. And now we have to get you home." The old woman touched the captain's arm.

Ardal gave Nagora a warm smile. "That's my task. It's the least I can do for you. We leave now."

The Bridge
Âsokan

Nagora was happy to have her weapons back. All the doors leaving the secret granary were open for them to leave. Three other men joined the captain at the mouth of the cave. Nagora and Keng followed them and the captain. Coyle and his men followed her.

The group traveled back down the narrow valley all the way to the forested land below. They turned left and stayed among the trees, following the contour of the mountain until they entered a valley.

The group followed the valley, came to a brook, crossed it, and kept it to their left until the valley began to climb and the brook turned into a series of cataracts.

Onward, they climbed the mountain to their right. By the time the sound of the rushing waterfalls had disappeared, the group reached a narrow plateau and followed it to the left until the captain called for a halt. "We'll wait here. Spread out among the trees above, bows at the ready. Have some rations.

"Edana, I want you no more than ten strides away from me."

Well, Tars, I hope you're not confused. I'm doing my best with this new name. I don't know about taking on Edana's role. We'll have to find out what those in charge of The Cause think about it.

As the men dispersed, Nagora turned to the captain. "Ardal, what are we waiting for?"

"Keallach, one of my men. He'll be reporting on what the mercenaries are up to at the lake village. His report will decide our next move." Ardal looked to the sky. Soon the sun would be just a pale shadow on a gray sky. "If he's not here in two counts, we'll leave."

"For an alternate destination?"

He looked around to the positions his men had taken before answering. "Yes." It didn't seem to please him.

Just as Ardal signaled to Nagora that they were about to leave, she pointed to a man running up the plateau's slope. The captain signaled his men to hold their positions while he moved down to the plateau to meet Keallach.

Nagora followed and kept close enough to hear. When Keallach arrived, he bent over to catch his breath before speaking. "They're everywhere. Forty more showed up at dawn. No way we can go there. They have men on the water too."

Something's not right, Keng. He's only looked at me once. He keeps looking at you when he bends to catch his breath. Maybe he's afraid of dogs. He's not wearing a shred of uniform. Why would that be?

Ardal spit. "I feared as much. We don't have a moment to waste. We'll double our pace from here on."

Nagora stepped over to the captain. "Where are we going?"

"We'll be taking you to a bridge. You'll be the only one to cross it."

"Why? Where does it lead to?"

"To the Stone Standers' domain."

Maton's words jumped up. "Wait! But only Stone Standers can go there. I'm not a Stone Stander."

"That's right. If anyone stands a chance of setting foot there, you do. It's that or try to fight the mercenary force."

"Ardal, I had the impression The Guard was a sizable force."

"That's what many think. Half of those who bear arms are here with you right now. The other half guards the granary."

Her stomach tightened. This isn't looking good, Tars.

"For a thousand gold coins, the mercenaries will do whatever it takes to find you. If they catch you, they'll turn you over to the prince. You've seen Acindor's justice in action. It's your choice."

Not a choice, is it, Tars? "Take me to the bridge."

Ardal gathered the men to explain the situation.

She took hold of Keng's collar and looked at Keallach. "You keep ahead. I'll keep my dog away from you."

Keallach nodded and looked away.

Coyle and his men took the lead, followed by Keallach. Ardal ran just behind Nagora. "Don't worry. We'll get you there. Or die trying."

Tar piss! What's he not telling me?

Now that they were on a steep climb, their pace had slowed as it was beginning to rain. Nagora was careful to follow Keng. He had a knack of avoiding the loose stones and finding good footholds.

Keallach kept glancing back. That, and the fact he kept a hand on his sword hilt, bothered her. He's itching to use it. I don't like his eyes.

Ardal spoke from behind Nagora. "After we reach the top, it'll be downhill all the way to the bridge."

She looked up ahead as far as possible, but couldn't determine how much further it was to the top. Coyle looked back at those behind him. He smiled and held up two fingers when his eyes met hers. Two more counts to the top?

Coyle was right. As Nagora came over the top of the ridge, the wind slapped rain into her face.

Ardal pointed down to the right. "If it wasn't raining, you'd be able to see the gorge below, and possibly the bridge."

She touched the side of her head and held her fingers up to her ear. "Possibly see the bridge?"

He yelled into the wind. "You'll understand when we get to it."

The going was steep and slippery and slow. It kept Keng on his haunches, and the climbers went down sideways with their bows in their downhill hands. All of them, except for

Keallach. He was armed with his sword and a dagger at his belt.

Good man that Coyle, right, Tars? He sets an even pace, especially on the descent. His brief stops are just enough to give my knees and ankles the rest they need. That Keallach though. He's got his sword out to support his uphill hand while he rubs his knee with the other. That's dangerous, Tars. And a sure way to ruin the blade of his weapon, no matter how much his knee hurts. If I were his captain, I would order him to return the sword to its scabbard.

The group came to a section of the slope that wasn't as steep, but big boulders were scattered along its surface. Probably from the side of the mountain above the ridge we just came over, Tars. As the line moved into the boulder field, Nagora lost sight of those ahead of her as they wound their way among the big rocks.

Nagora had just switched her bow to her right hand so she could lean forward on her left as she came down around the boulder. That's when Keallach swung his sword at her. Luckily, Nagora was able to ward off the blow. It struck her bow's brass handle, just above her fist. She whipped her bow's limb up to Keallach's wrist, bringing his sword hand up, and at the same time, she pivoted to kick him in the ribs. When his arm came down, Nagora struck his wrist with her hand and knocked his sword to the ground. He fell down, scrambled to his feet, and ran down the slope.

Keng had been behind her during the attack, but now he was on Keallach's heels. Nagora drew an arrow, nocked, and loosed before any of the others could react. Her arrow struck Keallach's shoulder blade and brought him down.

Nagora drew another arrow and ran toward him.

"Edana! Wait!" It was Ardal's voice behind her.

Keng had Keallach covered. The man was on his belly, screaming, and trying to reach back to grasp the arrow. Nagora stopped next to Keng. "Good dog."

Nagora struck Keallach on the side of his face with the curved horn of her bow. "You bastard! You sold us out to the mercenaries, didn't you?" She struck him again. "Didn't you?" Nagora drew her arrow. She aimed at his eye.

Ardal put a hand on Nagora's shoulder. "Don't. You're probably right. We need to find out what he's done. We might be walking into a trap."

Ardal's men gathered around as he went down on one knee next to the fallen man's head. "Keallach, what'd you tell them?"

Keallach grimaced and shook his head. "Nothing."

"Nothing?" Ardal reached for the arrow and flicked it with a finger.

Keallach screamed.

"That hurts, doesn't it? What'd you tell them?"

"We were tracking the rebel, headed for the lake. Lost his tracks. Picked 'em up on the other side of the river. He had to be headed this way."

"How much did they offer you?"

"Twenty gold coins alive. Ten dead."

Nagora pressed the tip her bow into Keallach's neck. "So why'd you try to kill me?"

Keallach shook his head.

Nagora lifted her bow to swing it at him.

Keallach winced. "To be sure to get the reward. Others have been sent to the bridge."

Ardal touched Nagora's arm. "He wanted to wound you so you couldn't cross the bridge."

Nagora narrowed her eyes. "What do you mean?"

"When you get to the bridge, you'll understand."

Ardal sent two men along the slope to scout the pass where the mercenaries would have to enter to get to the bridge. Nagora had given the scouts her last whistle arrow. "Warn us if the mercenaries approach," she told them.

Coyle and Brin had gone ahead to scout the bridge.

The others stayed to help bring Keallach down.

Just before they arrived at the bridge site, Coyle came out of the mist and pouring rain toward them. "No mercenaries at the bridge. But the chains were moving. Someone was on the bridge. Probably headed to the other side."

Chains moving? She had to ask. "Could it be a mercenary?"

Ardal shook his head. "No way. They know they're not welcome there. They'd be dead before setting foot on the other side."

"What about me? What if they take me for a mercenary?"

Ardal placed a hand on Nagora's shoulder and looked in her eyes. "You'll make it to the other side. What happens when you get there, Edana, I can't tell you."

"But how will the Stone Standers know I'm not a mercenary?"

"You'll be naked. There are no women among the mercenaries."

"I won't go without my scrip and my blades."

He pursed his lips and nodded. "Okay."

Coyle interrupted and motioned to the captain to join him. He explained something to him. From what Nagora could see, Ardal was pleased with what he heard. However, his brief smile disappeared as he returned to her.

"Come have a look at the bridge."

As Nagora approached the bridge path, the noise from the roiling river in the gorge below rose out of the mist and fog generated by the warm rain. She saw the chains. These are the bridge? I don't believe it. But sure enough, the closer she got to the ledge at the edge of the chasm, only two chains stuck out from the huge boulder into the mist above it. There was plenty of space on the ledge near the boulder, allowing her to stand before she set foot onto the bottom chain.

The long finger thick triangular links of the bottom chain were all set flat, so the top pointy end of one link was bent and wrapped around the wide bottom end of the next link. Each link was just wide enough and long enough for a person to place a foot on it.

The top chain, elbow high from the bottom one, was made of elongated links pressed together in their middles and open at their ends to accept other links. Each of those links was at least three hand-widths in length. They resembled long bones strung together one after another.

Nagora and Keng heard it before the others did. The scream of the whistle arrow had Ardal's men cowering. It had come down through the gray cloud surrounding them.

Nagora looked at Ardal. "What're you going to do with Keallach?"

He didn't hesitate. "He's going to become you. We'll put your pack on him. We'll keep your bow and quiver. His body will be in the gorge below. We'll say we captured the rebel, but he tried to escape across the bridge, so we shot him with his own bow and arrow. We'll have your bow with the gash in the handle as proof of our first skirmish before we unarmed him."

It wasn't making sense to her. "But they won't believe you if they don't find the body."

"They'll find it. Go out on the bridge until you see the ledge below. I want to know if you can carry his body that far."

"Are you crazy?"

"First, go look if you can see the ledge. Believe me. You'll be able to do it," said Ardal.

"Can't you send someone with me? To help me?"

"The bridge is ancient. We've no way to tell what weight the chains will hold. We can't risk breaking it.

Ardal held out his hand. "Give me your pack. Now. Quick. Go."

Nagora handed it to him and stepped onto the chain. There's no way I can carry him. She moved along it tentatively. This wouldn't be an easy task. The chain was slippery under her boots. Will it be like that when I'm barefoot? She kept moving until the top of the ledge came into view. It was barely visible below in the mist and spray of the rushing water splashing over it.

She returned. "There's no way I can carry him. It's too slippery."

Ardal pointed to Keallach. He looked unconscious. His men had rigged a rope harness to him. "It's your rope. We'll tie a loop of rope around to the top chain. All you have to do is pull him along, reach behind, cut this rope here. He'll fall free down to the ledge. We'll pull the rope back. You continue on to the other side."

Nagora swallowed as she looked at Keallach. "I think I'd rather push him. In case he comes to."

Coyle made a quick motion with both his hands at his own head. "He won't."

Tar piss! He's dead!

Coyle and his men carried Keallach over to the chain.

Nagora stripped, tied her belt around her waist, and let the sheath of her knife hang down on her backside. She slipped the strap of her scrip over head onto her shoulder and let it hang at her hip. As she slipped her sheepskin vest over her blades, she looked at Keng.

I haven't forgotten you. You know you can't come with me. "Here, Keng." Nagora bent to let Keng lick her face. Pearls of raindrops covered his coat. Nagora scratched behind his ears and hugged him for a last time as she whispered, "Protect Erin and Moreena."

She stood up straight. "Keng, find Quinn." Keng disappeared into the mist as he headed up the mountainside.

As soon as Keng was out of sight, Nagora grabbed her boots, tied their laces together, and hung them around her neck. She rolled her leggings, undergarments, and shirt into a ball, handing it to Coyle.

Coyle stuffed her clothes into his scrip.

Ardal stepped up to Nagora. "I wish I could take you all the way to your home. Even if I could, I feel I'd still be in your debt. Open your mouth."

She did not see what he had put in her mouth. Three coins?

"Don't drop them! Only open your mouth when you get to the other side. Three gold dragons just might buy you safe passage. Good luck, Edana." He walked with her to the bridge. He gave her the dragon-chord salute. The others did the same.

Nagora returned their salute and took hold of the top chain before stepping onto the bottom one to lean against Keallach's chest. The loop from the rope harness held Keallach so the left side of his neck rested against the top chain. She avoided looking into his lifeless eyes. She pushed, and Keallach's dead body moved ahead one link. Nagora's bare feet on the chain had more grip than the leather of her boot soles.

"Faster, Edana!"

Pushing against Keallach, keeping some flex in her legs, and just hanging on in the pouring rain took all her strength and concentration. I don't think I can go any faster. I'll try to push him ahead two links at a time. Tar piss! I just put some bounce in the chain. Nagora slid her feet forward and pushed Keallach, then slid and pushed his dead weight again, trying to do so as fast as possible. Now the misty spray from below surrounded her. Was it the force of the falling rain that pushed the mist up? The ledge came into view. About ten more links would do it.

The chains sloped slightly because of the weight on them. Pushing Keallach seemed easier. Because of the slope or the wetness of the chain links? She rubbed the links to remove as much of the water from them as possible. Did wiping her hands on her sheepskin vest help or hinder? Droplets of water were no longer just clinging to the surface of the fur, but penetrating it.

Nagora reached behind for her knife. Don't drop it. Okay, now how do I do this? How much were the chains going to move? The top one would move the most. Tar piss! Am I going to be able to hold on? Don't worry about it. Just do it. Both his feet are on the same side. Now cut.

The cut rope harness released Keallach. She didn't watch him fall. She reached out for the rope dangling before her with her knife hand and wound her arm around it as much as possible. The top chain lifted, but not as much as she thought it would. She released her arm from the rope and slipped her knife back into its sheath.

Just then her right hand felt a vibration in the top chain as her arm extended and her feet were pulled up off the bottom chain. Tar piss! Am I going to fall to the ledge too? Noooo! Not now! Nagora hung on with one hand. Tar piss! Don't swallow the coins! She clenched her teeth and pulled back her lips to suck air in through her mouth. She swung her left arm up and grabbed onto the top chain. Tar piss! Why didn't I put those coins in my scrip? Not enough time?

The bottom chain struck her shins. Ouch! She had almost opened her mouth to scream. Tar piss! Lose those coins and you'll only have what Bardas put in that pouch. No curraghs in Stone Stander territory.

Nagora pulled her knees up in pain and hung on as she tried to locate the bottom chain. She looked over her left shoulder. The bottom chain barely moved. The top chain had settled. She set one foot on the bottom chain, then the other, and steadied herself.

Nagora looked out at the chains in the mist. The top chain was in motion again. This time she was ready for it. When her arms extended, she managed to keep her feet on the bottom chain. Good. It'll stop soon. She moved to the next links to leave the rope loop free to be pulled back. Immediately, it disappeared.

Nagora looked down at Keallach on the ledge. He looked so small. Water streamed onto the ledge against him. If it kept raining like this, would the river rise enough to wash him off? Probably what Coyle hoped would happen before an attempt to recover Keallach's body.

She looked back at Ardal and Coyle, pointed down, and held up her thumb. They held theirs up and waved her on.

The waves in the chain had receded. Nagora moved on as fast as possible. I hope arrows won't follow me into the mist.

The next time Nagora looked back, all she saw was foggy mist and all she heard was the raging river crash through the gorge below. The rain was still warm, but the mist was cold and the chains colder.

How much further? The bottoms of her feet ached from the irregular pressure of the cold metal links. If ever I make it off this bridge, I'm sure I'll feel these links in my every step for days. She pressed on and kept swallowing the spit in her mouth that the coins seemed to pull into it.

A vibration ran through Nagora's feet and hands. She froze and readied herself. Probably someone out on the chain to go see Keallach's body—the rebel's body.

Tar piss! Let them believe it. Good man that Ardal. He had most likely listened to Coyle's idea. He's no Pug that one.

Nagora flexed her legs with the wave on the chain and counted as she waited in the rain. Tars, they won't want to stand on the bridge too long. The vibrations came again, followed by another wave. I'll wait a little more in case they're watching the chains. Coyle will most likely make sure they're distracted.

On her next move Nagora came out of the mist. The chains extended further ahead of her to a huge boulder. She was almost there. She kept moving. We're going to make it, Tars. No one in sight yet. Someone must be watching, even in this rain. We'll find out soon enough.

The Stone Standers
Asinîy Chimataw

Nagora stepped off the bridge onto solid ground. She crinkled her nose as she looked at her feet. They wanted to rise by themselves as if they weighed nothing. Her hands were cold. She rubbed them together for a few moments then crossed her arms to pin them to her sides. A shiver ran through her. She bent over and pressed her legs together as she stared down at her toes. Maybe I won't be as cold if I put my boots on.

She pulled her wet boots from her neck to untie them and froze.

"Look what we 'ave here, Garret. Think she's a Stone Stander? Or is she the one we've been looking for?"

Nagora looked up at the two men in their rain-soaked clothes. They must've come from behind the boulder. One carried a spear, and the other had his sword drawn. *Ka asweyihtamihk Ka Peyakot Mahihkan.* Another shiver ran through her. Beware Lone Wolf. She dropped her boots and took a balanced stance. Are they Stone Standers? They aren't dressed as mercenaries.

The one with the sword licked his lips and grinned as he slowly approached. "We're going to be rich, Garret. You and me. Equal share if she's the one. I told you it was worth crossing at daylight. Are you glad I convinced you to wait a while longer? I tell you, Garret, when I get a feeling, I always trust it."

Mercenaries? No. They don't look trained. Something about them was familiar.

"No way to tell, Miach. If she don't match the description. She's no boy. We can't count on the mercenary reward yet. She might have something of value on her. We can split that."

"If she doesn't, we can take her before we bring her back for questioning. At least we'll have 'ad us a piece o' tail," said Miach."

Heat returned to her hands with each breath she took through her nose, and those breaths were coming faster and faster. The mercenaries enlisted you two to do their dirty work? I can't believe it.

"She doesn't like that. She's barin' her teeth. She's gonna give ya a good ride. He! He! You take her first. You like 'em with some fight in 'em," said Garret.

Miach grabbed his crotch with his free hand. "Well, lass, I think it's time for you to put your hands on your head and get on your knees."

Garret's spear was now within reach. "Do what he says, lassie." He jabbed the spear point at her belly and pulled it back. Now I see it, the burn scar on the side of his face, no hair around his yellow scarred ear. The two with hammers and nails I followed in Windhaven.

Slowly, Nagora raised her hands. Miach's eyes were on her legs. Garret looked to Miach. When her fingers touched, she spit the gold coins from her mouth. They flew to the ground between the two men. One of the gold pieces rolled past them. In the time their wide eyes followed the coins, she had pulled her big blade from its sheath, lunged forward, and swung at the spear, cutting it in two along with Garret's thumb and two fingers.

Nagora shifted her weight as she brought her big blade back up to block the swing of Miach's sword, kicking him in the balls as hard as she could. It knocked him back. He doubled over, clutching his crotch with his free hand. His right hand wanted to go there too. Too bad. Mistake. Nagora swung her blade down and cut off his sword hand. Blood squirted across her legs and then onto Miach's crotch and legs as his left hand clutched at the spurting stump, and he went to his knees.

Nagora looked to Garret. Tar piss! He was crawling on his knees with his right hand stuck into his left armpit, chasing the coins. He had managed to pick one up and hold it in his fist.

Nagora stepped over to him. "Drop it, Garret, if you don't want to end up like your friend."

He looked up at her, over to Miach, and then over to Miach's hand still gripping his sword where it had fallen. He opened his hand, looked at the gold dragon, let it drop, and watched it roll away and fall over next to one of the others.

"Now you pig, the only chance you and your arsehole friend have of ever hoping to get a piece o' tail is to get back on the bridge and head for the other side."

Garret's jaw dropped as his wide eyes looked at her, then back to Miach. He shook his head and moved his lips, but could only croak. He swallowed hard and this time his words came clear. "There's no bloody way we'll make it back!"

"I know that. At least you'll have tried." Nagora tapped the top of his head with her blade. "Or if you choose, I can hack your tails off and feed them to you. Your last piece o' tail before you die. Won't that be something to joke about?"

Garret waved her blade away.

Nagora backed off and Garret crawled over to Miach, whose eyes were squeezed shut. Most of his teeth were bared in a grimace. His left hand was wet with blood as it did its best to stop the flow.

"Miach, you heard her. We gotta go. Come on." He was on one knee and trying to get Miach to stand. "Come on, Miach. Let's go."

Miach opened his eyes, looked over at her, and tried to say something, but his locked grin didn't let him. His tears forced his eyes shut again as he twisted his head and brought his chin to his heaving chest.

Garret was on his feet now and pulling on Miach's shirt. "Let's go."

Miach growled at him and leaned onto one knee as he set a foot flat on the ground. His breath came in spurts and he spit before staggering up on his other foot. He bent over, cradling his stump. His eyes must've opened and seen his sword. For a moment, he could twist his neck and blink the tears from his eyes to glare at her.

Nagora gave him her best smile. *You poor bastard. If you don't get on that bridge, I'm going to make you regret the day you ever set your dirty eyes on a woman.*

The two moved toward the bridge. Miach said something to Garret. He stopped, reached for Miach's belt, unfastened it, and removed the scabbard.

Miach held out his arm. With Garret's help they were able to wrap and tie the belt around the bleeding stump. Then it was Garret's turn. He pulled his shirt off, and they used one of his sleeves to tie a knot around his wrist.

Miach motioned for Garret to go first. He followed close behind, holding one end of his belt between his teeth as best he could to keep his arm up.

Garret reached for the top chain and as he stepped onto the bottom chain, he looked back at Nagora before speaking to Miach. "Come on."

Miach grabbed onto the top chain. He seemed to be waiting to catch his breath before stepping onto the bottom chain. Once he did, Garret moved forward, one link at a time.

Miach growled something between his teeth. *Saying good-bye to me, Miach?* Whatever it was, Garret ignored it and moved on. He was four links ahead of Miach. The growling became louder. Garret continued on and gained another link. Miach let go of his belt. "Wait!"

I hear desperation in your voice, Miach.

Miach tried to close the gap. His handless right arm swung back and forth. His neck twisted down to his shoulder as his chin tried to stop the swinging. The arches of his feet turned across the bottom links as he tried to crab-walk.

Their moves were no longer in time, and the chains were reacting to the alternating shifts in weight. How would the bullies react to the coming waves? Nagora got her answer as the two wounded men neared the mist. Garret held on as the first bounce hit, but Miach panicked as the chain bounces collided from opposite directions.

Miach lost his hold of the top chain and in desperation, twisted and lunged for Garret, catching hold of his pant leg. Garret's legs split, and he came down hard on the bottom chain, bounced as he tried to grab hold, but Miach's weight pulled him away. They both disappeared, screaming into the mist below.

Before slipping it back into its sheath, Nagora wiped her blade on her bare thigh as the bouncing waves in the chains receded. As soon as her hand left the handle of her blade, cold metal pressed on her neck just below her ear. A sword!

"Stay as you are. Don't you move."

Nagora obeyed. The voice was old. It sounds like a man's, but I can't be sure, the words are so soft spoken.

The speaker coughed and spit. "Hear me out and you'll know I mean you no harm."

It was a man's voice.

"Spending my day in the rain watching those two was not my idea of enjoying myself. Waiting to see if you would come our way, though, made it bearable." He paused a moment to take in a long breath and cough again.

"Yesterday, our eyes on the other side sent an arrow warning us of their coming. It came on the heels of one bearing a message of your exploits and the price on your head. From the way you dispatched those two poor buggers, I don't doubt you are the one from that first message. I want you to know you're welcome here." The sword left her neck and the sound of it returning to its sheath reassured her.

Slowly Nagora turned to look at the speaker. She stared up into a face surrounded by cropped gray hair on its forehead and a neatly trimmed gray beard on its chin. Under an equally gray cloak, which reached below the man's knees, only his boots were visible. His sword was concealed. His blue eyes held hers for a long moment before he spoke.

"You're lucky to still be standing where you are. No one comes here unless they are from here. Or, on rare occasion, invited. You are neither. What is your name?"

Nagora or Edana? Not *Ka Peyakot Mahihkan*. "I'm called Edana."

A hand appeared from the middle of his cloak and reached up over his heart. His fingers splayed to form the dragon chord, and he saluted her. "Welcome to our domain, Edana."

Nagora's sight blurred with her tears. Could it be true? She was safe.

"My assistant, who usually guards the bridge, is on his way to Council with the arrow that brought news of your exploits. He and I thank you for taking care of the mercenary fodder.

"Do you know how to ride?"

"I do." How did they ever get horses over here?

His other hand appeared as a fist. He held it out to her and opened it. "I believe these belong to you."

She took the three gold dragons and dropped them into her scrip.

"Get your boots on. Let's see if we can get you some clothes."

...

Nagora followed the man past the boulder, up along a path that leveled out behind more big rocks where two small horses waited. They were even smaller than the ones in her part of the country, with the same brown coat that turned to black on their legs, and with black manes and tails. One was saddled, the other not. It only wore a bridle.

"You'll want that vest under your bottom as you ride Fester." He untied a rolled-up blanket from behind his saddle and handed it to her. "It's a short ride from here. A fire'll be waiting to warm you. My name's Grimrod. You can call me Grim."

She took his advice and set her vest on the horse's back, then grabbed onto its mane, and threw her leg up and over. She patted Fester's neck and leaned over closer to his ear. "Fester, you're so docile. I like you already." She pulled the blanket up over her shoulders.

Grim climbed onto his mount without a problem and set off right away.

Nagora pressed her knees into her new friend's sides and followed Grim over rocky ground and through winding passes, leading into a small valley that rose between mountains. They came to a cascading stream and followed alongside it up the easy slope of the mountain to a green plateau spotted with folded mountain flowers.

A small stone hut sat in the distance. A thin line of smoke from the chimney pushed against the rain. Already in her mind, she sat before the fire inside.

...

Nagora stood in front of the fire with a dry blanket over her shoulders. She stared at the open pot of soup Grim had hung from the hook above the flames. Her vest and blades rested on the back of a chair on the other side of the fireplace. Merna, Grim's wife, had told her to warm herself well while she hunted through the old clothes she had stored away.

They had raised three sons who had all grown so fast that, even if the clothes were handed down from one to the other, they had outgrown them before they wore them out. "I'll put a kit together for you in no time," said Merna.

The hut reminded Nagora of home. The only real difference was the precision with which the stone walls here were put together. Not even the smallest knife blade could be slipped into the cracks between the stones. And three of the walls had animal likenesses made of stones of different colors set in their walls: a howling wolf on the chimney just above her, a mountain ram on the wall to her left, and a bear on the wall to her right.

A sense of security had settled over her. *I could curl up right on the floor in front of the fire and fall asleep.*

Grim tapped on her shoulder and handed her a long-handled wooden spoon. "Edana, give the soup a good stir. Once you're dressed, we'll have some. Then I'll give you some time to rest. The rain might let up. Even if it doesn't, I have to take you to Council. We'll be there before nightfall. They'll decide what we'll do with you."

"They'll decide?" *That doesn't make me feel so secure now.*

"A formality, you know. They'll have lots of questions, and then it'll all come down to what we can do to help you."

Tar piss! That's a change. Almost too good to be true.

"He! He! See here what I found for you. Should be something to your liking in this pile." Merna dropped the clothes and two pairs of boots on the floor next to Nagora. "Now Grim, let's look the other way so the lass can choose and not feel embarrassed." She had Grim by a shirt sleeve, showing him to his chair and making signs for him to turn it around.

Nagora had chosen the socks with the smallest holes at the toes, the brown linen pants with worn knees, and two shirts with worn elbows and frayed sleeves. One had been black but was now mostly gray on the front, the other was pale brown. Merna had insisted she take the long coat even if it was almost twice her size. "It'll fit over what you carry. It's colder here in the mountains, all year round. Take the black tam too. You won't regret it."

"Thank you, Merna. I'll pass on the boots. Mine'll be almost dry by the time we're ready to leave."

Nagora had a big bowl of soup, some fresh bread, a piece of cheese, and some goat's milk. It was tasty. Merna had spoiled her like when Pare kept her for a meal. I can't wait to see you, Pare. I have so much to tell.

When she had finished eating, Grim touched her arm. "You rest now because I am tired too. We'll have a long ride ahead of us to get you to Council."

She had not needed further coaxing. Merna had hung a hammock for her not far from the fire. She curled up in it and fell asleep.

When Nagora awoke, she was under a blanket. Merna stood at her side, gently brushing the hair from the side of her face and smiling at her. "Time to go. Rain's almost stopped. Wind's come up. Be sure you wear your tam."

Grim came over. "I'll saddle my horse. Will you be okay on that sheepskin, or should I stop to borrow a saddle for you?" Before Nagora could answer, he answered his own question. "We'll borrow a saddle. What was I thinking?"

Had Merna made a face at Grim? As soon as Grim left, she looked to Merna who wore a big smile on her face. "I don't know how to thank you, Merna. I'd like to pay you." She reached for her scrip.

Merna waved a hand and placed it over hers. "We've no need of coins of any kind. You keep that. Someday, if you're back in these parts with a dragon, fly over and give us a wave. You'll make our hearts happy if you do."

Nagora took Merna's hands in hers. "You have my promise." I'll have to remember that, Tars, if ever I get to sit on one. Think it'll happen?

Nagora was glad they had stopped to borrow a saddle. It made the ride up and down mountain passes so much easier. Now they were on a long, wide plain. A lone mountain grew out of it in the distance. "Almost there, Edana."

They were Grim's first words since getting her saddle. He picked up the pace with his little horse, Renny. Fester didn't need any urging to do the same.

...

Deep wide trenches lined either side of the unmarked road. See that, Tars? Buildings and dwellings carved out of the rock on this plain. All of stone. Not a single one made of wood.

Nagora caught sight of people. What business they were about, she could only guess. Right now I want to know more about Council.

They had made good time because the sun would be in the sky for at least three more counts. When it set, it would be to her right. I'm guessing we're less than a count from the mountain. Well, right now, I'm headed in the direction of home. How far away can I be? How many days?

Wow! Tars, look at the size of the stones in this mountain pass. They're huge. Probably carved from the rock of the plain. How did they ever set them in place to build this mountain?

They came to a wall. The carved way could take them to the right or to the left. Grim went left.

The walls in the pass grew higher, but the sky was still visible above their heads. The way turned sharp to the right and then to the left. Turns in the pass succeeded each other many times until the sky above disappeared and they rode into darkness that only lasted a moment.

They rode into a man-made cave lit with oil lamps, many of which were recessed in the stone walls. The others all hung from iron hooks screwed into the stone.

A young man appeared from one of the many doors along the wall to Nagora's left. "Welcome, Master Grimrod. I'll take Renny."

"No 'Master' and 'Grim' suits me fine, Cyril."

Cyril nodded as he took their reins. "Merrik's at his usual post, last door. Err ahh, Grim?" He was waiting and glancing at Nagora.

"Yes, Cyril?"

"Is this—?" He looked down at his feet. "You know, Grim."

"So sorry, Cyril. Yes. Edana, meet Cyril. He's our head groom. The stables wouldn't be the same without him."

Cyril bowed awkwardly. He didn't seem to know what to do next. He finally looked at her and saluted. "Honored to meet me, err, you."

News sure travels fast around here. She smiled at him. Was he blushing?

He looked to the horses, then back, and gave a shy wave.

Nagora followed Grim to the last door along that wall. He rapped it with his fist and didn't wait for an answer. "Merrik, you old fart, are you awake?"

Nagora followed Grim in. Merrik sat with his back to them. Long white hair fell to his shoulders. When he turned in their direction, a matching white beard framed the rest of his face. He must be older than Grim, much older.

"Ah! Grim! My old friend. You made good time. Thought you would when the rain stopped and the wind came up. Lucky for you, your old stone bones aren't piss soaking wet.

"Oh! Pardon me. Pardon us for speaking that way in your presence, Edana. Welcome to our domain's seat. Council is so looking forward to meeting you.

"Grim, I tell you what. While I go to announce your arrival and they assemble, you two can go relieve your bladders and stretch your legs. You know where the chamber is. Bring Edana when she's ready. There'll be food and drink for everyone."

"We'll do that Merrik. Will you be attending?"

He was slow in getting up, but once he got moving he made it over to them in two blinks. "Why, of course. Wouldn't miss it for anything. And the food. Oh! The food will be something good. I won't tell you what it is. Ha! See you there. Take your time. By the time I do the rounds and they all assemble, well, you know how it is.

"Oh! Grim, a word, please. Excuse us, Edana." They moved just past the doorway. Merrik whispered something in Grim's ear.

Grim put a hand on Merrik's shoulder. "I'll do that. You go do what you're paid for. We'll take care of ourselves."

Merrik's eyebrows leaped up as did his hand. "Oh! And Grim—wine. There'll be wine too!"

"It's the least I expected." Grim pointed at Merrick.

Grim's look was solemn as he returned to the room.

Now what?

He bent his head and scratched the back of his neck. "Edana, this will sound silly to you, I'm sure. But I have to test you."

Nagora's eyes narrowed. "Test me? How?"

"Just another formality." He waved a hand. "You do know how to use a sling, don't you?"

Nagora took a deep breath and smiled. "Yes. It was my very first weapon until I was big enough to handle a staff. About the same time, Uncle put a bow in my hands."

Grim raised his arms and smiled. He seemed most pleased with her answer. "Stone Standers pride themselves in the fact they've chosen the sling as their weapon of choice. If ever called to battle, it'll be with their slings and their battle stones. Succeed the test, and chances are you'll be made an honorary Stone Stander. Come."

He led Nagora back into the stable area. "Cyril!"

His head popped out of a stall. "Yes, Ma, err, Grim."

"Your sling, a bag of stones, and the usual targets."

"Yes, Grim." He disappeared.

"Cyril needs to practice. A lot. How long since you've practiced with one?"

Nagora looked up. "Hmm. Seven … no, eight years."

Grim's eyes opened wide, and he lost his smile.

"But the last time I used one was last year, about this time. I haven't lost it."

His smile returned. "Cyril!"

"Coming, Grim." He had a bucket in one hand, with a broom tucked under his arm. His other hand carried the bag of stones. The sling hung on his shoulder. "Where do you want me, Grim?"

Grim held out his hand. "Your sling to Edana. The bag to me. You with the bucket down there, in the middle where the ceiling's highest and you're away from the lanterns on the wall."

As Nagora took the sling from Cyril, she looked in the bucket. "Fresh horse turds?"

Cyril wore a smile as he skipped away with the bucket.

"Cyril. When I give the signal, you lob. Edana will sling." Grim held the leather bag open. "They're all the same. Cyril will throw a—target, in the air. You try to hit it before it hits the ground."

Nagora looked at Grim as she took a stone from the bag and loaded it into the leather sling. "That's it?"

"That's it. Ready?"

"Aye." Uncle's words came back. "Trust yourself. Don't think. Follow the target with your eyes and just let it go." Nagora had proved him right thousands of times with both standing and moving targets.

Grim raised his hand. "Lob!"

The turd exploded. Cyril's jaw dropped. He stared at Nagora. "Lucky shot."

"Lob!" Another turd exploded.

After the tenth one, Cyril set the bucket on the ground and walked over to them shaking his head. "How'd you do that?"

Grim laughed. "I told you, Cyril. It can be done. Any advice for Cyril, Edana?"

Nagora repeated her uncle's words.

Cyril's eyes blinked. "Just that?"

She handed Cyril his sling. "It won't happen right away. It's all in the trust you put in your eyes to follow the target.

Your arm will know when to release to hit it on the path it'll travel. In a few hundred tries it'll happen."

Grim tapped Cyril's shoulder. "In the meantime, you've got work to do with your broom."

Nagora entered the chamber ahead of Grim. No one else had arrived yet in this amazing room. Could she ever in her life have imagined such a place? No. It was longer than it was wide. Its two long walls curved inward and met in a point at one end. The door she had come through was at its other pointed end. Almost like the shape of a ship.

Along the wall to her left, was a single long bench carved out of the stone. It stood almost a full stride from the wall and stretched almost all the way to the other end.

In front of that bench, a long curved stone table, also carved right out the rock, followed the same curve as the bench. Both the bench and the table were well worn. Wow! How long has this place existed?

All along the center of the chamber's ceiling, oil lamps hung from hooks. They lit up the relief carvings on both chamber walls. The reliefs were all detailed. They must be of the works of the Stone Standers. For there it was, on the wall opposite the table, the Twin Rivers dragons, drawn with all the details the original statue must've had. Proud Stone Stander art, defaced and destroyed on the orders of vengeful Queen Raganora. How could she be so stupid?

Nagora stopped before one of the relief carvings. Beautiful pillars stood in a ring, with images of dragons carved upon them and on the stone lintels spanning the tops of the pillars.

Grim placed a hand on her shoulder. "Ever see something like this?"

"In a field on my way to Gallanford, I saw rough pillars standing, some on the ground, only a few had the top slabs on them. I couldn't see any dragon images."

Grim sighed. "Defaced. Destroyed. Nothing on the inner ring of pillars either. Right?"

"Nothing. Just rough chipped surfaces. What were they?"

"Dragon rings. Dragons from all parts of the land would fly to meet at the rings. They brought their eggs, placed them in the middle ring, and perched on the outer ring to watch their babies hatch."

He pointed to the carving they were looking at. "It was one of the biggest of the dragon rings. There were many others in the land. Most were smaller though, but well-loved by the dragons. Those times are no more."

His words sounded heavy with loss. They even seemed to press down on his shoulders.

But then he straightened up, took a deep breath, and looked at her. "But today you are here Edana. You bring us hope."

Now the weight of his words were on her. What have I done? How can I ever bring back such greatness?

Grim touched Nagora's arm. "I'll be gone for a few moments. I want to check on Council. They should be here by now. Can I leave you here?"

She was still admiring the different reliefs. "Sure, Grim. Take your time."

She stood before a most intricate relief. It was a maze. Could she find the way in before Grim returned? She picked one opening on the outer edge and let her eyes walk into the maze. She blinked and lost her place. She returned to the starting point she had chosen and focused on the path.

"Does your leg hurt?" This time, Grim's words pulled Nagora from the maze.

I was almost there. "No, my leg doesn't hurt. Why?"

"I saw you rubbing your thigh as I came in."

"I was? I didn't realize it. I was trying to find the way to the center of the maze."

"Not many can." Grim pointed. "Look. Council arrives. Stay with me until they're seated."

They filed in, old men and old women, all with hair of white and wearing robes of white. Silently, they walked along the space between the bench and the table. When they stopped, they all turned to sit at the same time.

Merrik came in and sat at the end of the bench, near the door.

Grim leaned close to Nagora. His breath touched her ear. "I will sit at that end. You see that space in the middle. That's where you'll sit in a few moments. Everyone will see you as you tell your story. It'll be easier for you than if you stand here to tell it. You decide when you want to stop to eat or drink something, or to get up to stretch your legs."

Nagora took a deep breath as she looked at all the people before her.

Grim took her hand. "A little afraid right now, aren't you?"

She squeezed his hand. "Yes."

"That's a good sign. It means you have a good story to tell, and all these people want to hear it. Trust me, once you sit down and start, all your fear will disappear."

"But aren't they going to question me first?"

"Oh! No! Afterwards, probably. Not until you've told your story."

"Where do I start?"

"At the beginning. You know, as far back as you can remember. Tell them all the interesting things. The things you think are important and they should know about you."

Grim let go of her hand. "Council, Edana will tell her story." He walked to his seat at the end of the table. Before sitting down, he smiled at her and with a quick circular motion of his finger, motioned her to go take her place at the table.

Merrik winked at Nagora as she walked by. The chamber was silent except for her footfalls. She stepped over the stone bench, sat down, looked at the wall opposite her, and placed her hands on the table. She took a breath, looked to her right and then to her left. Grim winked.

She began. "Mum died giving birth to me … "

Grim had been right. Once Nagora got started, she was at ease. Her story went on into the wee morning. She called for food and drink and pauses for people to go refresh themselves. Her audience listened, and laughed at times, and cried at times, and to her astonishment even cheered. They had all examined her blades, and she had let them all touch the gold dragon coins.

She had answered all their questions and when they had no more, they had all wanted to touch her, to hold her, and to wish her well.

They had agreed all would retire for some sleep and, after rising for a communal breakfast in the chamber, Council would announce what it would do to help her make it home.

Nagora stood before them in the chamber after breakfast. The first announcement was that Council would spread Edana's story, limiting it to the events in Windhaven to protect her true identity and the identities of those who had helped her.

Next, Council announced it would too, like The Guard, honor the rightful king's call to arms when he was ready to fight for his crown. They promised to commit all their slings.

Then Council made her an honorary Stone Stander as Master Grimrod had attested to her skill with a sling.

And finally, Council announced Master Grimrod would, first, see that she was equipped with a new bow, a quiver full of arrows, and supplies to last her on the final leg of her journey home.

Second, he would guide Edana through Stone Stander territory to the edge of the high cliffs where he would make arrangements to get her lowered safely to a spot near the Little Snake River.

According to their maps, Yhorgal would be only five days travel on foot from that spot.

Good fortune smiles on me this day. I can't believe it.

Nagora and Grim had traveled for three days on their little horses before reaching the edge of the high cliffs. They dismounted, and Grim stood behind her and pointed off into the distance. "Look straight ahead along my finger. You see those three mountains that appear tight together?"

"Yes, I do."

"If you were standing on one of those three, and looked down, you would see Yhorgal and the sea beyond."

Her heart leapt in her chest.

"I live on the coast. I'd be able to see home."

"Most likely. Now go peer over the edge. Tell me what you see."

"A river. It's so far down!"

"If you follow it back that way, you should be able to see part of the shore at the top of Great Snake Lake."

"Council said something about getting me lowered down. How's that going to happen?"

"We'll have to find help from one of the lookout stations. We should come to one if we go in that direction." He pointed across the low shrubs and grassy fields of the plateau to where they met the rusty winding edge of the stone surface of the high cliffs.

Nagora smiled at Grim. "That suits me. It's on my way home."

He laughed. "You'll be Tars again."

Just over two counts later, the lookout station came into view. Two people came out, one of them running, lifting a cloud of orange dust as he did. The runner must be a young man. By the way he jumps as he runs toward us, he's happy to have visitors. The one who followed waved.

Grim pointed at them. "They haven't been home in over three months. I hope they'll be happy with what I brought."

...

Not only did Tosh and Rame seem happy with the letters, the jars of food, and cured meats Grim had brought, they also seemed pleased with the task he asked them to perform. They already had a hoist of sorts ready to be rigged, since they sometimes used it to lower either one of them down to go hunt in the forest below, or fish in the river.

Two tall posts were planted in holes bored into the rock, about two strides from the cliff edge. At their tops, the posts held a pulley in place, and two more between them about knee height off the ground.

Big metal brackets were attached to the sides of the posts, at their base near the ground. These brackets held two long movable posts, with a pulley between them at both their ends.

Stout rope went through all the pulleys, and when the long posts were moved out beyond the edge of the cliff, the rope could be used to lower a person to the valley below, or raise them. The men used a horse to make this job easy to do.

Tosh, the older of the two, was eager to explain as he pulled up the end of the rope with the harness on it. "Edana, we're very strict about when we go down and for how long. Down just before dawn. Stay for three full counts. Then back up again."

Rame added his preference. "I prefer to go down for the counts before nightfall and come back up just before dark. I set snares. Tosh checks them the next morning. When do you want to be let down?"

She didn't hesitate. "Just before first light tomorrow."

Tosh held up the rope harness. "Good. I'll show you how the harness works now. It'll be easier than doing it in the dark.

"It's these two loops for your legs. Pull them up to your rear end. This big loop around your back and under your arms to the front." He pointed. "Walk down this path over here right to the edge. Hold on to the rope, let yourself swing out easy, then when you're stable, down you'll go. I'll give the signals to Rame. He'll control the horse. Try the harness on now."

Nagora removed her pack before slipping into the harness. "Like this?"

"You got it. Tomorrow, you can put your pack on and hang your bow from your shoulder."

She slipped the harness off and looked at Grim. "I can't believe how close to home I am."

"You're not home yet. Keep a weather eye until you are.

"Rame. Are your quarters clean and suitable for guests?"

Rame had his eyes on his boot as it scuffed the ground. "Give me half a count and I'll have it ready for you."

Grim winked at her and Tosh as Rame made a run for the station house.

Tosh pulled at his ear. "The young ones are all the same. He's good though. Hardly ever complains. Some it's every day. Can't wait for their stints to be over."

Nagora was the first to rise, have her bedroll packed away, and use the latrine. Tars, I don't know about you, but I feel like I hardly slept.

On her return, Grim roused Tosh and Rame.

After their silent morning meal, Rame went to the stable to fetch the horse. Tosh and Grim, with candle lantern in hand, accompanied her to the lift.

Grim verified the rope was securely attached to the horse. When he gave his approval, Nagora slipped into the harness, pulled her pack on, and slung her strung bow over her shoulder. She was ready. She looked over at Grim. "Thanks for all your help, Grim. Tell Merna I'll keep my promise."

Nagora smiled at Tosh and waved to Rame. "Thanks for your help. I trust you'll get me down in one piece?"

"No worry, we've got you covered. Have a safe trip, Edana."

Grim held the dragon chord over his heart and winked at her. She smiled and held back the lump in her throat as she headed down the little path to the jump-off spot near the edge of the cliff.

The Chain
Sakâpihkan

Nagora stood on the edge of the high meadow. This was familiar hunting ground for her and Uncle. If she stayed in the forest, she would cross a brook and begin a climb up the mountain to its top where she could see Yhorgal below. But if she crossed the high meadow, she would not be far from a trail that would take her to Cairnmase. She could easily be there before sunset.

What do you say, Tars? Cairnmase tonight, home tomorrow? We've been away for one hundred and one days. I know this pretty lass in Cairnmase and I've missed her so. I'd like you to meet her. I think I told you about her once before. Who knows, Uncle just might be there on a visit.

Nagora had come down the woodland trail not far from Geirador's forge in the early evening. She had not come across anyone from Cairnmase. She walked into his forge. It was quiet. The ashes in the hearth were cold. She walked to the door of the stable. No one there. Over to the other end to look in the corral. The horses and mules were there. They must be having supper.

Tars, I've got an idea. We'll have some fun. It made her smile.

Nagora skipped back to the forge, took off her pack, her quiver, and her vest. She pulled off her blades. Now where can I hide these? I know, under the bellows. Then she leaned her bow and quiver in the space between the wall and a big wooden cabinet near the door to the stable.

Now this. She reached into her scrip, pulled the hidden flap aside, and removed the chain. She let it drop onto the hearth ashes, took a poker, and shook the ashes so they buried the chain.

She put her vest back on and slung her pack over one shoulder.

On the doorstep of Geirador's hut, Nagora stood and listened. Humming. That's Pare. Wait till you see her, Tars.

A voice said: "But we don't know it's her." That's Geirador.

Uncle said: "Who else could it be? Who else could've done that and then got herself killed? I shouldn't have sent her."

Oh! No. She was about to open the door.

"Dangor."

That's Pare.

"Stop blaming yourself. Anyway, you don't have proof it's her. Wait for confirmation from a sure source."

"Thanks for the meal." A chair moved. "Time I head home. So Geirador, you going to buy back that young stallion?"

Young stallion?

"No, Dangor. Not right away. I've got a feeling Nagora's on her way home. I think that horse is just right for her. In no time she'll break it in, train it to do whatever she wants."

She was about to cry. My own horse.

"I wish I had your optimism. I'll saddle up Jarra and go home. Thanks again." Uncle opened the door.

Nagora threw her arms around him. "Not without me!"

Dear Reader,

Thank you for reading *BANISHED*. For the benefit of future readers and to help me as an author, you would truly warm my heart by leaving an honest review at:

www.hnhenry.com/testimonials

OR wherever you purchased this copy of *BANISHED*.

Sincerely,

H. N. Henry

P.S.: Here's a **SPECIAL OFFER** for you:

Get the first chapter of *BRANDED* for **FREE**:

Find out how on the next page.

ABOUT THE AUTHOR

Other than writing, his passions include kayaking, baking bread, and trying to learn how to play guitar. He shares the profits of his work with a local community cause, *Point de Rue*. They help homeless people on the streets find meaning and passion in their lives. Learn more about it here: http://www.pointderue.com/point_de_rue.html

To learn more about the author and the other books in the series, please visit: https://www.hnhenry.com

†

Titles in **THE DRAGON'S GAME** series:

BANISHED BOOK I

BRANDED BOOK II

BETRAYED BOOK III

BRED BOOK IV

BLAMED BOOK V

ACKNOWLEDGMENTS

The Dragon's Game books wouldn't have come about without the generous and invaluable support of these people throughout the creative process.

From the beginning, Staecy-Lee, my editor, gave my manuscripts tough, honest critiques. Her hard questions made me see my stories with fresh eyes for the benefit of my readers.

Randi, my proofreader, closely read the final formatted-for-publication texts, finding inconsistencies in details, descriptions needing clarification, and grammatical errors my own eyes could no longer see.

Staecy and Randi, avid readers of this genre, also offered truly valuable and insightful comments that have made me a better writer. Learning from them has been a pleasure and a privilege.

My passionate beta readers of the first original brick, in first name a-b-c order, Ann, Daniela, Danielle, Maria, Marie-Josée, Randi, and Staecy-Lee generously delivered invaluable feedback and constructive criticism that helped spawn *BAN-ISHED*, Book I, and from the volume they read, give birth to Books II and III of the series. I am forever in their debt for their support and encouragement.

To the stained-glass window artist, Guido Nincheri (1885-1973), who over ten years (1924-1934) created the beautiful windows in the Cathedral of the Assumption in Trois-Rivières, QC, Canada. From the photographs of those windows that I took on February 27, 2006, I was able to digitally manipulate images from two of the panels to create the unique dragons that appear on the covers of the first edition of my books, a humble homage to Nincheri's masterful work.

Though not referenced as Cree in the context of my stories, I have used Cree, in Roman orthography form, for the chapter titles and chapter numbers throughout the books in the series. More importantly, it is the " … strange yet familiar language … " Nagora, the main character, a.k.a. *Ka Peyakot Mahihkan*—Cree for *Lone Wolf,* hears in her mind and eventually uses to communicate with her dragon and other characters. At those times, when used, Cree is referred to as the *Language of the People*, in reference to the *First People* of *The Land* where my story is set.

The *Language of the People*, or "dragonspeak" as some readers of The Dragon's Game books call it, in a way, reflects the status of the Cree language in our land today. Though Cree is the most widely spoken Native language still spoken in Canada, it has yet to be recognized as one of this country's official languages. Similarly, in the fictional setting of *The Dragon's Game* books, the *Language of the People* is now only spoken by a few in a divided and renamed land where two different languages (those of the invading Outlanders) have become dominant in use.

To the Online Cree Dictionary Team: *Kinanâskomitin. Thank you,* I am grateful to you for making this resource available to all. It has been indispensable in helping me lend realism to that second language in my stories. I hope my readers will have as much pleasure as I do in discovering the living Cree language.

In the end, what appears on the pages of my books is mine, and I take full responsibility for any errors that show up in the final versions.